GIRL WITHOUT A VOICE

Chris Bridge

ISBN 978-1-78036-390-5

Published by
Peach Publishing

Praise for 'Girl Without a Voice'

"I jumped at the chance to read this book because I know how well this author can write, having read *Back Behind Enemy Lines* a few years ago. This book didn't disappoint. It is written in several significant parts. The author does an excellent job building the layers of suspense and tension, it was obvious just how much research had gone into making the plot and characters really believable."

Roses Are Amber

"Excellent read. A real page turner - I could not put it down. A first-class Book Club choice."

Edwina Derby, Amazon

"*Girl Without a Voice* is a gripping novel which explores, amongst other things, the devastating consequences of childhood trauma and emotionally coercive institutions on those least able to defend themselves from such predatory abuse. It is also, though, a testament to the resilience of the human spirit and to the power of love, demonstrating how selfless heroism can be ignited in the most unlikely people when a battle between goodness and evil can no longer be avoided."

Sylvia Cooper, Amazon

"From page one I was drawn into this intriguing story of a dysfunctional family overshadowed by a strange past."

Bob Wood, Amazon

"Gripping story and some lovely descriptions of places and nature. One of those books you are sorry to finish."

Christina Anderson, Amazon

"Chris Bridge is a writer who makes his readers really care about what happens to his characters. I highly recommend *Girl Without a Voice*."

Lorna Holborn, Amazon

"I absolutely loved this book. I found it hard to put down and read it in two sittings; I was intrigued to know what was going to happen to the characters and couldn't guess at the plot. The subject matter is dark and fascinating. The characters are sympathetically and realistically portrayed and the book left me wondering about the vulnerability of the human mind and how this can lead to extreme outcomes. An absorbing read - highly recommended."

Emma Bell, Amazon

"A highly enjoyable tale - a powerful story packed with superbly drawn characters - I guarantee you will not be able to put this down."

Simon Steward, Amazon

For Sheila

'I and the public know
What all school children learn,
Those to whom evil is done
Do evil in return.'

September 1st, 1939 WH Auden

Prelude

I was nine and Danny was five. We'd gone picnicking to our secret place on the North York Moors. It's a place Mum found and no one else knows about. We drove along a narrow winding road, parked the car in a meadow and walked down to the stream, then along its bank for simply ages. Julia and James were out in front, running races, hiding and jumping out at us. My mum, Izzy, was at the back with the rucksack. I was walking with Danny, chatting away, pointing things out. It was the day I noticed that Danny was almost as big as I was, and because he was almost as big, I wasn't having to wait for him, in fact I was struggling to keep up.

Heather was flowering everywhere. The narrow sandy path ran between banks of purple blossoms. I told Danny the difference between the pinker ling and the darker purple heather, which I'd been reading about. He wasn't listening. I urged him to sniff the air. The whole moor smelled of honey. Danny wouldn't close his eyes and sniff. So when I did, to fill my lungs with its sweetness, I found he'd got away from me, had already caught up with Julia and James, and that Izzy, following with the picnic, was about to fall over me.

I had to start running to catch up. But it was too late. Where the path widened, I saw that Julia and James had hold of Danny and were swinging him between them. It felt at once as if this baby boy who had always been mine was now theirs.

We reached the picnic spot. It was no more than a triangular patch of sheep-cropped grass, edged on one side by the stream and walled in on the other two sides by bracken. Inviting small sheep-paths led up the hillside.

'Come on,' I said to Danny, trying to lure him back, 'let's explore.'

He shook his head. He was bubbling over with happiness at being with the others.

'There might be beetles,' I said, 'or those shiny black slugs you like.'

To shut me up he began to sing his alphabet song. 'ABCD EFG, HIJK LMNOP.'

'Sometimes,' I said, 'you can find snakes higher up.'

I thought he might have forgotten the next line of his song, but he hadn't.

'QRST U and V,' he sang. He clearly had no intention of coming back to me.

I was aware that Julia and James were watching us.

'Snakes,' snorted James. 'Leah, you're the only snake in the grass that I can see.'

'Damn,' said Izzy. 'I've left the drink in the car. Julia, you're in charge. I won't be long.'

I turned round and she was striding away along the path, soon to be swallowed up by the bracken.

Just the four of us then in an area like an arena. That's how I remember it. They knew I could scream. Was that why they did nothing for a while? Did they deliberately wait until Mum was out of hearing?

I remember the silence, the way the insects in the blossoms grew louder until their murmur acted like a kind of film music. Then:

'What shall we do to Leah, Danny?'

'Shall we push her into the water?'

'Shall we make her stand in the middle and throw stones to splash her?'

'Splash Leah, splash Leah,' said Danny.

They came for me while Danny stood and watched, grinning, dancing up and down in excitement.

'Splash, splash her.'

I stood still and they grabbed me, one under each arm, hoiked me up in the air and dragged me towards the water.

I wasn't frightened then, just cross and unhappy to see Danny ditch me after all I had done for him. I remember I shouted, 'Put me down,' then added something Dad often said, 'For God's sake, put me down.'

At that we all heard a strange roaring noise coming from the bracken just above us. The ground shook and the water in the stream disappeared. It was like magic. It happened in a second. The bees stopped humming and the only noise was of earth running like sand and stones settling slowly somewhere beneath us. Then there was a profound silence.

They were stunned. Only I understood. Some of the bracken had gone, and when we ran up to look we found a hole that hadn't been there until the noise came. It was still moving, getting deeper. Triumphant, I turned round.

'I called on God and he heard me.' Our primary school was Catholic. 'Look,' I said, 'God's opened up the gates of Hell.'

The others were shocked and hung back. So I walked to the edge and pretended to look down. 'I can see smoke,' I said. 'I think the devils are coming to get you.'

Neither James nor Julia moved. Danny was the one who recovered fastest. He didn't want his moment with his older brother and sister to be over so quickly. 'Not splash,' he said, 'no water. Throw her into the hole.'

'You can't,' I said, full of my direct line to God Almighty, 'that'll be a sin.'

Danny seemed to find this funny. 'It's a sin, throw her in,' he chanted.

Julia had now reached the edge. She and James peered over.

Danny was still chanting. 'Throw her in, it's a sin. It's a sin, throw her in.'

From where I was standing I could feel the edges shake a little. I lost my confidence, began to walk downhill, shouting, 'Get away, it's not safe.'

It was James who tripped me. It was Julia who grabbed an ankle, then James immediately grabbed the other. I kicked out but they were too strong. Then they picked me up so my skirt hung downwards and everyone could see my knickers.

I was shouting and all the time I could hear Danny singing as if he hated me. My head was bumping the grass, then suddenly it was swinging clear over the lip of the sinkhole. I smelt the dampness, saw the crumbling earth and rock falling into nothing, knew if they dropped me I'd never get out. The earth was still moving with little stone falls. The hole was getting deeper. If they dropped me it would be impossible to climb up those muddy overhanging sides and the hole might close up as quickly as it had opened.

I thought I was going to die. Now I couldn't kick. Kicking might make them let me go. I hung there pleading, splurging.

'Don't drop me. Don't drop me. Please don't drop me.'

They pretended to drop me, letting me down and yanking me up so that for a while I bobbed at the end of their arms, my head getting closer and closer to the damp shifting soil.

I know I was crying. Then something else.

Danny spotted it, 'Look, she's peeing her pants.'

I remember the feeling of urine running down my chest, reaching my neck and dripping past one ear into my hair. It might have been the disgrace that saved me. I remember I closed my eyes and mouth. I didn't want it in my eyes. I didn't want to swallow my own pee. That's the moment I went silent.

And suddenly they swung me down onto the turf and let go. I rolled limply and then was still, face down in the cropped grass and the sheep droppings. I stayed motionless, too shocked, too humiliated, too miserable to do anything but lie there.

'Get up,' said James.

Normally I would have shouted back, but staying silent made me hear the fear in his voice. 'Come on, we're sorry. Get up. Please get up before Mum comes back.'

They were frightened now. If I stayed where I was Izzy would be bound to ask what had happened to me.

But I didn't want that. I knew this was my battle. I made myself get up, turn my back on them and walk slowly down to the stream. The water was running normally again. I washed my face in the stream in silence, took my knickers off, rinsed them, wrung them out then slipped them back on. They felt cold and clammy. The others crowded round me, worried. I held onto that.

'You're not going to say anything to Mum?' Julia's question.

'Only we never meant to frighten you.'

Somehow I knew that if I said anything they would relax. It was my lack of response that kept them nervous. So I stayed silent.

Danny caught the mood, went and found a yellow flower and held it out to me.

I didn't take it.

Soon Izzy came back and we pretended that nothing had happened. She never noticed the sinkhole and we never pointed it out. After my constant chatter Mum and Dad enjoyed my silence. The longer it went on the more powerful I felt. James and Julia treated me with increased respect. I told myself to do one more day, just one more day of staying silent, and the days stretched.

Part One: The Aftermath of a Funeral

'The thing I feel for her is physically painful. It's an awful love. A terrible love. It's a bruise being pressed, continually by a strong thumb.'

Eva Wiseman, *The Observer* 04.01.15

Chapter 1

I walk in last. The church is packed. All the pews are full and there are people standing down both sides and at the back. Would Dad be pleased, I wonder, or would he have turned to Julia and said, 'They've come to check I'm really dead,' before adding, 'This is what happens when you die before your time.'

Dad's coffin leads the procession. It sways rhythmically on the undertakers' shoulders. The movement gently shakes the many wreaths so that a single lily, freed from its floral restraint, sways and dances on top of the oak and brass-handled casket. My mother, Izzy, follows the coffin. She is supported by my older sister, Julia. Izzy, I notice, is quite upright in the way she walks. She doesn't seem to need support but Julia is clearly determined that she should be supported. Because Julia is taller than Izzy by half a head, she has to lean over to tuck her arm under my mother's. This makes it look as if Julia is the one bent over with grief. I know this isn't the case. Over the last week she has surprised me because I haven't seen her shed a single tear for the father I always thought she adored. I make a note to watch her later, in the crematorium when the curtains close. If she doesn't cry then, I will know.

Behind Izzy and Julia are my two brothers, walking almost in line, side by side for once. James's walk is an amble, slightly stiffened for the occasion but still the amble of a clever, clever boy who thinks effort has been reserved for the exclusive use of those who are less intellectually endowed than he is. James has put a suit on for the occasion, which looks suspiciously new. Just above the knee are two faint, horizontal lines that clearly come from a plastic hanger. I am surprised that he owns a suit. Did Izzy insist, give him money and send him to M&S? If so, he hasn't spent long choosing. The jacket isn't quite big enough on the shoulders and I rather doubt that he can fasten the jacket buttons.

James's hairstyle makes him look like the modern day version of a Viking god. His hair has always been dark and full but the recent addition of ringlets bulks it out so that it looks like the fringe of a heavy theatre curtain. He uses it in the same way. It's a look-at-me hairstyle. When he swishes it to one side his arm gestures are theatrical. His hair is parted on the right and on that side you can see his unblemished, almost baby like skin. He's carrying more pounds than he should. Does he think the bulk of his hair somehow balances this out?

Danny's walk is upright, shoulders back, neck fixed like a locked tripod. If he was a soldier he could not be more disciplined. His hair is close-cropped. His suit fits perfectly but then I know his lovely muscular body won't fit into anything off-the-peg. This suit is made-to-measure, expensive.

Eyes from either side sweep over us as we walk up the nave. They sweep like CCTV cameras, evenly and without real interest until they come to James, where they pause just long enough to work out that his hair must be permed. When they move on and reach Danny, those same eyes notice his beauty and brighten. They stay with him and reverse their previous movement so that I walk invisible at the end of the line.

It's always like that.

The pall bearers have reached the altar rail. From long practice they turn, come alongside, slip two of their number, lower the casket and slide it onto the rails. The wreaths stay where they are. The lily, as if recollecting itself, stops dancing.

Because the place is packed, only a single pew on the left hand side has been reserved for the immediate family. Izzy is ready to go in first but Julia holds her back as she marshals the others. Danny goes quickly to the end of the row. James follows him in, sits down and spreads his legs wide, the way he always does. I move forward to sit next to James, but am a fraction too late. My way is blocked. Julia is moving Izzy in to sit next to her older son. I don't understand and then I do.

She has forgotten about me. I try to slip in, but Julia moves too quickly. I watch her sit down right up against the carved end piece with its brass ring. She is Julia. She has pole position and I am left in the nave standing in front of the coffin.

I think of the car on family holidays, of the dinner table, of the bedroom arrangements when we moved house. There's room in the pew. There has always been room for me. I'm a rather small person. If they all moved down you could squeeze another three of me into that pew.

But no one moves. No one notices me. My family are all looking forward, ready for the service to begin.

I know I am different. I know I'm a nonentity and a silent one. But I thought that today, with our first death, I might have been accounted for, remembered. Instead Julia nods to the vicar, giving him the signal to begin.

The vicar seems perplexed, surprised by what has just happened in front of him, even upset on my behalf. I don't want that. I turn to my right and walk slowly, with what I hope is dignity, to the side of the church just past the coffin and I stand there.

The vicar smiles at me. Julia glances up to see what is causing the delay, glares at me as if it is my fault, then looks quickly back at the vicar. I see her tap her watch as if angry that the service hasn't already started.

We are soon underway. I look at the coffin closely, see from minute indentations at the joins that the oak is a veneer, no doubt stuck onto plywood. I am glad about that. Real tough oak, the kind of wood that fights against a saw and that sets like iron over the years, would be wasted if it was just to be burnt around my dad. A body is worth plywood. No human being is worth solid oak.

As I stand there, half listening to the opening prayers, I see the irony of my situation. I am close to my dad, physically closer to him than I have been for most of my life. Now, and only because he is dead, he is no more than two metres away.

When I was a little girl I liked to hold his hand, sit on his knee. He called me his Danger Mouse. Then things changed between us. Perhaps he saw the way the others treated me. I know he wanted me to be different. I used to catch him looking at me. Julia was upright and full of energy. James won prizes at school without trying. Danny was the sporting one, chosen for every team. I was the child who looked most like him and the one who most disappointed him. He couldn't brag about me to other people in the way he could about his other children. I did nothing special except for the fact I'd stopped speaking. I grew to hate the way he treated me, the way he'd look at me and shake his head.

So I kept out of his way. Of course, once it was clear that he really was dying, that there would be no more treatment, no further offer of wonder drugs, I used to creep in to watch him from the edges of the room. Sarah, the Macmillan nurse, saw me there, which Dad never did. When Sarah told me it wouldn't be long now and that I would probably find him already asleep I walked boldly into his room. Did I plan to touch him, to say goodbye? Perhaps. Did I still hope that he'd open his eyes and smile at me? Yes, I probably did.

I opened the door and walked in. He wasn't asleep. He was sitting up, looking irritated. Irritated was his default position. For the man who made things happen, for the man who was always in control, a little matter like prostate cancer, when it has reached the final stage, is bound to irritate.

I felt sorry for him. His face was pulled down with fatigue, as if gravity was not of universal strength but particularly strong round him, in the way that a gust of wind can seem to pick on a single person. Once I realised he was awake I wanted to turn and leave, but he'd seen me. His eyes had locked onto mine and I wasn't prepared to show him any weakness. I stood still. I stood in silence. He stared at me, trying not to flinch at the pain, at the way his body had turned against him. When he'd made himself more comfortable he spoke. We both knew this was an unnecessary waste of energy. I knew what he would say. It was what he always said. He'd said the same thing continually most of my life. Did he know the end was imminent and that this might be his last chance to say it?

His lips were grey. I saw them come together, then part. I watched his tongue move forward in a hiss, then stick to the roof of his mouth. I moved nearer to his bed, moistened his lips with a wet towel as I had watched the nurses do, and let him suck a little water. Then he slowly forced out the old mantra. Each word fell between us in that room and made no difference. He had to say it and he knew I wouldn't respond.

'For God's sake, make something of yourself,' was what he said.

I thought that was it, but he wasn't finished. He had something else to add and this time he whispered so I had to move nearer. That meant invading his space, which he hated, but there was no alternative. I still hoped for warm words, something loving to remember him by. When I bent my head to his face, might he even touch me?

I leant in. His hand stayed clutching the duvet and I heard him slowly say, 'I know your secret, Leah.'

Then he closed his eyes as if he'd had enough of me, this time for ever.

Did I keep my face still? I hope so. Did I register how much he had shocked me? I hope not. I waited for a while. He might have closed his eyes with the pain. I waited for thirty minutes, timing it by the clock, but he kept his eyes closed.

Now at his funeral service, I know we can never be reconciled.

His coffin is very close. I could reach out and touch it. I imagine him through the wooden shell, conjure an image of him lying there, shirted, suited, still cold from the refrigeration. I imagine his skin with a faint blue tinge, already a little shrunken, and I ask myself, just what is a human life worth?

We are at the point in the funeral service when a member

of the family is invited up to talk about the deceased. It will be Julia. I see her rise to her feet, watch her walk across to the lectern, and wonder what she will say and how she will say it.

Julia is my older sister. She is the tallest of the family. I can't call her pretty but she is striking to look at. She has a long face and a waterfall of hair which she accentuates by sweeping it up from her forehead so that it forms a small triangular peak there before falling away. The hair is long enough to cover her breasts. She wears it in front on the left but always sweeps it back over her right shoulder.

Julia is *in* Human Resources. You can *be* a teacher, a fireman, an accountant. But everyone is a human resource so if it is your profession you have to be *in* it. Julia is in Human Resources in the same way that other people are in a bad temper or a minor war. Quite early on in her career, I think, it occurred to her that she who understands employment legislation will always have the ear of senior managers. I have heard her bang on about this. Her qualification, she claims, gives her two pieces of vital information: what you shouldn't do to employees and what it will cost you if you choose to do it anyway and end up in a tribunal. It's what Dad liked about her: their shared notion that you can be as ruthless as you like in business, provided you understand the costs and have the money to pay. And, she sometimes adds, 'a certain fluffiness of language to cover up the reality'. When James taunts her, as he often does, she turns on him. 'I got to be a senior manager because I play it right, I play it in the best interests of my employers. I don't ever play it safe.'

She is in position now, behind the lectern, one hand on each of the eagle's brass wings, ready to begin. The vicar turns to look at her sideways and I wonder if he notices what I can see from my unusual position in the church: the remarkable similarity between the eagle's beak and my sister's nose. We all have Dad's nose. It's like a family signature.

This isn't my first funeral. We say goodbye to people with

a few funny stories, a brief summary of a career, and then we lace the final family section with emotion. Are we British so bad at families that we have to laud them at each and every funeral?

Julia has her notes on the lectern. Only two pages. This won't take too long. She looks up. 'Gary. . .' she begins.

Yes, I think, that's just what she would do, use his first name, give him a name she has never called him by. It both distances him and puts her in control.

'Gary Stephen Goulden was born in Hull in 1944, just as the war was coming to an end. He grew up in the post war years, played on the bomb sites, watched as the fishing fleet declined, always wanted better for himself than the back-to-back streets that formed him.'

Her notes are spread on the lectern but she isn't looking at them. To do so would spoil her performance.

'After school he went to Nottingham University, to its marble fronted buildings, its lakes and lawns. There he studied Business. This was a less fashionable subject back then and he studied it in the less fashionable buildings, affectionately known as the cow sheds. In his final year, on his way to the cow sheds when he was late for a lecture, he ran into a first year student called Isabel and nearly bowled her over. Literally became metaphorically.'

Only a small smile, almost a shy grin, betrays her enjoyment of her subtle joke.

'That girl became the love of his life. Only two years later they were married and nine months later, virtually to the day, I was born.'

You can't hear smiling but I see the congregation react. She is doing alright.

'While some young people struggle to know what to do after university, Gary never did. He'd completed a placement at Boots as part of his degree, working in both the factory and the stores. Back then, as some of us remember, to buy what you wanted you had to go to several different shops. Boots stores were excitingly different. Sainsbury had got as far as Birmingham but no further north, and when it did finally reach Nottingham Gary spotted at once that it was a store from the south and had too much of the south about it to be really successful up here. He went into retail, working long hours to make his first shop a success, then quickly expanded into the Goulden chain. The rest, as many of you who worked for him know, is history. Gary was a pioneer. He sold cheap and he sold plentiful. The kind of people he had grown up with loved Gouldens. They still do.'

'Those who worked for him know he was a proper boss. He managed the expansion himself. He kept control of his own creation. He didn't sell you out to speculators or to hedge funds. Under his honest leadership Gouldens blazed its own path and has continued to do so.'

Honest leadership. I have to give her that. She has a point. At work, at home, Dad was a bully. He led by bullying. He bullied Izzy. He bullied everyone except Julia, but he never disowned his rages when they subsided. He was never contrite because, in his own mind, his anger was God-like, justified because it was necessary, because it brought results. I suppose you can call that honest.

So far Julia has sketched his career. Where will she go next? Danny is watching his sister carefully. I still love Danny because he's the most straightforward of my siblings. You can see what he is thinking. It's written on his face. James has his eyes down, and whatever he is thinking is hidden by his hair. I suspect he is only waiting the time out until the service and his family obligations are over. And my mother, Izzy, what is she making of this? She is looking intently at Julia. Her eyes are aimed at her daughter, but there is that look on her face. I call it her inward look. It's the one she adopts when she needs to think and wants no one to follow her private thoughts. It used to drive her husband mad.

'So Gary was a man of business. He was also a family man. . .'

I am urging her on. Tell them, I'm thinking, put into words what they already know. They are his friends and his workers. They know about the anger, the bullying and the control. Tell them the truth. It will be cathartic for all of us.

'. . . and an excellent husband and father.'

You think you know someone and then they take your breath away. Excellent father, okay. She might just get away with talking for us children, but how does she know what kind of a husband he was? How does she know what Izzy's needs were and if he met them? I look at my mother and think, how dare Julia even go there.

'We were brought up to know the difference between right and wrong.'

No, the difference between right and might. That's what Dad taught us.

'We weren't pampered and overindulged.'

Say that again. Say it over and over.

'Not every child can claim that. He was a good father to us all.'

Has she forgotten what comes next? She seems to pause, but it is only to change her tone.

'For a man so full of life and energy it was particularly cruel that by the time he was diagnosed with cancer it was too late.'

Too late because he wouldn't go to the doctor. Izzy told him to get himself checked, but he wouldn't. By the time they knew it was prostate cancer it had spread into his bones. The radiotherapy was meant to hold it at bay but he hated the side effects and refused, he said, to be turned into a woman by hormone therapy. 'I'm not growing tits,' I once heard him shout at Izzy. 'We all have to die one day so I guess I'd better just get on with it.'

Julia couldn't know that. By then I was the only one still living at home.

'Gary was well cared for. He faced death bravely. When we came to visit he was still his cheerful self. It was a privilege to visit him, to be there at his side, to see his fortitude.'

No comment. There are no words.

Then because her fame slot is drawing to an end, because she has to use this opportunity to the full, she turns to face the coffin.

'So Dad. On behalf of all the people in this congregation I want to thank you for the way you have enriched all our lives. We will miss you.' Then she bows her head and holds her own short but significant silence before walking, head still bowed, both sides of her hair now falling forward, back to her place in the front pew.

***

The moment we are outside we forget about Gary Goulden and remember the weather. They are already saying that it is shaping up to be the coldest December for decades. The snow that began to fall on 30th November is still covering the churchyard. Layers of frost cling to the gravestones even though it is already midday. It's just too cold to stand outside for very long. People queue up and Izzy shakes hands, carefully chaperoned by Julia. Danny stands back. James leans against the wall. Then we go to the crematorium, where Gary is consigned to the flames with almost indecent haste.

I watch when the curtains close. Julia's face goes very still. Izzy knows that her husband is about to be burnt. She reaches for a handkerchief, dabs at her eyes. Her face puckers, her bottom lip quivers. She stays like that for some time, looking at the closed curtain. Even Julia doesn't rush her, allowing her time to say goodbye.

It is as Izzy turns away that I notice the change in her. It is like watching a butterfly emerge from a chrysalis. Her grey lethargy splits and a younger, more energetic Izzy steps out of her previous self. She stands upright, walks back to the car with such determination that Julia has to struggle to keep up. I find myself sitting next to Izzy and all the way back she stares ahead of her, following the headlight beams down dark Yorkshire roads as if she suddenly sees a future that has possibilities. When we get back she leaps out of the car and almost runs into the house. She's moving with a sense of purpose I have never seen before. I catch a glimpse of her eyes as she turns from hanging up her coat. Where I would expect sadness and perhaps relief that the funeral is over I see a kind of wild hopefulness that makes me frightened for her.

Chapter 2

The wild hopefulness isn't a hysterical reaction. It continues. The moment we are all back, Izzy hurries up to her room.

Any death has its energy rhythms. The moment the death happens, you have people to tell and a funeral to plan. Your life is governed by lists. For days afterwards there are the condolence cards and letters. But when the funeral is over all that activity is replaced by silence.

In contrast to Izzy I sense my siblings are listless. The funeral is over. We've now done everything we came to do and I can sense an itch to get back to normal lives. My siblings have agreed to stay the night, but I know they are already regretting that decision. They decided to stay for Izzy's sake, recognising, in a rare moment of thinking about someone else, that she might feel particularly low after the funeral and need her family round her. But, if they are listless, Izzy is re-energised. If my siblings want to go, it soon becomes clear to me that Izzy has something to get on with and she wants them gone.

As soon as we get back to the house I busy myself. I light the fire which I laid this morning. Then I make tea. Julia and James choose and open a bottle of wine. Danny has gone for a run. I put cups and saucers on one tray, wine glasses and peanuts on another, and carry them through. Izzy is back down and working fast. She has already laid a table in the dining room and is bringing out the salad, cold meat and cheese she's got ready on big serving plates. She stands looking at the table, quickly checking it over, then dives into the fridge for dressings and pickles. When all that is done the energy seems to drain out of her and there's that same faraway look in her eyes that I noticed at the funeral.

Our politeness stretches. We eat. We drink. We watch

the news. They talk about Dad, sharing memories. Danny even congratulates Julia on her address. I find I am enjoying myself. I am being acknowledged. The incident in the church is forgotten. Danny refills my wine glass and I smile at him. He smiles back.

Then, quite soon after the end of the meal, Izzy announces she is going to bed and I have a decision to make. I would usually go too, leaving the others, but there are no bad vibes, which is rare, so I decide to stay up. My wine glass isn't empty and I carry it over to the fire and sit on the floor as I used to when I was a child. I want to be part of this family circle again. Now Dad is dead I wonder if that might be possible. I don't hold my breath.

But the moment Mum goes upstairs the mood in the room changes. James begins it. 'Quite a performance that, Sis,' he says to Julia. 'Bravo. You'd make a politician.'

James is his mother's favourite. She has always indulged him, much to Dad's disgust. His suit is a case in point. I'd put money on the fact that Izzy paid for it. I wonder if he is thinking he can now take control through his only surviving parent, push Julia to one side.

She is sitting in what was Dad's chair, a glass of white wine in her right hand. Her eyes are questioning. She is checking if the compliment might be real. She decides it isn't. Her mouth forms a reply, but then she doesn't say it. Instead she takes another sip. There are traces of lipstick on her wine glass. She must feel the day has gone alright. Perhaps the wine has mellowed her.

James is surprised. His chubby right hand pushes his hair to one side so you can see his moustache and beard. There is something cruel about his face when viewed from the side. It is partly the contrast between the pale skin and the dark hair, but he also has a sneer which never used to be there.

'And you are sitting in Dad's chair...' James lets the sentence hang, then completes it '. . . with his ashes not yet cool enough to collect and bottle.'

'It's a chair,' Julia says, instantly forgetting any choice she made to stay aloof. 'It's close to the fire. It has a high back. You bottle plums. Ashes are placed in an urn.'

'His chair.' James replies at once. 'If I remember rightly he hates. . .hated anyone sitting in his chair.' James says this softly as if he is musing, talking to himself, taking both sides of the conversation. 'Of course, you'll say it doesn't matter. A ghost can't occupy a chair. He's no longer here to object. I just thought. . .' He drifts off into silence, examining the bottom of his whisky glass, which is nearly empty and reflects the fire.

'Thought what?'

I knew Julia wouldn't be able to leave it alone.

'Thought, Sis, that you might have waited, just for a day or two.' He says it with some force, then smiles at her. The smile is insincere and childish.

I notice the wine and whisky glasses are nearly empty. I get up and walk across to the table where I pick up both bottles and then turn. James is further away, but the whisky bottle is in my right hand, and as I am right handed I go to him first. I part fill his glass but he wants more. He taps my elbow and this time I fill it nearly to the brim. 'Thanks, Leah.' The words are whispered but that's what he says.

I turn towards Julia and lift the wine bottle. She shakes her head. She seems annoyed and then I realise that she expected to be served first, as Dad always was. I offer the wine bottle again. This time she speaks.

'No.'

'Manners Sis,' says James. 'If you are going to sit in that chair you'll have to . . .'

It's what James does. He needles.

'Have to what?'

Julia's manner has changed. She is sitting upright now, fully alert, and I know that she's feeling threatened. She's had a good day so far. She's in Dad's chair. Her feet are already into his shoes and she doesn't want to be dislodged.

'Be as clever as he was,' James pronounces.

I find I am shivering. I know the pattern. They will hammer away at each other and then they will unite and turn on me. I finish my wine. I get up to go. It's Danny who stops me.

'Another glass please, Leah, 'he asks. 'I think I can afford that. I've been for a run. Mind you, I'll have to work it off tomorrow.'

Because he asked me, because he used my name, I get the bottle. I fill his glass and then I surprise myself by filling my own. I offer the bottle to Julia but she shakes her head, and with a full wine glass I have no option but to sit back down. I suspect this is a mistake, but I can't resist kindness, however slight. I take a sip, move a fraction further back away from the fire and into the shadows. We all settle again.

'And being as clever as he was may challenge even you, Sis.'

Julia writhes. 'Is that what you think?'

'Actually, it's what he thought.'

And suddenly, after the wine interlude, we have reached a new level of internecine struggle with Dad's words as weapons, each now tipped with a nuclear warhead because he's no longer with us and his words can never be gainsaid. They will always be his final opinions.

'And do you want to know what he thought about you?' Julia's challenge.

'Only a mild interest, Sis. And anyway, I'm not sure I'd trust your memory. You're not exactly renowned for listening to other people.'

'Listen to yourself,' Julia spits out. 'Just listen.'

'I do. It's the only way I can get a half decent conversation.' He takes a slug of whisky, emptying half the glass. Then he throws his head back and turns to face his sister.

'If you want to take his place, okay, go for it, but don't expect us to pretend it isn't happening.'

There is silence and I find I am breathing again. That

sentence sounded like a conclusion, even a throwing in of the towel.

I take another sip and wait. I know James.

'Okay, Sis, what did he say about me, just out of interest and to keep the conversation going?'

Julia is backing down too. She doesn't want to use what she knows. She hesitates. 'Go on,' James says.

I understand what he's doing. Now it has been hinted at, it has to be said. Only if it is said can it be neutralised. Until it is spoken Julia will have her weapon.

I want to tell her not to say it. I want to stop her but I don't talk. James is right. She isn't clever enough, but she is determined.

Julia clears her throat. 'He once told me that the trouble with James is that his intelligence is unattached.' She smiles when she's said this which is another mistake. Her insincere smile is a batting back of his.

And I see that James is deeply hurt by the remark, that he would rather Julia had stamped with her heels on his foot or slashed at him with a knife. He looks crushed. He has withdrawn his face inside its curtain of hair. His hurt is so naked I wonder if this is his own judgement on himself and whether he is often unhappy.

Danny suddenly lurches into the conversation. 'Why are we?' he asks.

Julia and James turn to face him, each irritated that someone else has entered what was their arena, gone off on a tangent.

'Why are we what?'

'All of us, unattached?'

Julia says, 'At least I have been married once. At least someone asked me and we stuck it out together for just under nine years.'

James rallies. 'I've had partners, quite a number. You've not met the latest. Her name's Roz.'

'How many years younger is she?'

'Several, I don't exactly know.' James doesn't want to go there and Julia, having made her point, leaves it alone.

'How about you, Danny Boy?' James asks.

'I've been in love.'

'With yourself or someone else?' Julia is out to prove she can be both clever and incisive.

'Look at you all,' Danny says. 'James is getting positively fat. You, Julia, are not yet forty but beginning to stoop, and your muscle tone looks as if it needs ratcheting upwards. If I was you sister, I wouldn't leave it too long. As for Leah, she slouches and takes no care of her hair. She probably mistakes skinniness for fitness and they aren't the same thing at all.'

Their eyes suddenly swivel in my direction. I look down at my wine. When James begins his reply I glance up again. No one is looking at me any more. They never do for very long.

'So answer your own question, Danny Boy. If you are such a wonderful specimen of pectoral perfection, why aren't women flocking round you, or do you beat them off with your own narcissism?'

'Just not interested.'

He's not in the least hurt by what has just been said. It's a funny thing with Danny. He has a natural resistance to being got at. It's a kind of immunity, and I wonder again how two parents can have four children and the genes be so mixed that each child turns out differently. Dad's drive and ambition went to Julia, bypassed James completely, and mutated into a search for physical perfection in Danny. Izzy's passivity took the limelight in James and was eliminated from Julia. The moment I have thought this I wonder if what I've said is true. You see, I don't think we know our mother very well. She's always lived in Dad's shadow. There is, I suspect, a fun-loving side to her nature which attracted her to him but which she had to suppress when we came along. I suspect she needs someone to love who will love her back. I suspect, but I don't know. Dad's moods rang through the house. Izzy always internalised her feelings. For all his anger I wonder if he was cold inside and I don't think she is. I'm not sure if he really loved her or even if he could really love anyone. Is that why Julia stayed dry eyed today? Is Danny really like him in that way? Is that why, as far as I know, he's never had a relationship?

I look round at my siblings. Only Julia earns a decent salary. Danny is a fitness coach. James is an innovations consultant. I still live at home. We can be as we are because Dad was rich. He bought this house. He owned the company. We don't like each other very much but it will soon be Christmas and we will all be back. We will be together on Christmas Day. If Dad had been poor, would we bother to keep in touch? Is money the best family glue and when the money has been distributed will we stay as close? They don't know how much he was worth or how he left it. James probably needs to know most urgently. He doesn't do much work and he has a lifestyle to support.

I look at Julia. She is an executor. She's read Dad's will and knows who will get what. She is sitting there smug in the knowledge. The energy is flagging in the room but she wants to play her master card to cement her position.

'Ahem.' She clears her throat again, waits for their attention. 'In my role as executor I do actually need to consult you all. I do need to know if any of you has an interest in running the company now Dad is no longer able to.'

She looks round. I do too. No one nods. No one volunteers. No one looks at me.

'Nor do I. Far too much hassle,' Julia pronounces. For the second time today she has their attention. 'In that case I suggest we sell it, employ the right people to get us the best possible price. Agreed?'

Has she asked Izzy, I wonder. Has anyone thought of asking our mother? Those who are often overlooked need to support each other.

They nod. I see James light up. He has found a way to get

at the knowledge he needs.

'Excellent thought, Sis. But shouldn't we do as they do in auctions and put a reserve price on the asset we are about to sell?'

Julia reaches down to her bag, snaps it open and takes out a notebook. 'Dad gave me the figure. You need to understand that although he owned the company there are a number of bank loans involved. Expansion is always expensive. There will, of course, be capital gains tax and inheritance tax, unless Mum survives for seven years.' She pauses, enjoying herself. 'And, before I release the figure, you also need to know that the will has a small number of significant bequests, so not all of his fortune will eventually come to us.'

I've only been half listening up to that point. Money of itself doesn't interest me but I sense the rising tension in the room. I hear the oak beams move in and listen, the window panes tremble. The tiles on the roof are suddenly glad of the hard frost which has pinned them silent in this gusting wind so they can hear every word. We are all involved.

Julia has the floor. 'Now, I won't be held to this figure. It is a ball-park number, a best guess at most but, if I can manage the sale as I expect to, you should each receive around three and a half million in due course.'

I see the satisfaction on their faces. It's reflected in the way they finish their drinks. I get up. It's time to go to bed.

***

Pronouns not verbs are often the most important part of every sentence. I know that. I have seen the will. I found a copy in Dad's desk. I have read the notebook with the valuations. I found that too. I have therefore seen the figures. I know that Julia is lying and I wonder what she is about.

You. A small, all inclusive, three letter word. She means Julia, James and Danny. Not me. His disappointment was so acute that Dad wrote me out of the will. I am to receive only a life-time allowance and the house.

You. All the money goes to Izzy in her lifetime. Izzy is only sixty-seven. She has probably got a lot of living in front of her. They will be kept waiting. Oh, and the figure is wrong. Gary's own calculation was that his estate will be worth just under £20 million after tax. Even I can divide twenty by three. They stand to inherit well over £6 million each. Why has she told them the much lower number?

The others help themselves to another drink. Julia has her place as head of the family for as long as she can draw out the financial settlement and for as long as Izzy will do as she says. I wonder about that as I leave the room. No one wishes me goodnight.

I climb the stairs alone and notice Izzy's light is still on. It's some time since she went to bed. Has she left it on and is she fast asleep? If so I could go in and check. I walk towards the door, have my hand on the handle. It's then I hear noises: rustlings, a drawer being closed, the sound paper makes when it is shuffled. Then footsteps and something being dragged across the floor. She isn't in bed. I listen for a while. The noises are continuous. I step quietly away from the door, go part way back down the stairs and then come up again, making as much noise as I reasonably can. By the time I have reached the landing Izzy's light has been turned off. Whatever she is up to she doesn't want us to know. I am suddenly alarmed.

Chapter 3

It's about 10.30am on December 10th. I am standing outside my home, waving goodbye to Julia who is the last of my siblings to leave. It's wonderfully cold and the garden is covered in snow. I wonder whether to wrap up and go for a walk. It won't get dark until 3.30pm. I can walk to the town across the fields, look in shop windows, visit the bookshop and then come back along the old railway line. I often walk by myself and think nothing of it. Immediately the thought comes into my head I decide not to. They have gone. My father is dead. I want to listen to the house. I want to know what it's thinking. I want to know why Izzy came to life the moment her husband vanished behind the curtain at the crematorium.

Our house is Arts and Crafts. I love it and am thrilled that one day it will be mine. It's made for living both inside and out. It looks especially wonderful in this crisp winter light. The snow has melted from the steepest part of the roofs, revealing the soft orange reds of the tiles. Where the angle of the roof slackens the snow is still thickly piled. I follow the snow/tile line with my eyes. It's almost exactly horizontal as if the architect designed that too. A mistle thrush which has been feasting on the crab-apples is perched on the gutter, its flecked and speckled breast stands out against the snow. I have exceptional eyesight and it thrills me to see it there. Below the thrush the low sun picks out the brickwork, highlighting the way it caps the windows and marks their indentations.

It's very quiet now my siblings have all gone. Behind me a large blob of snow escapes from the holly and slides to join the snow on the ground. The two come together like a wet kiss.

I shiver and walk back to the front door silently. At a certain point where the sun has already reached the ground my feet crunch through to the gravel. That noise accompanies me until I step over the threshold.

Here I stop and listen. I want to know what the house is feeling. The perfume of wood-smoke from the fire mingles with the scent of wax polish. The grandfather clock's unhurried travel continues to give a pulse to the house. I step into the hall in time to its beat. The sun has followed me in. It spills across the black and white tiled floor, is reflected from the wooden panels. When I close the door the colours of the stained glass pattern the floor. I hear new words in the clock's relentlessness. It is saying, 'not here, not here, not here.'

I walk over to the jardinière. Its wreath of oak leaves circle the bowl and never repeat. Two silver acorns are followed by three, then one on its own. Each copper leaf is different. I flick the rim carefully with my nail and hear the ring and its echo. I listen but the sound doesn't come back purely. The discordant note is still there. When I last made this test, did I have the door open or closed? I don't remember. As soon as I have closed the door I try again, but with the same result.

I expect to find Izzy in the sitting room but she isn't there. It doesn't feel as if she has been there either. The room has the same notes as last night. My siblings drank more after I went to bed. No one cleared up. The glasses and bottles are still on the table. Even though I am looking for Izzy I collect them on a tray and carry it through to the kitchen. I leave the glasses by the sink and go into the scullery where I put the bottles in the green container for recycling.

I check Dad's study. I look into the dining room. There are no other possibilities. Izzy will be in her bedroom. I climb the stairs but I can't go straight in there. We have this unwritten, unspoken rule. Our own rooms are sacrosanct. If we need each other we have to knock. I stand outside the door and listen. I hear the same noises as I heard last night. She is opening something and I know at once that she doesn't want me to know what she is doing. It's as if she is aware that I might be listening. Her movements seem stealthy. What she is opening isn't a drawer. I hear it fall back into place, as if it has a lid. I hear a minute click that isn't a drawer closing. It sounds more like a lock or a catch. Then there is the noise of something being pushed back along the carpet.

Part of me thinks, 'She is my mother, of course she will have papers to deal with. She must be the other executor. She probably has a copy of the will. There is nothing unusual happening here so I can still knock.'

I reach up and do so. The room goes very still. Then I hear her say, 'Wait.' Immediately I know the house was right. Something is happening that has made it uneasy. The source of its unrest is here in this room. It has lain here for a long time and has just been disturbed.

She says, 'Wait,' and I am waiting. Sun through the stained glass window patterns her door. I see red and yellow smudges on the oak, then purple and green. She is taking her time. I think better of it and go away. Before I am at the bottom of the stairs I hear the door open. I expect to be called back but no one calls me and I hear the door being closed again.

I make the coffee anyway. The jar is empty so I open a new bag of ground Italian, pour it into the jar and transfer three heaped spoons into the cafetière. That aroma fills the kitchen. The smell has always been the best thing about coffee. I open the kitchen door. I want the scent to fill the house, to mingle with the savour of wood-smoke. Coffee and fires on a winter's day, the sky clear and a faint grey-blue, blackbirds stripping the last fruit from the crab apple tree, what could be better? The kettle boils and I fill the cafetière. The scent again assails the kitchen, creeps up the stairs. I stir it and balance the cap back on, settling the plunger just at the liquid's brim. I hear a door open.

I find a packet of custard creams and put them on a plate, get two plain white mugs from the cupboard and the milk jug from the fridge. Then I sit and wait. There are footsteps on the stairs.

Izzy walks in. 'I thought I smelt coffee.'

I smile. I love my mother but I no longer think of her as a mother. She has become my friend. She has become Izzy. That happened when the others left home. Dad was at work so Izzy and I rattled round this house together. Then Dad went to hospital and came home to die. Now we are back together and no one else will be coming home except for brief visits.

I plunge the cafetière. I pour a mug for Izzy and one for me, push over the custard creams and watch her take one.

What is it with biscuits and people? What is this idiolect of biscuit eating? Izzy usually nips at the top of the custard cream to dislodge the biscuit top. If it doesn't come off cleanly she nibbles round the edges in order I suppose to maximise the ratio of filling to the bottom biscuit in the final mouthfuls. It needs concentration.

Today she is distracted. There is no doubt about that. She bites off a whole corner. Her eyes look towards the window but, as in the church yesterday, they see nothing. The blackbirds are squabbling in the crab apple tree, but Izzy is looking beyond them. I am sitting close to her. I reach over and touch her hand. Normally I wouldn't allow myself to do this but after the funeral I feel I can. Her skin is cool.

She starts, pats the top of my fingers and then puts both her hands round her mug. Whatever searching she was doing upstairs has made her hands cold. Her quarter eaten biscuit is abandoned on the table.

'I was miles away,' she says.

I'm here if she wants to talk.

Her eyes drift out of the window. She's holding the mug in front of her face. Her thumb and the first finger of her right hand are squeezing the handle, the other fingers are folded over. Her left hand is round the mug.

And the index finger of her left hand is tapping on the rim. Two beats then she stops, a pause, then two more beats. Repeated, then again. She is saying something too, saying something to herself. Her lips silently form a word that goes in time with the tapping. I can't catch it. I think it begins with p.

It's as if she is praying. I am fascinated. I have never seen her like this. She sips the coffee, taps and speaks a two syllable word. Normally she would sit and chat, totally relaxed. Today she is anything but. I have never seen her so intense. Is that what the house is reacting to?

Suddenly she shakes her head, remembers I am sitting there.

'I think it went alright yesterday,' she says. 'James wore a suit. I managed to arrange that. I thought Danny looked very smart, and Julia . . . enjoyed her father's funeral. They are, were so alike, those two.'

She drifts on and it is almost but not quite what it was before Dad came home and died. She mentions the names of those who were there and those who didn't come. She suddenly notices her abandoned biscuit, looks at it when she picks it up as if she is surprised by its shape, then goes back to eating it as she normally would, neatly lifting off the top. She talks about everything except what's on her mind. I am tempted to ask a question but of course I don't. It would take much more than that to make me interrupt the flow of my continued silence.

It is the other thing that alarms me. It's the kind of electricity she is giving off. It's as if Dad's death has brought her back to life. We are, to all intents and purposes, exactly as we were a couple of days ago before the family came, but we are also utterly changed. The more she tries to impersonate her normal self, the more uneasy I become.

My mother, my best friend. Izzy the calm, Izzy the passive, Izzy the accepting, is now needy and full of longing. She has a new hope and it's hurting. I feel protective towards her, but if I am to protect her I need to find out what it is that she isn't telling me. When she goes back upstairs, taking her cup with her, I begin to make plans.

***

Izzy is going out. I see her coming down the stairs. She has her hat and coat on, picks up the car keys. Normally she would come and tell me where she is going and when she will be back. Today she doesn't. I hear the car start, snow compacting, gravel crunching, acceleration out onto the road, then silence.

I have my chance. I tell myself that Izzy is in a vulnerable state, that she needs protecting. I repeat my idea that if I don't protect her nobody else will. It is probably nothing to worry about, but her going out like that has increased my worry. How can we be normal together until I know?

I leave the kitchen and climb the stairs. I'm not certain I will go into her room. I tell myself I might go up to my own bedroom, use the chance of her being out to wrap the presents I have already bought her for Christmas. But, of course, there is no need. Our bedrooms are sacrosanct. Izzy would never just walk into mine. I can wrap presents any time.

My hand is on the handle of her door. It's as if the whole house is holding its breath. I turn the knob. The door opens a fraction. It isn't too late to stop this breach of etiquette, to close the door and go away, but I don't. I'm inside the room and listening hard. How do I know where she has gone? How do I know how long she will be? If she should catch me?

But I may not get a better chance.

Everywhere I look there are signs of a search. The drawers have all been opened. The wardrobe doors have been hurriedly closed. I know that because the edge of a green skirt has been caught in the doors. Even the carpet has tracks in it, as if something has been pulled out from underneath the bed. I remember the noises I heard. I look under the bed and there is a large wooden box I have never seen before. It has a lid. It hasn't been pushed very far back so I can easily reach its handle. I pull it out. The dust round the clasp has been disturbed. What Izzy was looking for this morning and what she quickly put back is in this box. But it's locked. I think of the other noise I heard, that faint click. It must have been the padlock being snapped shut.

I look around. If I know her the key will be somewhere close by, in a small pot or just lying in a set place.

In the next few minutes I find lots of keys but none of them is small enough. I'm getting frightened. The more I search the more traces I will leave. The worst possible outcome is that I fail to find what is in the box and Izzy knows that I have been in her room. Reluctantly I push the box back along the same tracks in the carpet, leave it exactly where it was under the bed, then walk out of her room and close the door behind me.

I don't wait for her to come back. It is still a lovely day. I put my coat and woolly hat on, pull on lined boots with grips because it might be muddy where the snow has melted. I leave a note on the kitchen table, then I am outside and thinking furiously.

***

I walk fast. In winter there is always that initial stepping outside moment when the cold threatens you. I like to be too cold when I set off because I know I won't be too warm half an hour later.

What can she be looking for? That box is locked. Has the box always been there? Was it there when she shared the bed with Dad? Did he know the contents?

I think I can answer that. He didn't. The chronology is all wrong. Why this new alertness in her, this scarcely disguised longing just after the funeral? No, his death has let her think other thoughts, given her permission to explore long-hidden feelings. My best guess is that Dad didn't know whatever's hidden in that box.

There are still berries on the hawthorn. As I cross the first stile a hundred plus fieldfares fleer up from the thick hedge and fly along in front of me, the sun glinting on their pale bodies and the underneath of their wings. As they settle again they disappear from view.

I watch Poirot. I read Sherlock Holmes. I want to be Miss Marple. There has been no murder, but there is a secret, something from Izzy's past. The anger is gone from the house and it is now full of longing. What used to fill our lives has disappeared. Was the longing always there, just masked by the anger? I don't know and I need to.

The key to the box must be in Izzy's handbag. I have invaded her room and I hated the experience. I can't invade her handbag, can I?

***

I have reached the town now. I am heading for the bookshop. We still have one, an independent new and second-hand shop run by Martin. He spends money on the new half of the store but his heart is with the second-hand books. The shop is a model of his schizophrenic personality. The new section is smartly furnished and often freshly painted. Here the shelves are horizontal and they manage somehow to dominate the books. In the second-hand section the books bend the shelves and lie in piles in every corner. The stairs must once have been newly carpeted, but the carpet has worn away in places and the stair rungs creak.

I like the feel of this place. It's dusty, unkempt. On one windowsill behind the biography section are two old kettles and a cracked mug. Time has made them sticky and they are now coated with dust almost as if they are growing fur. There is no jardinière to flick but if there were I'm sure the notes would be muffled but chordant, if there is such a word. The place is harmonious, at ease with itself.

Martin is dressed rather like I am. He has curly, tufted

hair that he does nothing with. He wears the same clothes summer and winter. It's always cold in his shop. There is no heating to dry out and spoil the second-hand books. He wears a succession of faded jumpers and sits on a kind of throne surrounded by piles of books he has yet to catalogue. He watches the smart half of the shop through CCTV.

We know each other. We are occasional lovers. He has a flat above the shop. Sometimes he will close the shop early for lunch and we will go to his flat. Have you noticed that words can easily get in the way of sex? He hardly talks and I don't talk at all. If he fancies me he will put a hand on my shoulder. If I want him I do the same. Just occasionally he will follow me into the dark recesses of the second-hand shop and we will kiss wordlessly, clutching at each other, breathless, before we go upstairs. Only once did we make love there and then, reaching for each other in the most needy way possible. I think that was his favourite time. He'd somehow joined me to his books, united his passions.

I am walking to his shop. The pavements are treacherous because they are partly iced. I pick my way carefully. The cold is making me feel randy. I look at my watch. It is nearly lunchtime. But then I see Izzy's car. She has parked in the high street and must be somewhere nearby. It's about a forty-five minutes' walk from house to town and then I need to add on the time I spent in her bedroom. She has been here for at least an hour and I see that there are twenty minutes left on the parking ticket on her windscreen. For some reason I don't want her to see me, so I head quickly to the bookshop. Martin smiles as I come in, looks at his watch and taps me on the shoulder. My body wants him, but I smile and signal twenty with both hands. He looks disappointed at having to wait, and I know it won't be as good. The rush is part of the attraction. He is puzzled when I position myself at the window, hidden behind his most expensive second-hand books, but from here I can watch the car and much of the rest of the street. Of course Izzy may be longer than twenty minutes, but she hates getting a parking ticket.

Time passes. With five minutes to go I see her walking quickly towards her car. Has she come out of that green door? If so I don't know what is behind it. Izzy gets in the car and drives away. While I am trying to make out where she could possibly have been I see her coming back to a different spot where she parks up again. It's against the rules but must be worth the risk. When she's bought another ticket and placed it on her dashboard she goes back down the street and in through the same green door. My twenty minutes are up. Martin taps me on the shoulder and puts the 'closed for lunch' sign in the window. I am both needy and needed.

***

When I leave the bookshop Izzy's car has gone. I walk along the street and find the green door. It isn't a dentist or a beauty parlour or even a branch of the Citizens' Advice Bureau. It isn't an office or a shop. It seems like a normal house. It has a number on the door and a bell. There are lace curtains at the window.

I am thirsty and just opposite is a café, a branch of Costa. The window seat is empty. I dive across the road and put my coat on the chair to bag the table before I join the queue, which is mercifully short. I keep an eye on the house opposite as I inch forward, picking up a packet of stollen bites on the way. When it is my turn to be served I show the girl my mobile phone. I have the only mobile phone in the world unconnected to any network. I don't talk into it. I talk with it. The screen has two words: small cappuccino. I can say yes to chocolate sprinkles with a nod. No one goes in through the green door and no one comes out. With my drink in front of me I have time to concentrate. Other houses in the row are already sporting Christmas decorations. This one isn't.

I sit there for a long time making the coffee last but nothing happens opposite. I wonder whether to ask the waitress, using Notes, but it's too complicated. I take a last look at the house. It is as anonymous as it is possible to be.

Walking back along the railway line I interrogate my feelings. I am still warm from the sex. I am afraid for Izzy. I wonder at my siblings, at their self-obsession. Weirdly I find that I am also enjoying this little mystery.

A man is walking towards me down the railway line. This is a particularly narrow section and dark because it is overhung with branches. I begin to feel in danger. He's tall, about 6ft 2in; he has thick white hair and must be in his late sixties, about Izzy's age. He looks harmless but he has sunken eyes. He's walking quickly. His rucksack is reassuring. He gives me an odd look as he passes. It is a quick, acute, wordless appraisal. Suddenly I want to ask him what he thinks of what he's seen but of course I don't and I wonder why I thought that. I carry on walking. He is already a distance away.

***

It's dark when I get home. We are close to the shortest day. Izzy must have been back for some time. Her coat is hanging in the hall. She has lit the fire in the lounge and is asleep in front of it. The fire is already dying down so I put more logs on and rattle a little coal over them. I expect her to wake, either with the noise or with the slight temperature change, then I will make a pot of tea. But she goes on sleeping. She must be exhausted. Her mouth is open and she is snoring slightly. Her handbag is a little way from her and in the handbag will be the key to the box under her bed.

Now is as good a time as any. She is fast asleep and I can easily pick up the bag and take it away. I won't even need to put it back here. I can leave it near her coat in the hall which is where it would normally be. Slipping the key back into the bag will be much easier than extracting it. There is very little danger, I tell myself.

I am about to lean in towards the handbag when my silent preoccupation does what my noisy banking up of the fire failed to do. It wakes her.

Izzy has been deeply asleep. She comes to and is groggy. I'm certain that she suspects nothing.

'You're back,' she says, 'and I have something to tell you.'

Adrenalin mingled with disappointment pumps through me. I'm convinced she is about to tell me her secret but I am also disappointed that I won't have the satisfaction of discovering it for myself.

I hold one flat hand vertically and balance the other at right angles making a T sign.

Izzy shakes her head. 'No, open a bottle of white wine. Bring two glasses.'

She is both eager and fearful. When I return I have the sense that secrecy is no longer an option, that the words are threatening to speak themselves if she doesn't speak them. That is why I present the bottle to her as if I were a waitress in a restaurant, trying to make her laugh.

All I get is a half-smile and a 'Yes, fine.' I undo the screw cap and pour two glasses. I hand one to her, take mine to the chair on the other side of the fire and get ready to listen.

Now she has got to this point I can see that she doesn't know how to begin. I know I am leaning forward so I sit back, stretch out my legs to the fire, enjoy a sip of wine.

She begins speaking slowly. 'I have been trying to find the right words, but I don't suppose the words matter very much, Leah. There is something I want to tell you about me, something even you won't have guessed.'

I note that 'even you'. She's no fool. She knows me as well as anyone.

'I feel I can tell you because you will keep this to yourself. I don't mean to be cruel when I say that. I mean I can trust you and, after this morning, I must tell you.'

The slight emphasis is on the last word, you. I realise she has already told someone else. I think again of the house with the green door. Her face is down. She holds her wine glass by the stem and seems to be studying the fire through it. My mum, my friend Izzy is still beautiful. She's more than half way through her sixties but she carries the younger woman she once was in her features. Her face is lined but the tiny folds do nothing to detract from the symmetry of her features. She seems very calm now.

'When I was nineteen I fell in love. It was 1968. It was easy to find love then. The world seemed newborn and hopeful.'

Suddenly I guess what she is going to tell me. I've done the calculation. She married Dad in 1972, the year Julia was born.

'I won't tell you his name. We were young with all the eagerness and none of the constraint that comes later.' She's talking slowly as if she's remembering, but if I am right she will never have forgotten. 'Soon I found I was pregnant and he,' she paused, 'abandoned me.'

Two words, a world of feeling, a commonality of experience, every woman's fear.

'I'd thought the man I loved was so grown-up but he wasn't at all. He was still a little boy, a musician who sang of things he never really believed in, things like peace and love and Aquarius. Believing him was my mistake, my failure.'

I have another sibling, a half brother or sister. Do I mind which?

'My parents were appalled. It was your grandfather really. He insisted on adoption. I was sent away to have the baby.'

Pain floods her with this memory. Izzy wasn't alone. I know there were hundreds of others. I have heard such stories. You think you are worldly, that you know, but Izzy is crying now and it's as if I'm hearing this kind of story for the first time. I'm also wondering about my grandfather, the one we never met.

'There we were, a few girls with similar tales to tell, confined in that home and waiting to be delivered of our shame. We talked of freedom, of being able to live our lives again, of the hope they would find a good home for each of our children. We cheered ourselves up by talking to each other of the kind of future our children would now have, the kind of future we could never give them.'

'He fought against me when the time came. I was in labour for thirty hours. The pain went on and on.'

A boy then. I have a third brother. I see a tear drop into the wine, slightly discolouring the surface. I want to reach out and touch Izzy, wrap my arm round her. I put my wine glass down on the hearth and start to get up but she waves me back into my chair.

'He was so beautiful. They let me hold him and I felt bewildered. He wasn't shame. He was life. He was mine. I was taken over by this awful love. Every time I fed him, every time I changed him, every time I rocked him when he cried I hoped they wouldn't be able to place him, but they did.'

She's back there, reliving the moment. How many times has she done this, I wonder. Does she wake in the night? Did she lie next to Dad thinking of her secret son?

It's as if she knows what I might be thinking.

'I want you to understand that a bit of me died the day I handed him over. I loved your Dad and I love you, my children. You have to believe that, but I love you with what was left over. I just hope it was enough.'

She looks at me then, raises her eyes and looks straight at me. If I talked I would have to say something. Being mute I can only nod and smile. I nod vigorously. Her need is so great I can't deny her that.

'I went back home. I abandoned my parents, got a grant and went to university, met your father, had four children. Enough, you would think, to fill any gap.'

She smiles weakly. I realise I have always known that there

was sadness about her. I used to think she was passive, let my Dad walk all over her, but perhaps she was only unhappy.

'I could never tell your father. I've kept this secret for forty years. I've felt guilty for all that time. I need to stop feeling like that. That is why today I have started a process to find him.'

The visit to the house with the green door. Clearly, giving information and explaining details took longer than she had allowed on the parking ticket.

I get up then, go over and hug her. I put my cheek against hers, feel the wetness on her face. I lift her wine glass, urging her to drink.

You don't need words to lie.

'And if I find him will he want to meet me? If he does do you think he will be able to forgive me?'

I don't say anything. I have no answer to her questions.

'I want to tell him I am sorry. I want to tell him why, explain that I didn't have any choice.'

I hold her tightly, hug her to me. She is rocking with pain. I find her wine glass again and urge her to take another drink.

***

I never knew my grandparents. Or did I? A memory comes back. Danny in the pram, me holding onto the side, Julia and James out in front. We went to a house behind a high hedge, knocked on a red door and heard a dog barking. We were all silent, I remember, all tense, especially Mum. A woman came to the door and asked if she could help, then suddenly recognised Izzy, called her Isabel, said something about how she couldn't, she really couldn't. Julia was holding James's hand. I talked in those days so I stepped forward and announced that I was Leah Mary Goulden. The woman squatted down and put out her arms. I remember I looked at Mum and lurched forward into the embrace.

Then a voice from inside the house. 'What's happening,

Norma? Who is it?'

Did Mum say, 'Hello Dad,' as the man walked towards the door? Have I made that up?

The woman who was hugging me let me go. She turned to the man who must have been my grandfather and said, 'Just this once. Just once. It can't do any harm.'

Then the door was closed on us. We were left outside. Mum was herding us towards the road. A woman was wailing from behind the door and a man was shouting, 'Do you want to be cast out?'

Were they Izzy's parents, my grandparents? Is it a memory or a dream?

***

Izzy is pulling herself together. I feel I can let go.

As soon as I release her she dives into her bag and takes out a photograph, looks at it again and then hands it to me. Her look is racked with hope.

I take the black and white picture. It's pristine. Is this what she was looking for last night? Was it in the box under the bed? It shows a little boy, rather fat of face. He's less than one year old I'd guess and is wearing an old fashioned nappy, the cloth kind you wash and re-use. The boy is standing up, holding onto a chair with one hand, balancing himself. The nappy is bulky. It makes him seem heavy hipped. I look from her to him, tracing a link, fail to find one.

'He doesn't look like me. I know that.'

If I spoke I'd ask for details. I want to know more, but that can wait. She will tell me, not because I ask, but because she needs to. Asking is for the impatient.

I smile. The baby in the photo is smiling. His chubby face is grinning up at whoever is taking the photo. In his other hand he holds a rabbit toy. He has it grasped round the neck which looks uncomfortable for the rabbit, but it is clearly the thinnest part of it and so the easiest hold. The rabbit is a very simple toy, possibly home-made, just a stuffed shape with ears as big as its legs. The eyes, nose and mouth are sewn on. The inside of the ears is lined with thin checked material. Part of the check is white.

'It's the only photo I have,' Izzy says.

I mouth, 'He's beautiful,' and give the photo back.

'Thank you,' she is saying. 'Leah, thank you so much.'

I leave her sitting with a nearly empty wine glass in one hand. I've put another log on the fire. It's quite dark outside so I close the curtain behind the front door and put the lamp on in the hall. I don't ping the bowl because I know what the echo would tell me. For Izzy's sake I want her to find my older brother. I feel generous in even thinking that because I'm not sure, even at the great age of thirty-four, whether we can ever be really unselfish. Can a wife who realises her husband has fallen in love with another woman be happy for him even though she has been made miserable? I am hoping Izzy finds him. I am also hoping she doesn't. One mum, four children is complicated enough. I am also telling myself that if she searches and fails, at least she will have tried and the regret might be lessened. I can't bear to see her this unhappy but I am also afraid what happiness might do to her. Sit out a crisis is the usual advice. Don't move or make sudden changes until you are certain what you want. Is the day after you have buried your husband the best time to start looking for the son you gave away, I wonder.

Then another thought strikes me. Who has Izzy contacted about her lost son? If I wanted to find someone I'd look for them on the internet. I'd trawl through birth records and write letters to adoption agencies. If I was desperate I might employ a private detective. Is that who she was talking to behind the green door and if so, why was there no indication on the door itself? Private detectives need to advertise.

As far as I know Izzy has made no phone call. She has not

written any letters. We live in each other's pockets so I would know if she had. The computer we both use is in Dad's study, but Izzy doesn't like computers. I go there and look up the search history and find nothing unusual.

So why has Izzy gone straight to a green door to begin her search? What does she know that she isn't telling me?

Chapter 4

After Izzy's revelation nothing happens except more snow. It falls for several days and then we are cut off, waiting for the snow ploughs to get through. Only when we run out of milk do I don boots and trudge across the fields. This white embellishment to our landscape is banked against the hedges, so keeping to the paths becomes impossible. In several places I am forced to walk out into the fields, across the spring wheat, in order to skirt drifts that are waist high.

I note redwings perched on the snow banks to peck at rose hips. I spot everywhere the pristine un-melted snow that clings to north facing banks. It's such hard work walking through it, having to lift your legs when you're used to sliding them along. I find myself thinking about my other errand. We got the phone call a few days ago. Normally we would have gone at once but the snow prevented that. Izzy has asked me to go to the undertakers and pick up Dad's ashes. I know I pulled a face, used my hands to ask how big the urn is. She didn't know. She didn't know how heavy either. I would have thought Dad's ashes could wait but Izzy is probably feeling guilty and she wants me to bring him home.

I've warmed up now. It's nice being out. I have to say it's also nice to be away from Izzy's longing which has filled the house. When I last pinged the bowl a filtered echo came back as if it was making its way through a kind of fog. My home feels different. There's an art nouveau vase in one of the big windows. It came with the house and belongs to it. Whoever created it built up the coloured layers: the blue of a landscape, the yellow and white of a rising sun, then blue sky that darkens until you reach a rim of yellow at the very top. Irises are superimposed on these bands of colours, their blue petals overlapping that final yellow line. I've always loved it, found it serene, calming.

Not now. The iris blossoms seem to be straining out of their leaves. In my mind sunrise has become sunset and the yellow at the top is like a falseness, a dream as impossible as heaven, or making a relationship with a child you gave away. Izzy's longing is changing everything, re-setting the norms.

Out here the snow is fresh and very clean. I have the world to myself.

Is it a Martin day? Definitely.

I see he has a customer so I go to the undertakers first.

The ashes come in what they call an urn, but it is in fact a green plastic container. It's about the size and shape of a Roses chocolates jar. It's heavy. They hand it over in a dark plastic bag. As I take it, a little hesitantly, the contents shift and there is a granular sound like dry sand.

Carrying 'Dad' I feel important. It's nearly lunchtime so I go to the bookshop. I can tell that Martin is pleased and surprised to see me. His throne-like pile of books is much reduced and I know that he's had few customers during the snow and has been cataloguing. The shelves are tidier and I can tell how bored he must have been. He locks the door, puts the sign in the window.

I've put the bag down on the shop floor but now I pick it up again. It seems wrong to leave Dad in the shop so I take him with me as I climb the stairs. Martin's eyes widen when he sees me pick up the bag. He has a half-hopeful, intrigued look. Perhaps he thinks I have brought something for lunch. He can't think I am about to dress for sex, can he, that I have been to Ann Summers to give him an early Christmas present?

The flat is cold. I put Dad down in the small kitchen. In the bedroom Martin has switched on the convector heater. We both stand in front of it to feel the warmth on the back of our legs then strip quickly, throwing clothes anywhere, and dive under the duvet. Martin has remade the bed since last time. This isn't the one he sleeps in. The underneath of the duvet is so cold it hits us like a slap, and at first we grab for each other just to keep warm. I feel Martin's pent up need and we are soon conjoined. Then I remember that Dad is next door, just the other side of the wall. I feel like a naughty school girl and wonder what Dad is thinking from inside his plastic jar. Suddenly I'm giggling at the thought. From nowhere I find my body in the wrong kind of spasms. Then it's too late. I'm helpless. I want to say I'm sorry but I can't.

Martin is upset, but later I show him the contents of the bag, unscrew the top of the urn and mime listening so that he understands. He seems satisfied. Ours is an easy relationship. We don't demand very much from each other or put any pressure on each other's emotions. It'll last for as long as it's fun. But today he kisses me goodbye and I realise that sharing my Dad's ashes has subtly changed our relationship.

***

I go to the supermarket with my bag and buy two bottles of milk. Each is two litres. That should last us until the snow is cleared. Two is possibly excessive but one might not be enough. The checkout girl says, 'I see you've already got a bag.'

I nod and wedge a bottle either side of Dad.

It's time to head back. The bag is heavy. Even before I'm out of the town I have to change hands. The awful thing about plastic bags is the way weight sharpens the handles which then dig into you. I know this weight is stopping the circulation in my fingers because when I swap hands I feel the pain of the blood forcing its way back.

I slog my way up the first field, swopping hands frequently. I am now hot but my hands are getting colder because of the weight. I have a rest, blow into both gloves, clap my hands together, then set off again.

I should have brought a rucksack. Then all this weight would be on my shoulders and my hands would be okay. I stop again, take the ashes out of the bag and jam the urn under my arm. Then I pick up the bag with the other hand. For a while it's better but the sheen on the green plastic bottle means it keeps slipping and I'm in danger of dropping Dad.

I stop yet again to think it out. I could cache Dad in the snowdrift, but would we ever find him? I have this image of the family cursing me as they scour the hedge bottom looking for him. I could scatter a little of Dad here and now, just enough to lessen the weight. No one would know, and it can't matter if he isn't all in the same place, can it?

For all practical purposes Dad is already forgotten. Izzy has moved on, almost gladly, and is totally occupied by her long lost son. Julia, James and Danny have been taken over by their daily lives and routines. They don't know how much ashes weigh. The scattering will be just another ritual to please their mum.

I know it is totally irrational but I can't have him separated. I can't scatter part of him here and part somewhere else. He must remain whole.

I put Dad's ashes back in the bag and get everything home by counting steps and having frequent rests. I put the milk in the fridge and place the urn on the oak pedestal in the hall. I smile at the irony.

When Izzy comes downstairs and sees her husband there she doesn't get the joke. Later I see that she has moved him into the lobby, put him with the boots.

***

Every day Izzy waits for the post. She lights the fire in the lounge and sits so she can see the front door. When the post comes she scampers across. I watch from the top of the stairs, see her discard circulars, requests for donations, insurance offers. We no longer trust each other. She doesn't want me to know about her obsession, and I have to be on my guard because I don't want her to see me observing her. This is our new ritual.

Yesterday, when she was sure there was no letter for her, she replaced the circulars where they fell and went upstairs to her room. Today she scoops up the post and finds what she is looking for. The circulars drop from her hand. My heart is pounding. I don't try to guess what she is feeling. I know what I am hoping. Let it be a no. It's like a prayer but it isn't. Let it be a no. Everything about our family depends on this letter.

The sun comes out as she stands there. Colours from the stained glass are on her hair and, when she turns, on her face. At that moment she stops being first and foremost my mother. She is another human tortured by hope.

I keep expecting her to look up, check I'm nowhere around, but she doesn't. Her hands are trembling. I know she is trying to stay calm. She slips a finger into one corner of the envelope and slits the flap, takes out the letter. I see the envelope drop to the floor. I note that the envelope is hand-written.

I know I am intruding, that I shouldn't be watching. This moment belongs to her, but I can't pull myself away. She has the letter open now and the right way up. She scans it, then reads it more slowly. Her face changes. In the light from the stained glass window it is like a benediction. I know it is a yes, that her son has been found. I observe the moment her fear switches from 'I may not find him' to 'he may not forgive me'. As always, when an immense change happens inside us, the physical world ignores it. House, sun, snow remain exactly as they were before this missive arrived.

Izzy reads it a third time, just to make sure.

Now I am filled with foreboding and I wonder if she will show me the letter.

She picks up the envelope and places the rest of the mail as if it has just arrived. I have time to get away from the rail before she heads upstairs. Quietly I go back into my room and close the door. I expect her to call my name but she doesn't.

She goes into her bedroom and stays there.

I leave a decent interval and then go downstairs. I try to keep everything normal. I pick the post up as I do every day. In her hurry Izzy hasn't seen the gas bill. I put that on the hall table and take the rest of the post through to the recycling bin. It is while I am checking each item through before binning it that I find the photograph. It must have fallen out of the envelope when Izzy opened the letter.

I've done nothing wrong, but now I have a dilemma. The letter can't mention the photo or Izzy would have looked for it. I could take it up to her. It must be the one thing she most wants to devour. I could go back to the hall immediately with the rest of the post and put everything back, let her find it or not. I make a mental note to put the gas bill back too.

What if she doesn't look for it? What if she clears the post and doesn't find it and it gets recycled?

If I give it to her she may guess that I have been watching her.

If I keep it how will she recognise him? Oh yes, it must have been sent because a meeting has been set up. This photograph is proof of that. If I give it to her, shrug my shoulders as if this isn't important, she might tell me, show me the letter.

Instead of deciding I find I am studying the photograph. It's passport size which is surprising and there's no discernible background. Wouldn't you send your birth-mother a better shot than this? Doesn't everyone have a favourite photo of themselves, one taken on holiday or at a wedding? Wouldn't you want to send a first photograph to your birth-mother that gives clues about you in the form of the room you're in, the person you're with, or the front of your house? Everyone has a mobile phone, don't they? It's so easy to take and send photos. I want this to go well. I tell myself that perhaps he wanted to reply quickly and this was the first photograph he found.

I think of the baby photograph and try to match it with the adult. It doesn't match, but not all adults look like they did when they were babies. He looks nice this half-brother of mine. He sits very straight. He's wearing a shirt and tie but not a jacket, and he's smiling. I stare at the photograph trying to remember every detail. I'm already on my way back to the hall where reluctantly I let the photo go, put the gas bill on top of it, and then pile up the rest of the post.

I'm pretty certain Izzy hasn't watched me do any of this. Now I must wait.

***

It continues to snow. Izzy tells me nothing. That is surprising. Why did she tell me about him in the first place if she now wants to hide their meeting? I know she found the photograph because she left the rest of the post on the floor. I need to know when and where Izzy will meet her long lost son. Strictly speaking it is none of my business but I want to be there. I feel protective of her and I like the house being hers and mine. I'm sure a meeting has been arranged because Izzy has been shopping, bought new clothes, and booked to have her hair done.

I've made my own preparations. I know what I shall wear by way of a disguise. I've even practised in front of the mirror.

I don't want to miss the reunion, so when Izzy goes to the hairdressers I slip into her room again. Her bag isn't there and I expect the letter is in her bag. But her diary is on the dressing table. I find a circle round 22nd December with the word Costa and 10.30. She's going to meet him in the café opposite the green door on 22nd December, three days before Christmas. The café will be packed. The town will be full of shoppers. I can be there before they are and dawdle over my coffee so that I hold my table until they arrive. I will be disguised so no one will ever notice me.

We decorate the house, make up the beds for the rest of the family. James is bringing Roz with him which will be different. As we make the preparations I feel Izzy's tension rising. I know she isn't sleeping. I can hear her walking round the house during the night.

***

On the 22nd December I go out early, head for the swimming baths. I pay and go into the changing room, shower and do my hair with lots of conditioner, then tie it back in a bun. I put on the smart dress and the new shoes that give me extra height. I spend time doing a full make-up. I'm nervous and I'm glad I've practised. Then I stand back and a smart young professional looking woman stares back at me. I am quite unrecognisable even to myself. The hat completes the transformation.

I'm there before they are. The café is already full, but when I've got my coffee there is a table to one side which is free but needs clearing. It will do fine. Now I only have to wait.

It's odd being this new me. I receive admiring looks. When I get served the staff are more attentive. I know what it means now to conform and be accepted. Is there a part of me which would like this every day? I blank my mind to check what I am feeling and yes, there is a speck, somewhere deep inside me, acknowledging that one day I might like to find my way back into this normal world. Meanwhile, it is enough to know that I could, that all it takes is make-up and a proper dress.

Then I see him. I see Patrick and other thoughts fly out of my head. He is the man in the photo and there is immediately something odd about him. It's the way he dresses. He looks younger than he is but he's dressed like an old man: plain blue shirt, v-neck pullover, chinos with a crease. He looks, how shall I describe him? He looks wholesome and nervous.

He's also at a loss. There are no tables free. He glances at the queue as if he is working out how he can manage this. When he sees a woman putting her coat on he goes and stands too near her table so he is almost harassing her. She looks up at him, moves quickly out of the café and he sits down without clearing the table. Now he has his table I can see he's not at ease in here. I can understand that but he doesn't only glance at the door, he also continually looks round the café.

Does he know what Izzy looks like? Has she sent him a photo? I can see her outside now. She looks as she always looked when Dad shouted at her. Her face is shrunken, pulled in with more than the cold. For just a moment I think she is going to walk away, then she sees Patrick and opens the door.

It happens in slow-motion. He rises but stays near the table as if he is frightened that someone else may rush in and take it. She has to walk towards him. She raises both her arms and I see that same look on her face that I noticed when she read the letter. Something makes me think that he doesn't know what to expect but he goes with it and there, not fifteen feet from me, my mother is hugging her long lost son and crying.

And I empathise. There are tears in my eyes too. I mustn't stare but I can't pull my eyes away.

I find myself wondering what kind of upbringing he's had. I think of him being adopted by older parents, perhaps sent to a private school. How else could he dress like that as if he has no idea about trends? I see his diffidence and think of an adoptive mother he has come to love. He has the look of an unfaithful man. I saw that look on my dad, more than once. Does it feel wrong to hug another mother?

Then she is by herself and he has joined the queue. My mother gazes after him and he keeps turning to look at her. I don't think he's been to Costa before. He orders their drinks and then comes back to the table as if he expects to be waited on. Izzy has to send him back and then, most surprisingly, he comes back with only one coffee.

I wonder at this. Even if he isn't thirsty you'd think he'd need something in front of him, something to pick up and use to cover awkward moments.

As soon as he sits down she reaches her hands across and

takes his. Then she leans forwards and I know she is asking forgiveness, explaining that it wasn't possible to keep him as a baby. I see such earnestness in her expression. His face is hidden from me but as he speaks I see her relax and I feel a heel for watching such a private moment. She's found him and he seems pleased. I need to leave them to it.

I've finished my coffee and am getting up when I see him open his wallet and pull out a photo. He hands it over and Izzy whoops. She dives in her own bag and even across the crowded noisy café I can hear the word, 'Snap'. He has the photo of him as a baby. They laugh. I walk past the table, see the two photos there like mirror images, and then I go. There can be no doubt. The tension seems to have gone from each of them. I have no reason to be here anymore. They no longer need my supervision.

Chapter 5

On Christmas Eve the rest of the family arrive. Danny first, then Julia. James has said he will be late.

'And he's bringing Roz? What do you think she'll be like, Jule?'

'Young; too young for him.'

'That's not a guess, he told us as much. Try again.'

'Mouldable,' says Julia. 'She'll be pretty of course, in a small boned way. I suspect someone who resembles a china doll, or an Asian bride.'

'Do you think he might have bought her over the internet, Jule?'

'Your turn, Danny, What are you expecting?'

'A big girl. James is going to fat. He'll want someone who can eat and drink as much as he does.'

Even Izzy joins in this speculation. 'Big or small,' she says, 'the only really important thing is that she should worship the ground he walks on.'

'Mum!'

'Too cruel.'

My siblings are shocked. Izzy has always supported her children, even me. But James is clearly her favourite. Until now she's always defended him. I see looks pass between them. They have no idea.

Dinner is being held up so we are all drinking. Every family get-together has its honeymoon period, that time when hopefulness temporarily overrides knowledge.

I watch Izzy carefully and see something else. She hasn't talked to me about meeting Patrick. She's kept that to herself. They must have talked after I left. I had plenty of time to wipe off my make-up, change my smart dress for my usual scruff. She came back as if she had been nowhere special. When she did talk to me it was about beds and meals and whether I'd come to help with the big Christmas shop.

She slept well that night and I heard her singing as she came down the stairs for breakfast. Now I wonder about her James comment. She has another son, Patrick. Does that already mean that James can be jettisoned?

***

'And this,' James announces, 'is Roz.'

I won't speak for the others. What I see is a young girl with long black hair echoed by stern, dark-rimmed glasses. These are rectangular and designed to make her look serious. She has slight dimples and, seen from the side, the line of her throat comes straight up to the point of her chin. She has a delightful turned up nose. Its angle runs parallel to her throat. Are the glasses also worn to make her look less pretty than she really is?

'And these, Roz, are my family.'

'I'm Julia.' Julia steps forward and seizes Roz's hand. Then she takes over, introduces everyone else. When it comes to me I notice Roz looks nervous and I wonder what James has been saying.

'Hello,' she says. Her hand is cold, its grip fragile.

I smile back and nod.

When she talks it is to be apologetic. 'Mrs Goulden, I'm so sorry we're late. James wants me to say it was traffic but it wasn't really. He was late picking me up.'

So they don't live together.

We give them time to take cases up to the spare room and then we eat.

Roz has a thing with her hands. When the table is cleared she clasps them together with some force. When she unclasps them I can see slight pressure marks which vanish quickly as the blood returns to her skin.

'So,' says Julia, as if she lived a hundred years ago and is asking a young man about his prospects. 'How did you two meet?'

Roz answers at once. 'At university. James bought me a coffee.'

James looks embarrassed. I can see that at this moment he doesn't know if it was a good idea to bring her. 'I'm doing a Masters.' He says this as if it is a confession.

'In what?' The tone of Julia's question tells Roz that she should have let James answer. She stays silent.

'Business Management. We're on the same course.'

'Business Management?'

'I need some more letters after my name. The course is two years but I aim to complete in one. Then I might go for a Doctorate.'

I remember Julia's retelling of Dad's comment, 'The trouble with James is that his intelligence is unattached.' I take another look at my brother and think I see a new seriousness there.

Roz is smiling as if she is proud of him. 'He's getting good grades,' she tells us.

'So are you.' They exchange glances.

'Good on you both,' says Danny.

The compliment makes James flinch. 'Well, why not?'

Julia isn't finished. 'So who asked who out first?'

The question is unnecessary. James wouldn't risk rejection. He'll have engineered it, made a possible suggestion of meeting up, something like that.

Roz is proving delightful as she at once confirms my guess. 'It kind of happened,' she tells us. 'Your brother doesn't do precisely worded invitations.'

She smiles and I begin to like her. She looks sideways and gives me a little grin. I wonder about that. Does she see me as another outsider?

We don't quarrel that night. Izzy sits a little withdrawn. So far she has said nothing. James drinks less than he used to. We all turn in around midnight.

Before I go to sleep I hear sounds of sexual passion. These come in a series of throaty cries from James. What point is he making? Who is he trying to impress?

Then it's Christmas Day. After a cold December the weather has turned milder and the snow has melted. I'm first up. The rest of the house is silent, so I avoid the creaking steps as I make my way downstairs. I'm standing in the hallway when I notice a movement by the gate. A car is parked just outside the house. Two men get out. One of them is Patrick. What's he about? Has he bought a Christmas present for his birth-mother? I stay quite still. I'm sure I can't be seen. The two men walk a little way down the drive. They stop exactly where they can see the house in all its glory and stand there staring. Patrick smiles, except it's more like a grin. Then he says something before they go. Just before they vanish from sight Patrick turns back for another look and I notice the same grin.

Upstairs I hear a toilet flush so I ping the jardinière. As a family we are at peace. Izzy has found her son. James has Roz. What Patrick was doing outside I don't know, but probably no more than checking on where his mother lives. It's Christmas. I expect a clear echo but the house sounds troubled. The note jars and I wonder why.

It's at the end of breakfast that Izzy makes her announcement. It's always been the tradition in our family that we open presents straight after breakfast. That's why everyone is down on time and everyone is still sober. We've stopped eating and are sitting back drinking coffee. James has pushed his chair to one side in just the way Dad used to. Danny is tapping his fingers and wants to get on. No doubt he wants to go for a run before eating an enormous Christmas dinner. The mood round the table is relaxed. Roz has received a number of knowing looks, so I wasn't the only one who heard them last night. I feel she is embarrassed so I smile at her.

'Just before we open presents . . .' Izzy says.

It's great to have information that other people don't have. I watch for reactions as she tells them about her unwanted pregnancy and the older brother they didn't know they had. Concentration is intense as she describes her pain at handing him over, her joy at his forgiveness. I see my siblings listen and not understand. Only Roz seems to have grasped what Izzy is saying, but then she has nothing to unlearn. Izzy is watching their faces as she speaks, looking for reactions but there are none. 'He wants to meet you all,' she says. 'I've invited him here tomorrow. I hope that's alright.'

'Of course.' Danny is the first to react. He sees fewest implications.

Izzy looks round at the others.

'Are you sure about this?' Julia begins with a question. It's no doubt one she uses professionally. 'I mean, are you sure that he is who he says he is?'

Izzy nods. 'He had the same photo of him as a baby. How else could he get that?'

'Then wonderful.' It's not what Julia is thinking. 'You must be so happy.'

'How exciting.' Roz is being unguarded again. 'How really exciting to have a brother you didn't know about.'

'Tell us more, mother dear,' James says. 'How old is my half-brother?' The emphasis is on the half. 'Who was the father? When did you meet?'

My questions and someone else has asked them. You really don't need to talk. We lean in. James pulls his chair back to the table. Presents are forgotten.

'Patrick was born in 1967. He took the surname Barr when he was adopted. He's five years older than Julia which makes him forty-three. I've not told him who his father is so I'm not sure I should tell you.'

Does that mean Patrick didn't ask? I remember the uncertain man in the cafe who had to be cajoled into a hug, the man who thought keeping the table was the most important thing.

'I was nineteen and living at home when I got pregnant.' She pauses. 'To say my parents didn't approve would be an understatement. They insisted that I have the baby adopted. I had no money and Patrick's father only sang about peace, love and a new world order. When I told him we had made a new world order of our own and that it was growing inside me he was horrified.'

She paused. 'So I did as they demanded.'

I thought of the woman crying and the man shouting at her. Do Julia and James remember? I look at the others. Their faces are rapt. Did they hear the obfuscation being formed? Have they sensed the trace of what she will not say?

'I think you know the rest. I went to university and met your father.'

'And never told him.' Danny is the one who has to spell things out.

Izzy nods.

Roz intervenes. 'He didn't have the right to know.'

I'm cheering but Julia takes Roz on. 'Of course he did. He was married to her. It was a material fact, one that might impede the marriage.'

Roz disappoints me by looking round at James as if seeking permission. He shrugs, then she says, 'There are things I've never told James. There are also questions I've never asked him.' She waves a hand to stop Julia. 'I know you are going to say we're not married, but the way I see it is this.' She pauses. 'What we do, the choices we make, the experiences we live through are part of what makes us who we are. It follows then that if someone is attracted to us, part of that attraction must be to the life we have already lived, mustn't it? And if that is true, then our secrets are already discounted.'

Izzy smiles, pats Roz on the hand. The others work out what she's just said.

Danny flings his hands in the air. 'Okay,' he says. Then he turns to his mother. 'Thanks for telling us. That can't have been easy. I'll look forward to meeting my older brother.'

Julia is scowling. I see Izzy turn to face her. 'You must feel let down because you didn't know. I'm sorry about that, Julia. I'm sorry you are no longer the oldest.'

That last comment is a real kick and Izzy realises it. She adds, 'But I couldn't tell you what I hadn't told Gary.'

Julia's hurt is driving her on. 'Did Leah know?'

'No, not until just now.' Izzy lies well. She shakes her head to reinforce the misinformation. She knows I can't contradict her.

Julia appears mollified when Izzy turns to her. 'In one way you are still my oldest child. The oldest that I mothered and brought up. No one can take that away.'

'Presents,' says James.

For now, at least, the talking is over.

***

But I hear snatches of conversation all the way round the house for the rest of the day. Izzy's news haunts Christmas like the music for a carol whose words you have long forgotten.

'Clever girl, Roz.'

'I hope you didn't mind my joining in. I just thought Julia was bang out of order.'

'Always was.'

'And how do you feel about it, James?'

'Intrigued, surprised. Julia doesn't seem to have noticed that I'm no longer the oldest boy and I'm not making a fuss. Surely we're adult enough to take the news calmly. Except for Leah we all left the nest a long time ago.'

'I thought boys and mothers stayed attached.'

'Anyone would think you read psychology.'

Then after a big Christmas dinner I hear another

conversation. I'm small and nobody thinks I matter. Or is it that, like Izzy, they don't mind if I overhear because they know I can't say anything?

'Good run, Danny? Will it have done the trick?'

'I hope so, Julia. I kept saying to myself as I ran that this mile will let me have second helpings of turkey, this stretch will let me have Christmas pudding and brandy butter. I'm not sure how much wine I drank. I'll know when I weigh myself in the morning.'

'So today's news didn't put you off your stride?'

'Julia, as far as I'm concerned you're still head of the family.'

'Thanks. I just don't know what to think.'

'I wonder what he's like. Will he have the Goulden nose?'

'I doubt it. That comes from Dad's side.'

'Mum must be so pleased to have found him after forty years.'

'I wonder what's in it for him? I mean, I can understand a daughter being really happy that her mum has got in touch. Do boys do that sort of thing?'

'I don't think I'd bother.'

'Perhaps he's a nice man and he's doing this for her. Heaven help him meeting us lot.'

Later still I catch Izzy singing and I know she is back in an earlier time, remembering.

> *'Come writers and critics who prophesize with your pen*
> *And keep your eyes wide the chance won't come again*
> *And don't speak too soon for the wheel's still in spin*
> *And there's no tellin' who that it's namin.'*

When she sees me and realises I'm listening she suddenly stops and looks embarrassed. It must be a song Patrick's father sang. I know the words. When she stops I go on singing them in my head.

'For the loser now will be later to win,
For the times they are a changing.'

Who will be our loser, who will win? For us the times are certainly a changing.

***

Before Patrick arrives on Boxing Day we scatter Dad. We've chosen to do this in the garden at the back of the house. There is a spot where the snowdrops are already showing as thin green prongs. It's where he used to look out over the fields. Even when ill he often walked out this far and just stood there, letting his eyes take in the pattern of fields divided by hedges and small copses. This for him was England and he loved it. It was also the proof of his hard work and success because he would then turn and look at his lovely house before walking back inside.

We family do the scattering while Roz stands in her winter coat, watching. Izzy goes first. Then the urn is handed on in order of age, except that James hands the urn to Danny and only at the end does it comes to me. There isn't much of Dad left. I get to spread the last dregs, upend the urn and make sure it's empty. We stay dry-eyed as we all hurtle into this new world without him. Even as the last grains of Dad settle and moisten on the soil we are thinking of Patrick.

***

He is on time and alone. We are assembled. Tea is laid with an as yet untouched Christmas cake, iced and splendid at its centre point. The fire is lit and the lamps pool their light on carpets, on polished oak, on the decorations we have known all our lives. Then there is the Christmas tree itself with its myriad lights. It feels to me as if we are showing off and I am uneasy. Mightn't he come in and think, I have missed out on all of this. But the wealth came about because of Gary. Indeed, Patrick had to be adopted. His father had to abandon my mother before any of us could be born. We children are therefore the beneficiaries of his adoption.

Izzy goes out to greet him. We wait. Glances are exchanged.

They come back arm in arm and Patrick looks different. I realise I never saw his face close-to in the cafe. The wholesomeness is gone. His hair has grown and he has a couple of days of stubble. All this has the effect of making him look younger and trendier. No chinos and old man's v-neck sweater today. He's wearing jeans and a big off-white jumper that zips up to the neck. Both look new. The jumper has no bobbles.

Julia comes forward. 'Welcome to the family,' she says. 'I'm Julia. I always wanted a decent brother. My other two are such dead losses.'

How long has she worked on that line, I wonder. Then James is being introduced. He sweeps his hair to both sides before shaking hands.

Danny is sweating. The moisture beads on his brow. The room must be too hot for him. I know what he'll do. He'll test the firmness of his half-brother's handshake. Patrick seems surprised, then responds. That seems to be that. But then I see Patrick walk over to Roz and say, 'You must be Leah.'

'Roz, actually,' she says. 'I'm with James.'

Patrick looks around and finally notices me. I do stay near to walls. From ingrained habit I am standing in the shadows. He comes towards me and I can see his eyes. They are kind. In spite of his recent tussle with Danny he holds my hand gently so I feel reassured. 'Hello, Leah,' he says. 'I'm Patrick and very pleased to meet you...'

His voice is like being bathed in treacle. His eyes are soft and brown. His look is quizzical. He keeps hold of my hand, clasps it in both of his. Then he adds, lowering his voice, 'Our mother told me that you are the special one.'

We are all standing. Roz has moved next to James. There is suddenly everything to ask but it is too early for direct questions. Izzy has stepped back and is watching to see if the two parts of her family can become one. She pours tea. The others gather round Patrick as if they would corral him. Faces are animated, interested.

Our mother! Well I suppose she is now.

Patrick's taller than Julia, stands as straight as Danny. He is now showing a confidence that is both winning and alarming. He is at home here in a way he was not when they met in the café. But this is hardly surprising. It seems he is used to this attention, to having people round him. The words are nothing, just a blur of sound without consequence, but I sense my family like him. And he hasn't forgotten me. Every now and then he looks my way and smiles. It is as if he is drawing me in. I find myself helping Izzy hand round cups of tea, then taking mine and standing just outside the circle. When he sees me he looks at me and nods.

It is as if the genes we share are calling to me. I can't put it any other way. People say that blood is thicker than water and now I begin to understand. The faces of my siblings show in their separate ways that they are feeling it too. We have all shared the same womb and it does, it really does, seem to make a difference. Phrases rush into my mind: *Blood of my blood... I would know you anywhere... The ties that bind us.*

They have accepted him. I know that because they are telling him family history. And he is reassuring them by the way he responds that he comes to change nothing, just to join. Izzy has sat down and is watching us. Her face is radiant. The pain of giving him away has been redeemed. I am glad for her and not as frightened.

Cake is handed round. Because it is so difficult to stand and eat with a cup of tea in one hand and a slice of cake in the other we drift to chairs. This makes the conversation more controlled.

'So, Patrick, tell us more about yourself.'

'Well, I was adopted when I was a tiny baby. I always knew I had been adopted. The woman I used to call Mum told me I wasn't theirs.' He pauses. I wonder how they told him, under what circumstances. I sense the statement is loaded with just a little self-pity.

'I wasn't terribly good at school. I don't have the kind of brain that I gather James has. I'm more of a practical person. English was my worst subject. I wasn't creative at all, could never make up stories or imagine something as something else. I scraped some A levels and then went straight to work to earn money. Dad, I mean the man I called Dad, found me a job and I liked it, stuck at it. And I've risen a little way, though not nearly as far as Julia. I used to do a little sport, played a little football, but then I got old and out of breath. So you've got a failure as a new brother. I'm not as clever as James, as successful as Julia, as fit as Danny. I used to tell girls to stand next to me because it would make them feel better. It wasn't much of a chat-up line, and in case you're curious it never worked. I'm single. I have no children.'

He stops talking. He seems to have no ego. Even though he missed me out I am charmed with his natural manner and his openness.

'Oh, I forgot someone else. There is another comparison that is to my disadvantage. I am not as good a watcher as Leah is.' Everyone turns and looks at me. Temporarily relieved of the spotlight, Patrick winks at me. My family laughs. No one asks him what he means. I wonder if he saw me at the café but decide that isn't likely. If Mum didn't recognise me, what chance did he have?

Silence follows his modest statement.

'I see you are all feeling sorry for me,' he says. 'That's very thoughtful, but today I feel lucky. You are my new family.'

'Where do you work, Patrick?'

He describes a small company that makes specialist components for the engineering trade. Then he tells us that is just a fancy way of saying they make ball bearings. He talks about the four processes: the outer race, the rolling balls, the inner race, and the cage. He offers to talk about heating and grinding, the choice of steel, the minute tolerances. On our behalf James declines the invitation.

He stays an hour and then suggests it's time for him to go. Izzy shows him out and stays talking to him in the hall before we hear the door close.

'Well?' she asks when she comes back in. 'Anyone for more cake?'

We decline and Izzy sits down. 'You asked me about his father. I've just been telling Patrick so I can tell you.' I watch her carefully. I've never seen her so relaxed, so content. 'I feel I've carried these secrets round in my head when there was no need. Now I probably won't be able to stop talking about it.'

She makes excuses. She talks about the summer of love, *Sgt Pepper* on the juke box, anti-war demonstrations against the American involvement in Vietnam, *All You Need Is Love*. Then she tells us about her lover, how they met at the Communist Folk Club, how he seemed to fit the time, about snatched love-making at his parents' house and in the back of his car. I find I don't want this detail so I listen instead to her happiness, her sense of release. Patrick seems to have said all the right things to her. Before she stops talking I find I have stopped worrying.

I even think, this is what the house was built for. This has the same kind of truth to it that the oak panels and the brickwork show. The iris vase has settled again. But the jardinière still sends out a discordant note.

Then my siblings open wine bottles and eat cold turkey with pickled red cabbage. The talk is about Patrick. It is laced with approval and they include me, bother to notice whether I nod and smile. Only Roz, who also approves of him, adds, 'But he doesn't look like any of you and he doesn't look much like Izzy.'

'Next time he comes you must give him time to draw breath. I don't think he took a sip of tea or ate a morsel of cake,' is Izzy's comment.

Chapter 6

I have always liked the days that follow Christmas. Each year I feel the build-up hoodwinks me, catches me out, makes me believe that life can be better. Those expectations never survive the day itself, but in the backwater that is the period between Christmas and New Year the world goes back to normal. The family leave. Izzy and I have the house to ourselves. This year, following the cold spell, it becomes unseasonably mild. Sparrows sing and squabble in the ivy.

Patrick is a regular visitor and I have to admit to myself how much I like him. He makes himself agreeable. There, I've said it. He has a happy knack of staying modest. When he comes back in the middle of the afternoon on New Year's Eve, he starts by saying, 'Do the family want you to put me back in my box?'

'No,' says Izzy. 'They like you. You were a big hit.'

'But not with Leah?'

I smile at him and say nothing. He turns to Izzy. 'This daughter of yours, she gives nothing away.'

'She's the perfect daughter. She keeps me company and listens to me without making me listen to her.'

'Is that so?' He winks at me. His brown eyes appraise me as he does so. They slip from my face to my cardigan with its pockets where I keep everything I need.

'I suspect she has a mind of her own. I suspect that she watches us all carefully, finds fault.'

The comment makes me look at the floor. I'm contemplating a New Year's resolution: to be more accepting and less critical. I haven't got the wording yet. Do I add 'to reach out more'? Izzy has reached out to her lost son and is happy. I have Martin, occasionally, but he is the only person I have ever reached for. Before Christmas that seemed enough. Now I'm not so sure.

Patrick is relaxed, drinking tea, eating piece after piece of cake. He's shaved. He sees me noticing this and touches his face.

'It was an ordeal,' he explains, 'coming here and meeting the whole family. I needed some stubble to hide behind. Do you prefer me shaved or stubbly?'

Izzy thinks the question is for her. 'Whichever,' she says. 'I'm just glad you are back in my life.'

I prefer him with stubble. It makes him rougher, less controlled. I make sure I show nothing on my face. Anyway, he isn't looking. He goes over to Izzy and holds her hand. 'I'm glad too,' he says.

James, Danny, even Julia would never voice their feelings in this open way. Nor would Dad. The man who is now granules of matter among the snowdrops always kept his feelings to himself.

We children have both Dad's nose and his distrust of touching. The hugs of childhood dwindled quickly for us. Being adult seemed to be something to do with no longer needing physical affection. Izzy was part of that. Now I see her holding her son's hand as if she doesn't want to let it go. Patrick is looking into his mother's eyes. Then, as if he is aware of me watching them, he turns and grins.

'Catching up,' he says. 'We have lots of catching up to do.'

Is that a hint for me to be gone? I clear the plates and cups away, taking them into the kitchen and stacking the dishwasher. When I get back to the lounge they are sitting close together talking, so I simply walk out and go to my room. The sun is shining outside with that horizontal winter light. It's caught in the branches of the cherry tree whose red bark curls away from the trunk. These individual curlicues are now lit like rubies, as bright as Christmas tree lights.

Old year, new year. This segued moment marks something else for me now. I sit on the bed, staring out of the window as the sun balls and drops out of sight. Soon it will be New Year and I am being called out of myself.

My thoughts stall, go nowhere. I don't know what to do any more. Back then I was so certain. When I still wouldn't talk they took me to doctors and consultants, made me go to speech therapy. The private school my siblings went to wouldn't have me so I was sent to a special school with all the other casualties of the human form whose parents had money. There I sat through long years learning more about human beings than perhaps was good for me. The others were genuine cases. I knew why they were there. Because I didn't talk I didn't sing. Music was a large part of the curriculum. If it was Maths or English I finished first. That seemed to upset my teachers. They didn't want an exception so I used to begin slowly, to complete work only towards the end of the lesson. Even in that place of different people I was the most different. Defiantly silent I spent my days reading, watching and thinking. I was there long enough to see enthusiastic young teachers come in and treat us with professional respect as if they would change our lives. Then I saw the hope die in them. I watched them become routine creatures, wearied by repetition until they talked about us openly, forcing us to listen to our own inadequacies. Meanwhile life was easy. A taxi collected me. The same taxi brought me home. No one set me any homework or put me in for exams. I was allowed to drift as much as if I had been born into a wealthy family in an earlier age. I painted. I sewed. I read avidly. I read everything I could find. These were my accomplishments.

A knock on the door. I'm surprised to see Patrick standing there. 'I'm just going,' he says. 'I wanted to wish you a Happy New Year.' Then he adds, 'If it was midnight I would kiss you, sister, but without the excuse I suppose I'd better not.'

I've never been so close or so alone with him. His physical presence is surprisingly powerful. I frown and shake my head.

He is leaning against the door jamb surveying my room. 'Well, Happy New Year, when it comes.'

I make a rotating sign, whirling my index fingers round each other.

'Right, you wish me the same.'

I nod.

'Goodbye then.'

I wave my right hand and smile.

'Okay then.'

He goes and I watch him bounce down the stairs. It isn't like having a brother.

That dress is still in my wardrobe. Next time he comes I wonder if I should wear it, but then he might remember and know that he was observed at that first meeting. He called me a good watcher and I don't want to do anything to reinforce that idea, but he does make me want to dress for him.

***

Izzy and I see in the New Year together. We listen for the chimes and drink whisky. Izzy is bubbling. She tells me over and over how Patrick has forgiven her, how wonderful it is to have him back. A tiny part of me wants to add a comment of my own. Izzy has always stayed with me, lived alongside me. I used to be terrified by the intensity of her longing. Now I find I am made uneasy by her total happiness. Then I remember that Patrick said if he was with us at midnight he would kiss me and I find myself wishing he was here so that I could be kissed. It is a thought that occupies no more than the time between the first strike of twelve from Big Ben and the start of the fireworks, so fleeting I don't have time to ponder it.

I kiss Izzy, give her a hug, smile at the toast to 2011 and Patrick. Are James and Roz together? Where is Danny? Is Julia on her own, I wonder. Why is the family card game called Happy Families? Are most families happy?

On the way upstairs I make my New Year resolution. I will try to come in from the cold. Patrick may be the healing factor in the Goulden family. I can't talk but I will try to mimic the normal. That means I have to change the clothes I wear. This long cardigan and men's trousers will have to be phased out. A pity. They've served me well.

***

On 2nd January I go shopping. Sales began before Christmas and I am in time to catch the last throes of bargain hunting. I inspect the rails of heavily discounted stock. My posh dress was a disguise. What I now need is a kind of incremental change. I don't want, I mustn't make a fool of myself. I spend as much time watching other shoppers as looking at the clothes. In the end I buy nothing that's in the sale, partly because they don't have my size, but more because somehow it doesn't feel right to leap straight into brand new clothes.

In the hospice shop I find a pair of nearly new jeans and a grey fleece-like top. I try them on and they fit. I've paid and am on my way out when I see the jumper. It's multi-coloured with a high floppy neck. The colours are predominantly yellow and reds but there is enough blue there to go with the jeans. When I've put it on I find I am grinning at the mirror. I look so different wearing it. Even though I am small breasted the jumper makes me shapely. My cardigan used to flare down to the stuffed pockets. Now I look like a woman.

It's then that I realise my hair won't do. I pull it back into the bun I used when I spied on Izzy's first meeting with Patrick. That looks alright for now. Then I let it flop back, take off the pullover and revert to the person no one bothers with. I pay for my jumper and go out into the last of the afternoon light.

Shoes? I decide not to buy another pair. I can wear the ones I put on with the posh dress.

Back in the house I go straight upstairs with my purchases. I strip off and wonder that I never thought about new knickers and a bra. Perhaps next time. I put on the jeans, pick up the grey top but go instead for the colourful jumper. I was right. It goes with the jeans. I make sure it is right on the shoulders, position the neck so that it sits just so. It is then that I realise how much I slouch. Has that become part of my disguise? I spend a happy five minutes slouching and then pulling my shoulders back, seeing the difference, admiring the way my head comes up.

My hair is okay. It needs conditioning and drying properly, with a brush and a hairdryer. The days of washing it and letting it dry by itself are probably over. My face needs a touch of foundation. Then he might approve.

That thought again. I spell it out slowly, chewing on the words, trying to swallow them. For reasons I do not understand I want Patrick to think well of me. Why, when for whole decades I have forced my siblings and the rest of the world to disregard me, do I now seek approval?

I take the jumper off. I decide against trying on the new grey top. But I stay in the jeans, disguise them with the old cardigan, fluff out my hair a little and leave it at that. Even for Izzy I must make the change gradual.

'New jeans?' asks Izzy the moment I walk into the kitchen.

I put up two fingers close together. She understands.

'Seconds?'

I nod, then give her a twirl.

'Very nice,' she says. She stops, then cannot help herself. 'I wish you'd buy new. We could go shopping together. Patrick said. . .' She stops again.

I screw up my face, furrow my brow. I want to know what Patrick said.

Izzy is contrite. 'I shouldn't have said that. I'm sorry.'

I mouth the word 'what?' I raise my arms and splay out both hands.

'He said you could be pretty.'

My insides are doing strange things. I keep that hidden. I

simply shrug my shoulders.

Izzy is on a mission now. 'Could we go shopping together one day? I'd enjoy that.'

I smile without nodding. I want her to know that isn't a yes but it isn't a no either. Besides, if I need a new wardrobe someone will have to pay for it.

***

My favourite chair in the house is made of brown leather. It dates from 1910. It may or may not be by William Morris. It may or may not have come from his workshop. I've always thought it suited me when I sat in it because it is so unadorned. Now I find I am looking at it with new eyes. The structure could not be simpler. The joints are raised slots; the corners square oak; the side slats are vertical and unfussy. The back slants and the arm rests are the same width and depth as the sides. Plain, it shouts. Just take me for what I am, it announces.

But now I see that the wood has been chosen for its grain, that the pegs are decorations, that the diagonals play off against each other. Now I notice that the chair has artifice. I thought this house honest and it is, but its honesty is not plainness. Its honesty is about finding the beauty in everyday things.

Next time I am with Martin, I tell myself, I will strip and stand in front of him before diving under the duvet. I will let him see me as I am with nicely done hair. If Izzy takes me shopping I will buy some perfume and wear it for Martin.

***

I nearly miss Patrick's next visit. He is coming out of the house when I walk down the drive. It's a really bright day and the light is reflected from the wet road so I have to squint to check it is him. He is leaning into my mother, talking earnestly to her. Behind them is the door into the house, wide open, letting the heat out.

For a moment they don't look like mother and son. What I am watching is more like a door to door salesman or an estate agent with a client. Izzy sees me first and says something which makes Patrick unwind and walk towards me, holding out his hand.

'Nearly missed you,' he says. His hand is warm and envelops mine in a way that is comforting. 'So glad I didn't.' Then he steps back and appraises me. 'I like your hair. I hope you don't mind me staring at you, but I knew something was different.'

All this time he has kept hold of my hand and it seems rude for me to pull it away so I let him hold on.

'I'm just going. I have to be somewhere else almost immediately, or we could have talked.' Then he remembers himself. 'Well, I could have talked and you could have listened.'

He lets go of my hand and walks towards the car. He opens the door and spins round. 'Bye Mum.' He waves at Izzy who has stayed by the front door, gets in the car and blows me a kiss as he drives out onto the road.

I walk into the house.

'Such a nice boy,' says Mum. 'He likes your hair.' She takes the risk of a further comment. 'I like your hair too. Something is changing in you.' She smiles and turns away.

I walk in after her. The hall is calm, its linen fold panels are patient, as if they remember the slow growing of the oaks that made them. I need to dust. Sunlight through the stained glass window is staining the table and picking out the dust motes around the jardinière. I have always served the beauty of the house. Now I must look after my own as well. When he made that comment about my hair something happened I need to think about. Something in my stomach tightened and released. It seemed un-sibling like. I was both flattered and disturbed.

My problem is that I have nothing to compare it with. My brothers have not touched me since that day at the sinkhole.

When Martin touches me it is with purpose. Patrick held onto my hand and I felt a pulse in his that linked me to the beating of his heart. Yet when I looked down at our hands, his was quite still and purposeless.

It's that separation I focus on. Martin's eyes burn when he wants me. His hand and all other parts of him are focussed on wanting me. But I don't expect him to love me. It's lust that holds us together. If I ask myself, do I want to spend a weekend with Martin, the answer is no. I don't even want to wake up having spent the night with him in the same bed.

Now switch the question. Would I like to spend...

What am I saying? What am I even thinking? He's my half-brother.

It's early afternoon, too late for lunch time, but Martin will still be in his shop if I hurry. I wonder what he'll think of my different hair. I remember my resolution, douse myself in perfume, then I am out of the door before Izzy can trace the scent.

I walk fast. The brightness is already beginning to fade and the day is getting colder. It will be dark when I walk back. Never mind. I need this. I need to clear my mind. I know I'm pounding the field paths just to keep warm.

I slow down when I reach the town. I don't want to rush into his arms all sweaty.

Martin is very surprised to see me. The shop isn't empty but I stay, pretend to look at books as he serves an earnest looking older man. This man is after something on SOE in the Second World War. Martin is being very patient, taking him to the relevant section and pulling books out for him. Eventually the customer purchases *They Lived For Danger.* He must be a regular. They briefly talk football and where you can always buy a ticket. Then the shop bell rings and he is gone.

I come forward and touch Martin on the shoulder. I must be smiling because he smiles back at me. He looks at his watch and frowns. I wonder if I have timed this badly but he's choosing to close early. I see him lock the door and turn the sign round. Then I'm following him up the stairs.

When he switches the fire on I start to strip. He's looking at me which is what I want but it causes a hiccup. Previously we have always acted in unison. Now he is the watcher and I am the performer. I make myself go on. When I'm naked, and feeling it, I use both hands to bunch up my conditioned hair, then wiggle my hips.

For an awful moment I think he is about to say something, but he doesn't. Instead he comes across and hugs me, buries his face in my neck, inhaling the smell of me. Then he is tearing off his clothes.

I feel like I think a woman should feel. I'm in bed and I welcome him in. Sex has always felt a little furtive before. Now it has an openness as if, even unspoken, it is at least acknowledged.

Afterwards he reaches out and gently strokes my hair. I know I'm smiling. Soon his hand is moving all over me. There is a whole language of touch, and in this world Martin seems both multilingual and a native speaker.

***

It is getting dark when I open the shop door. The walk will be a strain. Izzy will be worried. I hurry away.

I take the old railway line. The light is leaking fast, and what has been distinct in the daylight now turns non-descript. The path is edged with a mixture of soft, dull browns and lichen greens. Only my walking feet make sharp and certain noises as the hillside bulges and passing trees swim over my head. I realise I'm happy, alive, enjoying the walk.

I am not entirely alone. Bubbles of rooks blow across the sky, then collapse to roost. They chatter for a while and then are still. The first stars shine. Looking up I see that winter twigs are fishing in the sky, corralling stars in nets. Walking here is like going back in time. I feel as if I'm in touch with something from an earlier age when Hardy heroines walked down lanes like these as a matter of routine.

Then I'm on the road and resenting the way car headlights snatch away the quietness and the intricate darkness of it all.

When I get back Izzy is pacing.

'I was so worried,' she says.

I throw up both my arms in defiance. Because I do not talk there will be no need to tell a lie about where I have been and why I am late.

***

So that's lust, but what does love feel like? The next time Patrick comes Izzy is out and I have him to myself. He is as good as his word. He talks and I listen.

I'm wearing the new jeans and the grey top when he rings the bell. If I'd known that he was coming I'd have put on the multi coloured jumper, but I haven't worn that yet, not even for Izzy.

I let him in. I expect him to look round to see where Izzy is, but he doesn't. He must sense that she isn't in because he concentrates on me.

'Hello, Sister.'

He holds me by the shoulders and kisses me on both cheeks. No one has ever done that to me before. Then, still holding me, he leans away and appraises me. 'Jeans, hair and now a smart top.' He sounds as if he likes this new me. 'You'll get yourself noticed, young Leah.'

I take in his height and the sheer force of him. His grip on my shoulders is gentle but I feel held. I break his hold by stepping back. Even as I do this I'm conscious that he has chosen to let me go.

'Is your mum in?' he asks.

I shake my head. I think this confirms his sense of her

absence because he nods. 'I must have mistaken the time. I came to see her, of course.'

That's not what I want to hear. I am his sister. Does it always have to be Izzy he comes to see?

I make the capital T sign with my hands.

'Would I like a mug of tea?' he articulates.

I nod.

'Fantastic,' he says. He follows me into the kitchen.

'It must have been a shock,' he says, 'finding out about me.' He looks at me closely. 'It was a shock to me,' he explains, '. . . a nice shock I would have to say. I was an only child and now to have a family like this is just the best.'

So he didn't belong either. He was adopted as a single child. Perhaps we are similar in outlook. Is that why he has always tried to include me? He watches me put the kettle on, leaning against the fridge door as he does so. He seems wholly at ease in our house.

I hold up two kinds of tea: Yorkshire and Lapsang Souchong. 'Yorkshire,' he says. 'Builders' tea as black as you like.'

I hold up milk and sugar.

'Just the milk.'

I add milk to the mug. I don't use a pot. I keep stirring the tea bag in the mug until the colour turns a dark coppery shade.

'Enough,' he says.

I hand it to him.

He makes no move, takes the mug and stays where he is.

'This is a lovely house.'

Just for a moment he sounds like an estate agent.

'Art Nouveau?' he asks.

I nod. But it's more than that. I have books on the Arts and Crafts Movement, but if I suddenly walk out and fetch one, will he understand?

'Beautiful,' he says. 'I loved it when I first saw it. It was almost magical walking in on Boxing Day.'

That isn't a lie, I realise, just two statements that don't quite join together. I shake my head. I am the old Leah, distrustful, standing outside myself and observing the world, still out in the cold. I nod so that he'll carry on talking.

'Big for just you two, but I imagine a good family house when you were all young.'

He stops and thinks. 'And you do seem a tight-knit family.'

It's like charades. No nuances. All I can do is nod or shake my head.

I shake my head vehemently.

He smiles. 'I guessed as much, and you are the one who would know, you are the watcher.'

This time I don't mind the comment. It feels like a compliment.

'Did they leave you out? Were you always the outsider?'

His words carry real sympathy. Suddenly I feel like crying. The tears gather behind my eyes as I remember. I think he has seen them there because he says, 'I had no siblings and so I also felt left out. It's like there is a whole world that seems raucous and happy but you are not part of it.'

Is he wanting to upset me? He's not even looking at me but down at his feet. I wish he wouldn't go on about my isolation, but then I realise he isn't. He's talking about himself. We are twinned by experience as well as linked by genes. Once he realised Izzy wasn't here he could have gone, but he hasn't. He seems to want to be with me. I start smiling.

'Yes,' he says. 'That's it. Now we don't either of us need to be alone.'

It's so simply said that I have to respond. I walk towards him and hold his hand. That's okay because he's my brother. He seems startled and hesitant, then it's as if he remembers at the same time.

'Yes. That's okay, why not?'

My silence is weighing on him. I feel selfish. I'm making him do all the talking. I also feel I'm crowding him. I leave him, make myself a coffee and sit down at the kitchen table.

He comes and joins me there. 'We are very similar. I felt that almost immediately.'

I nod enthusiastically.

'If I had always been your brother I might have been able to do something about it.'

I smile, shrug.

He is silent for a moment, touching his nose. 'Well, you've got me now.'

I turn my hand upward, splay my fingers and then point at him.

'You want me to tell you more about myself?' he asks.

I nod.

He thinks for a moment. Then, 'I believe in God. I suppose that's the first and the most important thing about me. I like going to church. It's where I feel most at ease.' He looks at me suddenly. 'I bet that surprises you.' He pauses. 'Yes, I'm a sad man, very sad. Even this finding my mother, to me it's as though God planned it.'

I want to nod again. He's looking for a nod but something stops me from that little movement of the chin.

'With God,' he says, 'you are never really alone.'

His innocence is sweet. I find I'm smiling and he begins to laugh.

'Shut up, Patrick,' he tells himself, 'you've already said more than enough.'

I shrug.

'It's like being interrogated,' he says. 'Do you know your silence is intimidating?' Suddenly he's horrified at what he's said. I see it in his eyes before he voices it. 'Look, I'm sorry. I know you'd speak if you could. I mean, it must be awful, like being trapped. The funny thing is that you don't seem to feel sorry for yourself.'

He looks at me to check he's not upset me. No one has ever made me feel like this. No one has worried about me so much or taken such care to engage with me, draw me in.

I mouth back, 'I'm not.' Inside I'm jubilant. My guess was right. My New Year resolution is the right one. Patrick is beckoning me in from the cold. I'm in touch with Izzy's longing and now with this humble man's deepest feelings, this lovely man who can do self-mockery, a skill the Goulden family has never mastered.

'I mean, what you must think of me. . .' he says. That thought alone is enough to endear me to him. '. . .telling you all this personal stuff, just blurting it out like that. I mean, Izzy indulges me but you don't need to.'

His mug is empty. I make the T sign again.

'More tea? No, this time I'd like a coffee.'

I put the kettle on, get out the rest of the Christmas cake. He nods. I cut him a large slice.

'Now I'll talk for you,' he announces.

This startles me. I wonder what he has noticed and what he hasn't. 'I don't know what stopped you speaking …' he begins.

So he and Izzy have talked about me. Izzy must have told him about the way I used to chatter.

'. . .but it may heal in time. I hope it does.' He looks at me again, a penetrating look that warms me inside. 'When I met you on that first visit I thought you were unhappy. You looked at me so suspiciously. Now I'm not sure if you are happy or not. At least you have stopped being suspicious.'

I can smile at that. I add a nod.

'Good,' he says. 'I suspect you are hard to win over. If you like me, then I'm pleased.'

I want him to go on. I enjoy this attention. He eats his cake, fruit and cake first and then the marzipan and the icing, another eating idiolect.

He's smiling at me and I smile back. 'I came to see Mum,' he explains. The word is now quite natural in his mouth. 'But I'm glad to have had this chance to meet you properly. I feel we can be friends, perhaps even allies.'

I'm not sure what he means by this but I nod, reach over and put my hand on his.

A look comes into his face which I do not understand.

'Do you know you are very pretty when you smile?' he says.

He's finished his coffee and his cake. 'Must go,' he says. 'Give Mum my love. Tell her I was sorry to miss her.' He grimaces. 'Of course, you can't do that. I keep being cruel. I don't mean to.'

There's paper for shopping lists and pencils. He helps himself and writes Izzy a note.

I walk him to the front door. He wonders whether he should, then kisses me on my cheek. The touch of his lips on my cold cheek is wonderful. I think about it but I don't kiss him back.

When I give Izzy the note she looks disappointed, then says, 'I told him I wouldn't be in this morning. He must have forgotten.'

She takes the note with her and something inside me exults that he is forgetful and that he found me on my own.

Chapter 7

That night I dream about Patrick and wake unsettled. About a brother it was the wrong kind of dream. It brings back my greatest fear, that the not speaking, the feeling different, the way I dress, are signs of something close to madness, if not of real insanity. My dream is filled with desire and Martin is nowhere. Sectioned, that is my greatest fear. I like independence, being free to move around, feeling the air on my face even in January. If I were insane, would I know it? Is sanity as relative as everything else in this puzzling universe? I get up even though it is early, shake my head to clear it, dress and sit at the kitchen table with a cup of coffee.

The thoughts don't go away. I tell myself to be objective, but an image from the night of myself performing for Patrick as I performed for Martin will not so easily leave my skull. Incest? Is that how depraved I am? Am I beginning to be in love with my own brother? To squash that thought I revert to my suspicious self. I switch on the computer, open up Explorer, type in his name. There are thousands of Patricks. There's a film, a saint, a French man who uses Twitter. I type in Patrick Barr. The name is there, but he's an Irish bank manager who fell from a roof and made it into Wikipedia. Another Patrick Barr is an orthopaedic doctor. A third has published material about whale distribution in the northern hemisphere. There is one on LinkedIn but it isn't my Patrick. This one is a surveyor. I go down list after list, each time I reach the bottom of the page I click on next. There are endless accounts of the sudden death of the bank manager but nothing about Patrick Barr, natural son of Isabel Goulden.

I type in the name of the company he works for and find it immediately. They make ball bearings. I scroll down. *Rollers is the complete, one-stop supplier to OEM's and to wholesalers sourcing high-precision, miniature ball bearings, bearing related products, and associated professional services including world-class engineering and design . . .*

I examine each photo in the slide show. All their operatives wear the Rollers logo. They appear to operate in laboratory conditions. They look straight out of these photos as if they know they are the best. There is something of Patrick's confidence in the way they look and in the text about their product, but Patrick isn't there. I sign up for their newsletter, then go onto Twitter. Half the world is on Twitter but Patrick Barr is not. He isn't on Facebook either.

Now I'm puzzled. Yes, he is a modest man who makes light of his achievements, but he is also socially confident. I remember how well he coped with my siblings, how quickly he pulled me in. Does his modesty extend to making sure that he is not to be found anywhere on social media?

I go to the electoral register. There are no Barrs registered to vote in this area. I realise I don't have an address. I presumed he was local but that might be wrong. The company is in Leeds. Without an address I can't get any further. I also don't have a date of birth.

I hear a toilet flushing, the shower turned on, a hairdryer and then footsteps on the stairs. I busy myself making breakfast. The kettle has gone cold.

Izzy is bustling. 'Your dad's will,' she tells me, 'isn't as straightforward as we thought because of the company. I've told Julia that there's nothing that needs to be done right now. Everything's been left to me in my lifetime, of course. Julia wants me to pass some on. She says that if I do you can escape death duties, provided I survive for seven years. Well, I've every intention of surviving for a lot longer, so what's the hurry?'

We have these one-sided conversations, especially in the morning which is Izzy's best time.

She's helping herself from the cafetière. The room smells of toast and coffee. Its noises are the scraping of knives buttering and spreading marmalade.

'What do you think, Leah? Do you think I should settle some money on each of you now?

It's a yes/no question. Izzy is good at those.

I point to myself and shake my head.

'Of course. You're not in the will, are you? For you it's the house and an allowance.'

I nod.

She won't ask how I know. It won't occur to her that actually no one has told me anything, that I've found the information out for myself.

I hear the crunch of my own toast. Izzy is chewing.

'I can change that, you know. Because everything is left to me during my lifetime, perhaps I can rewrite that part of the will.'

She looks at me. 'Would you like me to?'

I shake my head quickly. A range of possibilities occur to me and I don't want any of them.

'So what about the others? Do you think Julia is right?'

Again I shake my head.

'You're so unworldly. You get that from me. I married your dad for all sorts of reasons, not because I saw the pound signs in his eyes.'

I smile at her, nod my head. Izzy effortlessly reads my thoughts.

'Yes, he was rather good at it,' she says. 'Julia says he's worth £12 million, a hardly believable sum.'

I try not to show on my face that it's closer to £20 million.

'Funny,' she adds. 'I'm now a very rich woman. I could buy a great car, go on holiday anywhere, do anything, and all I really want is to spend time with my son.'

I point to my ring finger and then at her.

'Marry again, at my age. Why?'

I laugh at that, shrug and splay my fingers.

The toast is eaten. She's on her second mug of coffee.

‘When I finish this I’m going to the solicitors. I might then go clothes shopping. Do you want to come?’

I don’t want to disappoint her, but I slowly shake my head.

‘Pity, but you would spend a long time sitting around waiting. Solicitors talk too much, seem to keep conversation going for more than an hour so they can charge more. It always happens.’

***

The moment she is out of the house I go straight into her bedroom. I need Patrick Barr’s address. I want to find out more about him. I know where Izzy keeps her address book. There’s a single filing cabinet with a drawer in the top. It’s in that drawer. I pick it out at once. There’s nothing under Barr. I look through the Ps and there’s nothing under Patrick either. Izzy isn’t always tidy and there are pieces of paper lodged between the leaves. I go through these systematically, read every name and each address, but I still draw a blank. I put the address book back.

This worries me. Perhaps she doesn’t have his address. They met in a cafe. He has always come to our house. Izzy has been protected for years. Her unworldliness (even in the sixties there was good contraception) might mean she has never asked where he lives. Patrick is attentive. He is clearly pleased to be part of the family. But because I don’t speak I’m stalled. Anyone else could phone the company, ask for Patrick Barr. A moment’s regret that I don’t do that passes quickly. What would I say if they put me through?

It’s a clear early spring day, high pressure, no wind and the light is immaculate. I tell myself that I do need more clothes. I tell myself that if I bump into Izzy I’ve changed my mind and can have a lift back. Izzy will be pleased that I’ve come shopping. It’s a win-win situation. But I know why I am really going. The robin is singing. The first aconites are lifting their heads through the ground ivy. I need to feel normal. I need to feel sane. I can be there at lunchtime.

I go along the disused railway line. At this time of year the field paths are muddy and my feet get heavier the longer I walk. The light is lovely through the trunks and low branches. It makes patterns on the opposite bank. A squawking blackbird flies straight at me and I have to duck as the chasing sparrow hawk nearly slaps the side of my head. I feel the rush of disturbed air chilling my face. Turning, I see the blackbird escape into a tangle of branches. The sparrow hawk veers up and perches in a Scots pine, keeping watch.

Last time I did my strip for Martin. Today I will revert. There will be no show. I'm not wearing perfume. I am wearing jeans and the grey top. I need to know that I still want him. I need to wipe last night's dream out of my head.

But I don't. As I'm walking past Costa, Izzy hails me from the other side of the street.

'You came,' she said. 'You came shopping. Do you want a coffee?'

I nod. I'm thirsty.

'Cappuccino? Americano?'

Another nod followed by a shake of the head.

'Cappuccino then. I'll get them. You sit there.'

The cafe is half empty. Izzy points to the table she shared with Patrick. In spite of there being so many unoccupied, cleared tables I do as I'm told, go and sit there among the detritus. The waitress shakes her head as she wipes my table.

Izzy comes back with the coffees, a pack of stollen bites and a piece of rocky road.

'Let's begin at Next,' she says. 'My friend Carole tells me no one your age would be seen dead in M&S. If we don't hit lucky in Next we'll go to that Urban shop.' She's enjoying herself. 'Two hundred pounds,' she says. 'That's our target.'

I realise there's a big advantage for me. If Izzy buys, I can speed up my transformation because it will seem that she is pushing me to be smarter. She'll tell Patrick that, and there will be no danger of him thinking I am dressing for him. The thing I really want is lingerie. We're bound to walk past some. I can make that happen. But there will be no Martin today. That can't be helped.

***

Two days later Patrick returns to us and I'm ready for him. I bought skinny jeans and tall fur-lined boots. I'm wearing crisp new knickers and a fancy bra. I've put on the multi-coloured, roll-top jumper. My hair is used to being conditioned now and bounces on my shoulders. I stop at make-up. My face is me but already that is changing. My skin looks more alive. I'm standing better. I know I'm walking taller.

'Wow,' he says. 'Sister, welcome to the world.'

I give him a twirl, watched by Izzy.

'Your daughter is transformed,' he says.

'We went shopping,' says Izzy. 'I've been trying to get Leah to go shopping for ages.'

I bask, then go to the kitchen, put the kettle on, leave them to it.

Even above the noise of the kettle phrases drift in from the hall.

'Yes, she's beginning to make an effort.'

'How long?'

'Since the picnic. I don't know what happened. She's never talked since. She used to be a chatterbox.'

'Can she talk?'

'No. I used to think she was faking it but not anymore. It'd be one hell of an act of willpower to stay silent for more than twenty years!'

Before the kettle boils I put mugs, milk, tea and coffee on the table. I find tea spoons. I find small plates. I cut a piece of Christmas cake for Patrick, leave the knife in case Izzy wants some. Then I clap my hands.

They come in, help themselves. We sit round the table. There is a silence, then Patrick carries on as if I'm not there, asking about me at school. Izzy tells him I went to a special school.

I get up and grab a piece of the shopping list paper and a pencil.

I write: *Ask me if you want to know something. I'll write the answer.* I push the paper over to Patrick.

He reads it. 'Sorry,' he says, 'that was rude of me. Which school did you go to?'

I get another piece of paper. *St Chad's.*

I pass it over, then when he's read it I pull the paper back. I need to make this into a game. *It was awful.*

Now he's reading what I'm writing upside down. I see him smile.

Everyone except me was weird.

He laughs. *My birthday is 15th June, when's yours?*

Izzy joins in and answers for him, 'March 19th.' I have to remember that.

What's your address?

Izzy says, 'I need that. Write it down.'

I pass him the piece of paper and the pencil. He writes his address and gives it to Izzy. This time I read it upside down and memorise it. 48, Waterloo Terrace. He hasn't put the postcode.

Now he asks me something. 'Why didn't you learn sign language?'

I need a fresh piece of paper for this. It takes two. *No one else in the school used sign language and my family . . .*

The memory is strong. I break the point of the pencil, have to fetch another.

. . .refused to learn.

'We were wrong,' Izzy says. 'I've always felt guilty about that.'

Patrick looks at me. 'I wish I'd been there. I'd have learnt it for you.'

It is a criticism of Izzy and she drops her head. I reach out for her hand. It hadn't been her choice. It was Dad, Julia and James. While I hold her hand I smile at Patrick. I wish he had been there too.

Izzy has an appointment in town. After she's gone, Patrick comes to my room to say goodbye. 'I'm sorry,' he says again, 'for asking questions about you in front of her. That was wrong of me.'

I smile.

'I'm also sorry about the sign language thing. It's left you speechless for years. That must be so frustrating.'

I walk up to him and put my arms round him. It's the only way I can express my gratitude.

I feel his arms go round my back. Is he as moved as I am? Is this what normal brother and sister love feels like? We stand entwined for what must only be seconds. Then, in a single fluid movement, his arms come down the side of my rib cage. This makes me shiver. I think he must be feeling some of what I feel, the awkwardness of loving a half-sister when you haven't grown up together. I stand there thinking any moment he'll step away, say goodbye, but he doesn't. Then his fingers dig under my jumper, feel for the line of my knickers. He's too quick for me and I'm naked from the waist down. My new jeans and knickers are round my ankles and I still don't react. I can scream but I don't. Is this happening? What is happening?

Then I am lying on my own bed, still not understanding. He's yanking my jeans from my legs and is tearing at his zip. Then, brutally, he is inside me pumping away, and I know he has done this before, that I am not the first. I now know what he is. I know he is not my brother. He can't be. In a second of total clarity I realise we have let a cuckoo into the house, that Izzy's happiness is false.

He gasps, stops thrusting and I come back to myself. Ice cold now and shaking I throw him off, grab my clothes, run into the bathroom and lock the door. The lock seems flimsy. He could break it with a shoulder charge.

But he doesn't. Instead he knocks on the door. 'I know that's what you wanted. I hope you enjoyed it,' he says. Then he adds, almost casually, 'See you next time.'

***

I hear him walk downstairs. His footsteps are untroubled. I wait until I hear the front door shut and his car start. Even when I know I'm safe I don't move.

But I have the feel of him in me and on me. His wetness is still there. I run a bath and slide into the hot water. At least I can wash away any physical trace of him.

As I lie there I imagine him driving away, perhaps with a feeling of conquest, replete for now. He has somewhere to go and he can come back to this house anytime.

The understanding of what has just happened hits me continuously like the swell of a heavy sea. He was nice to me on purpose. I played into his hands. He will say I hugged him first. He will say I didn't resist. And whatever he says they will believe him. I'm back dangling upside down over the sinkhole, wetting myself. He could do that to me because I am mute. I, who never trusted anyone, trusted him. I close my eyes with the horror of it.

The bath cools and I don't reach for the hot tap. I find I can't or rather that I don't want to. Any sense of being an active, purposeful human being has vanished.

It feels like watching a film. Scarcely edited scenes cross and re-cross my mind. Shopping, rubbing conditioner into my hair, the damp spray from the perfume bottle, my New Year resolution, everything I did to encourage him. That hug. Especially the hug. In my mind I keep walking across the floor of my own bedroom and hugging him. I do it again and again, only it looks like another girl is hugging him and a part of me thinks, stupid cow, she asked for that.

The images relent and words follow them. I, who have always been wary, let him groom me. How could I have been so stupid? How could I have been so wrong?

I don't know how long I lie there before the anger kicks in.

Never again, I think. Never again. I look at the drop of water on the showerhead and the condensation on the mirror. I mouth, I know you, Patrick. I know what you are and who you are not. You are not my brother or there is no way you could ever have done that to me.

I begin to shape things and ask questions. I think about running hot water but the bath's now too cold for that. As I get out I ask myself, But if you aren't Izzy's son, who the hell are you? What enormous powers of self-delusion allow you to casually leave saying, 'See you next time'?

I quickly dry myself. I can't tell Izzy. I can't rob her of her newfound happiness. Even if I did tell her, would she believe me?

And if I can't tell her, I can't stay here. I won't let him do that again. I have to leave but where can I go? I have no money, no means of support. He chose his victim well, didn't he? Truth and power don't go together. I know the truth but he has all the power. I am nobody.

I unlock the door and step out into the corridor. I get a clean pair of knickers and put them on. I am cold now but it's not a physical coldness. I am turning to ice. I haven't talked for twenty years. I have considerable willpower. I can cope even with this.

I find Izzy's address book, copy out an address and phone number that I happened to notice as I flicked through last time.

Then I dress in clothes no one has seen me in, taken from the back of the wardrobe. I make my hair into a bun. I pack quickly. I don't have options. There is only one place I can go.

I write a note for Izzy.

I've gone away for a few days. I have a friend you never met. I've gone to stay with him. Don't worry. I'll write to you.

Love Leah

The house knows I am not coming back. I can feel it grieving. It too knows what happened here.

Part Two

Chapter 8

The questions I keep asking myself are: who is she, what's happened to her, why has she come to my house, muddy from walking across the fields with her suitcase, and what does she want from me?

I live with my books, loving the feel of them, aware all the time of their weight, of the knowledge they contain. I look at the stacks and think to myself, I haven't read any of those yet and each was a battle to publish, each has survived thus far, each contains fragments of the total wisdom of my species. Some of them may be the only surviving copies. A second-hand bookshop is part archaeological dig and part fishing trip. One day I will stumble across something that no one considered valuable and it will contain the kind of writing that transforms lives. That text, that MS, when I find it, will be my lost Michelangelo, my discarded Picasso.

I think of myself as a dissident. I know the canon. I read it at university. Even then I wondered which writers had been excluded. We were taught to worship Shakespeare and Dickens, Jane Austen, George Eliot, Hardy. They were the chosen ones. Then from the rest of the world came Dostoyevsky, Balzac, Victor Hugo, Tolstoy, Thomas Mann. We were told these were the greats. If I were a darts player I would have the face of F R Leavis on my darts board. How dare one man act as an arbiter of taste, just because he made a list?

A *list* of great writers. *Lists* were also once jousting tournaments. To *list* is to heel over. To *enlist* is to join. To be *listless* is to lack energy. You knew all those. But did you also know that *list* is the selvage on woven textile fabrics, that it is a division of parted hair, and that the word once meant to please, to have pleasure in, to desire, (use archaic).

Do you see why I am a loner?

All listing seems to me to be arbitrary. I am astounded by how good forgotten novels are, how much better often that the hyped, Amazon-exalted ephemera of today. I love old books and I only sell them because I have to. I don't like selling them, except when I have multiple copies, but even I know I will never read them all. I sometimes think that if the world began to run out of second-hand books I would become a hoarder and refuse to sell any. The only books I won't touch are those printed by the Folio Society. I will have nothing to do with books reduced to an act of social pretension.

When she first came to my shop I glanced at her clothes and thought them eloquent of not belonging. I remember she was wearing a lichen green T shirt which hadn't been ironed, faded grey chinos that were turned up above the ankle and pinched in by a belt at the waist, and a long grey cardigan with pockets that bulged outwards. She never carries a handbag, hence, I presume, the bulging pockets. Each item of clothing looks as if it doesn't quite fit her. She always wears flat shoes, usually black. She never uses make up.

I like that. I like that looks-don't-matter appeal that she has. She has a wonderful nose, but apart from that her face is long and nondescript. Her hair is mousy, naturally so, and ragged. I suspect she cuts it herself. Until recently it only varied according to the weather, as if she walks straight outside when it is still wet and just lets the wind tangle it. Everything about her says, 'I don't belong.'

That doesn't make us kindred spirits. There are a few ways of belonging and many more of not belonging. I saw her and thought, we dress for the same reasons.

She looked round the shop and bought a novel. It was *The Well of Loneliness* by Radcliffe Hall. I made a presumption then and I was wrong, but I thought the book went with the clothing and with something in her face that was internalised and withdrawn. I looked inside the front cover, told her it was £3.50. I pointed out that this one had student notes in it, that was why it was cheaper. I said there was another copy, priced at £5, if she wanted just the novel without the notes. She looked at me and she said nothing, just flicked through to see how much scribbling there was, then nodded and handed me a twenty pound note. I didn't have a £10 note in the till so I had to go into my wallet to find the change. I'm always doing that, muddling the shop's takings with my own money. It drives my accountant mad. Meanwhile, this differently dressed girl was patiently waiting for her change. She smiled at me.

'Goodbye,' I said. I live in Yorkshire so I probably added, 'See you later.'

She said nothing, just walked out. I thought her rude. I didn't expect to see her again.

Now she is asleep in my bed, this girl who became my lover without ever being my girlfriend. Even saying that seems inadequate to describe what has happened between us. It would be more accurate to say I became her lover. It feels as if it happened that way round. The roles are reversed. If anyone is using anyone for sex, then she is using me.

I'm used to that now so I look out for her. I'm always pleased when she walks into the shop. She adds a frisson to my life as a bookseller. I've even begun to make adjustments in case she visits. I keep the flat tidier. I change the bed more often than I used to.

She shocked me with that first seduction, especially after she had bought *The Well of Loneliness*. I did wonder if the first time was a one-off, a five minute stand just to make some kind of feminist point. Then I got used to the routine. Just lately I felt her melting. That day she brought her dad's ashes and got the giggles allowed us to laugh together. First there was only sex, but now there is laughter. Just no words. I'm getting used to that. I know she is mute. I don't think she's deaf. I've read about people like her, people who can't talk.

I have wondered if she actually likes me. I can't say I mind much either way. I need sex, it's a great release. I know enough about myself to recognise that, but she leaves me perplexed. It's as if each time she comes to see me she shifts the rules. I mean, the way she now dresses, the way she has begun to do her hair, and that rather pathetic striptease act. I've been looking for the right word to describe the whole experience. I find it unsettling.

But then this afternoon she turned up at the shop with a suitcase. I was pleased to see her, even with the case. I went to touch her on the shoulder but she pushed me away. That was when I noticed she was crying, crying in a cold, soulless kind of way.

The shop was empty so I put up the closed sign anyway.

I wanted to ask her what was wrong. But of course, with her, I can't do simple things like that. Instead I tried to carry the case for her but she held onto it, jerked it away from my hand and headed for the stairs up to the flat, went into the kitchen.

I followed her, kept my distance, put the kettle on, then waited.

I know hardly anything about her; I don't even know her name.

She accepted a mug of tea, cupped it in her hands as if she needed the warmth, hardly drank from it.

So we stayed in our positions for a long time, she sitting on the one kitchen chair sipping her tea, me standing, just waiting for what would happen next.

Several times I saw her shiver. I noticed too that occasional spasms of what looked like disgust crinkled her face. She seemed to realise this and smoothed out her mouth by an effort of will. I realised, at some stage in that long vigil, that she was pretty. Her face, apart from the nose, has very even features. Her skin is smooth like Desdemona's monumental alabaster. She drank slowly, sipping silently. I watched the level in the mug fall by degrees. My calves began to ache with the effort of standing still. I was waiting for words, for an explanation, knowing all the time that one would never be forthcoming.

I held on because I felt sorry for her. Was there something else as well? I'm not a decisive man. I like to consider permutations of possibilities and I rarely reach conclusions. Was she in trouble? She certainly exhibited symptoms of this. Why had she brought the case? She must be running away from something or someone. But why run to me? I'm a second-hand bookseller. You only have to look round my kitchen to know that I can just about cope on my own. I kept wondering, as I stood there, how desperate you have to be to find that the only place you can consider running to is my flat. I am the least practical, the least demonstrative person. I am the most staid and dull man I know, but then I have so few friends and acquaintances that the statement probably has no value because it can only call on a statistically insignificant number of comparators. The only interesting thing about my life is that occasionally a mute girl comes to the shop and we make love.

But she has picked me out. She is here. It was only mid-afternoon when she arrived and she has clearly come to stay.

That terrifies me. I've never had visitors. There was no food in and I was out of washing up liquid, very low on toilet paper. 'Stay there,' I suddenly said, smashing the silence. 'I'm just going out to get some things.'

I put my coat on, searched for my wallet and found it in with the shop money. I hesitated about whether to lock the door or not. I didn't want her to feel a prisoner but I also thought she needed to feel safe. In the end I locked it but made a mental note to be as quick as possible about my shopping.

I think it took me twenty minutes. I came back loaded down. She was still sitting in the same place so I moved round her, trying not to disturb her. First I found the tulips and put them in the only vase I have, where they looked oversized but colourful. There was no room for them in the kitchen so I took them through to the sitting room, plonked them on the coffee table, and lit the gas fire to warm the place up, make it look more cheerful. The books which had spilled over the table I piled up underneath. I thought all the time I was doing this that she's never been in this room and I didn't want her to see it like this. I'd bought dusters so I could clean it.

I put the wine in the fridge with the ready meal and the yoghurts. I smuggled the fairy liquid under the sink. I put the croissants in the freezer. I'd also bought proper coffee. I knew I had a cafetière somewhere.

Her mug was empty. 'More tea?' I asked her.

She shook her head.

I took the pack of dusters into the sitting room. It was warming up in there. Quickly I lifted ornaments and dusted. It's funny how much dust there is if you really look. I knew it was on the mantelpiece, the window sills and the coffee table. But it was also on the radiator and the skirting boards. I released so much dust I had to get the hoover out.

It was when I was vacuuming that I found her standing in the door watching me.

'Sorry,' I said. 'I didn't want you to see it like this.' There was the flicker of a smile and that was it. She seemed to be hesitating about what to do next.

'Come in,' I said. 'You've not been in here before, have you?' Everything was the wrong way round about our relationship. She had been in my bedroom many times but never in the sitting room.

I had to move more books from the settee so she could sit down. I stood for a while wondering where to put them, then decided to pile them all up under the window. I retrieved the ones from under the coffee table and added them to the same pile.

She came in reluctantly, touched the settee and then looked at her fingers.

'I'll see to that,' I said.

I used an attachment to clean the settee.

‘There, sit.’

She did so, neatly, legs pulled in, arms wrapped round herself. Before I put the hoover away I cleaned the lampshade, switched the lamp on, closed the curtains, thought the room looked okay.

I didn’t offer her wine. Instead, in an act of great daring, I poured her a glass and put it by her side. She could drink it or not.

I don’t have a TV. I do have a laptop. I need it for checking prices. I sell some books on eBay and I always need to know the latest prices for first editions. The laptop was downstairs but I fetched it up, put it beside her, earned myself another smile.

Then I went back to the shop to tidy up, do the accounts, close up properly.

***

When I got back her wine glass was half empty. She was sitting on the settee with the lap top open, engrossed. I didn’t glance at what she was looking at.

‘Are you hungry?’ I asked.

She nodded.

I put the lasagne into the oven, made a mental note to clean that soon. The lasagne from chilled would take forty minutes. The salad leaves were still in the fridge. It was too early to get them out. I went and took the other chair from my bedroom, wiped the table and laid two places, found the dressing and checked the sell-by date. It was out of best-before but smelled alright.

When all that was done I took the wine bottle into the sitting room and re-filled her glass.

I think she was waiting for me to come back in. She lifted the computer up and handed it to me. On the screen was a word document. I began to read it.

Can I stay? I need to be away from home for a period. I couldn't think of anywhere else to go so I came to you. I can't tell you why. I don't like to tell myself why. Maybe I haven't worked that out yet. No sex please. I may never do sex again. It is enough to say that I've made a terrible mistake.

Leah Goulden.

She's called Leah. I didn't even know that. Does she know my name is Martin? I thought her name suited her. All the time I read the screen I knew she was staring at me, and I realised that she wasn't certain about me, didn't know what a pushover I am. She looked desperate and she wasn't just taking me for granted. 'Of course you can stay,' I said. 'No question.' Then, when her face didn't change, something made me add, 'I have two bedrooms. You have one and I'll have the other.'

She relaxed at that, breathed deeply. I saw her shoulders move downwards. Then she was reaching for the computer, so I gave it back to her and waited for the next message.

She started to type something else. Then she gave up, cried, wiped her eyes on her sleeve, looked hard at me and took a long deep breath. I saw her tongue move in her mouth. It was as if she was rehearsing. In her open mouth I could see it advancing and retreating. Then it touched her teeth and I heard a fluttering sound, like wind through dried grasses.

If it was a word I couldn't catch it. No way would I ask her to repeat it.

I watched as she frowned and shook her head. Then she took another breath and this time the th sound was more distinct. 'Thanks,' is what I think she said.

Then she was moving her jaw as if loosening it. I thought of Frankenstein's monster coming to life. I wondered if she had really talked or if I had just imagined it.

I must have stared at her. She opened and closed her mouth

several times, then spoke again.

It was a strange sound with uncertain volume control. She said it once and then she repeated it. I think she said, 'I need a favour.'

It isn't every day that you experience magic. I suspect I was so flattered that I gushed. 'Anything. Ask away.'

The next sentence took a long time. She was exploring each sound and how to make it.

'If I need to go and see my uncle, will you take me?'

I think that's what she said. The unc sound gave her real trouble. Then more of these fluttering words followed that were such an effort.

'No questions?'

She nodded, then the fluttering words followed that were such an effort. 'He lives in Scotland, near Ullapool. You'll have to pay. I've no money.'

I'd been expecting something simple, something you could do in a few moments or at least in a half day. Ullapool is in the far north of Scotland. I journey most days from my flat down the stairs to my bookshop and back. That miniscule distance is my safety. I own the shop and the flat. I purchased both with the money my parents left me. The activity of settling on a price, going to solicitors and dealing with the searches, had seemed an adventure. It had left me trembling with uncertainty, frightened because I knew these noughts and numbers on a piece of paper were the only real money I would ever have.

Ullapool was at least eight hours away. Alright, she was talking. She was talking to me. I felt honoured, privileged even, but I don't know her. We've never spent any time together. Now I knew she could talk we'd have to say things to each other. What if I didn't like her?

She was looking at me. I had to find an answer. I remembered the comment made by a man who had picked up a girl on a nudist beach and invited her out for dinner that night. While he waited for her under the clock tower in Skopelos, he was nervous both that he wouldn't recognise her dressed and that he might not like what her clothes said about her. I didn't yet know if I would like what Leah had to say. Silence between us didn't matter when she didn't speak. And there might not even be sex. *I may never do sex again.*

She was watching me, staring at me all the time. I hesitated. I had to refuse. What she asked was insultingly demanding, impossibly self-obsessed. But her look was so needy and I have never been able to deal with other people's unhappiness.

'Yes,' I said. 'I'll go. I'll pay.'

I didn't even get a smile by way of response, just a further relaxing of her shoulders, a reaching out for the wine glass and another sip.

We ate in silence. She didn't eat much before pushing the plate away.

'Was it alright?' I asked, exasperated. I hate waste and wondered if it was okay if I finished her portion. I'd had no lunch and I would normally eat a whole lasagne and a big bag of salad.

Her head was down. The street below was unusually quiet or I would never have heard what she said. Having heard it I was transported so far out of my comfort zone that I wished we had never met, certainly wished I had never made her that promise.

'I let myself be raped this afternoon. . .'

I forgot about the uneaten lasagne.

'. . . and I think I'd like to go to bed. I need to sleep.'

***

Now she is in my bed. I hope she is sleeping but I am very wide awake.

I re-warm her share of the lasagne and carry it through to the sitting room. I eat it there with another glass of wine.

I can't put any music on as I usually would at this time of night because I don't want to wake her. So I pick up the laptop and wonder what she has been doing with it, whether there might be another message for me. There's nothing on Word so I go onto the internet and look up her browsing history. She, I must get used to calling her Leah, has been on Streetmap. I open it up and there's the address she has been looking for. It's in Leeds. Leah must have zoomed in because the structure of the streets is very clear. She's been searching a street of what look like Victorian semis with front and back gardens. It's called Waterloo Terrace.

I can't glean anything else so I go back into research history and find Leah has been examining electoral registers for the Leeds area. She doesn't seem to have found what she was looking for there. The next few items tell me a bit more. She's been on Linkedin, Facebook, Twitter. She's been looking for someone and my guess is that she hasn't found that person.

I go back to the electoral register and stare at it. Then the computer suggests Patrick Barr. It's there only for a second but I've got it. I type in Patrick Barr and find that he doesn't live in a semi-detached house in Waterloo Terrace, or if he does live there he isn't registered to vote.

'I let myself be raped.' It's such a shocking statement. Women don't let themselves be raped. Rape is a male weapon and it ruins lives. I wonder why she is blaming herself. I wonder who Patrick Barr is or isn't. Why does she need to go to Ullapool? Can't she just phone? How long will going there and back take? I have a shop to run.

I need to calm my brain if I am ever to sleep. From the pile under the window I pick up Merivale's translation of Homer's Iliad, published in 1869. It's a fancy version with an embossed leather spine, gold tooling and the portcullis symbol of the House of Commons. It opens stiffly as if no one has ever read it. I think of the generations who have found shelf-room for this elaborate book. Has its beauty saved it? I can't play music so I begin to read. Charles Merivale was Chaplain to the Speaker of the House of Commons. He had translated Homer's masterpiece into English rhymed verse. I try to read it but the translation is poor and the rhyming dire. No wonder this copy has survived in such good condition. No one has ever read it.

Before I put it down I realise that it is the story of a rape and the enormous consequences. I think of the armies who were sucked into those battles, of the way no one got home unchanged, of Odysseus travelling for years. Some lines from Yeats drift into my head. *The broken wall, the burning roof and tower / And Agamemnon dead.* Then I remember the rest of the poem. *How can those terrified vague fingers push / the feathered glory from her loosening thighs?* I find myself wondering about Leah's ordeal.

I am asking what I have let myself in for when there is a knock on the door and she comes back in.

'I can't sleep,' she says. Her voice still flutters but is becoming stronger. Then ... 'I've been thinking. . . you don't have to come. . . I've asked too much.' She is talking in short sentences. Each one is an effort.

She is wearing a long nightdress that comes down to her ankles and I'm reminded of the illustrations in a hundred novels. She is the victim and who am I? I'm not the hero in a leather jerkin with a sword thrust under my belt. I'm not a soldier with a rifle. I'm a second-hand bookseller. The only weapons I have to fight with are words. Falstaff is now in one ear reminding me that, *the better part of valor is discretion.* What am I meant to do to help?

'Have you been to the police?'

She shakes her head.

I push my luck. 'You should, you know.'

'I can't. It would hurt my mother too much.'

Then she cries, cries like a child would, throwing her head back, letting the tears drip, making no effort to be in control.

Her crying goes on for a long time. I mustn't touch her. I have to watch and wait.

We sit in silence. I'm panicking. What is the right thing to do? What does she expect? I can't put an arm around her, give her a hug. But I can't just sit here either, so I fetch a box of tissues, taking my time about it. I take it back into the room and put it beside her. Eventually the crying stops.

'Tell me,' I say. 'If you trust me, tell me what happened. If you tell me now it might help you sleep.'

She's much calmer but she still seems doubtful, so I hand her the laptop and suggest she writes it.

She waves the computer away.

'Tea, coffee, more wine?' I ask.

She goes to make a sign but then says the word, 'Tea.'

I have a teapot. I have a small silver tray that came from my aunt so I can do this properly. When I come back in with the tray I see that she's been back into the bedroom and is sitting wrapped in the duvet.

She begins to tell me and it is such an effort. Slowly, painfully, I learn about Izzy and her search, about finding Patrick, about how overjoyed Izzy was. She tells me about the first meeting with the family and subsequent meetings, that they all presumed he was Izzy's son but they had no proof. She quickly gets hoarse and her jaw must hurt so I suggest she stops there and leaves the rest until the morning. But then I realise there is one thing I need to know and perhaps one thing she needs to tell me before she can sleep.

'Was it Patrick who. . .' I can't say the word.

She nods and starts to sob uncontrollably again.

Every instinct in my body cries out that I should comfort her. There is room on the settee. Surely it would be alright if I sat beside her and put my arms around her. I have hugged her before now. We are not strangers. It is at this moment that I begin to realise the enormity of what Patrick has done and I hate him for it. Hatred is a sharp emotion and one I have no right to, but I hate him because of what he has done to us, more specifically because of what he has done to me, when he doesn't even know I exist. I know that is a selfish thought and I have no right, just now, to think of myself. So what on earth must Leah be feeling?

Because I can't act I start to speak, but before I do I fold my arms so that she can't get any wrong ideas. 'I'm so sorry,' I say. 'I just need you to know that you aren't on your own.' Why have I said that? Am I letting pity drag me deeper and deeper into this? Am I really prepared to help her put this right?

I go on regardless because I am simply appalled by her hurt and the sharpness of her dilemma. I feel the need to say something, so I start talking about myself. 'I don't have many friends, but you will find me a true friend,' I say. 'I want you to tell me what you need from me and perhaps what you don't need. Meanwhile, I've got some brandy somewhere so I'll pour us each a measure and we'll drink to the future being better than now.'

She is sobbing when I go out of the room and she is sobbing when I come back in. I hand her the glass. She doesn't take it. I can't bear to see her like this. I think she needs the drink so I gently unwrap her fingers to make her grasp the glass. She flinches but says nothing. I clink my glass on hers and go away to the far side of the room. I wonder if I should even have done that much. I ask myself if I am doing all this for her or for myself.

I see at once that she isn't up for the toast so I busy myself finding some music. I choose Copland Symphony Number 2. It's called *The Age of Anxiety* and that seems fitting. Its quiet start is scarcely audible in the room. Her sobs are louder than the CD. Then, as the music softens, her sobs decline and the steady beat calms her. It feels the right music to be playing. There are undertones of tragedy and passages of lightness. I worry as we reach the first crescendo, but it's quickly over and the gentleness of the piano soothes both of us. She takes a sip of the brandy and I know she is listening. The discords mount in the music and become more pronounced, but always the piano maintains a steady pulse, akin to something like hope.

It is companionable to be sitting together listening to the same piece. We sip the brandy in time to the music and I realise that even under these circumstances it is better to listen with someone else than to listen on your own. The music has both despair and yearning. The brandy is hitting the spot so I stop drinking. I mustn't make a false move of any kind.

Her glass is empty. When the piece stops she yawns, picks up her duvet and goes back to bed. She nods to me as she goes but I realise the moment she has left the room that she hasn't said, 'Goodnight.'

I wait to hear the toilet flush, then her door close. I count slowly up to one hundred before going to bed myself.

Chapter 9

The promise I have made wakes me at 3.40am. Questions rob me of further sleep. Where will we stay? What do hotels cost? We'll need two rooms. Has Leah any money of her own? Can I really be expected to pay for everything, and what are we going to Ullapool for that we can't do by some other means? It is never more than semi-dark in the flat because the shopping area keeps its street lights on all night to deter crime. I lie in this half-light and begin to calculate the costs and the problems. There is nothing in this for me. What we had together has gone. Sex will never again be the uncomplicated, unpredictable, joyous thing that it was. I know it will be a long time before she giggles again, if she ever does.

Patrick! Her half-brother! Is he? Can he really be Izzy's son if he did that to his sister? I have never even groped anyone but I think I understand what rape is. It's about power, it's about male dominance. It has something to do with gender revenge. But to rape your sister. Well, she can't be, can she? She doesn't believe it either, hence the searches which seem to have been inconclusive, but how do you ever prove that he isn't related, except through a DNA test? She has no samples from him and no possibility of getting any now because she mustn't go anywhere near him. Even if she could prove who he isn't, how does she tell her mother?

There is something else haunting my night. I feel in the presence of evil. Not the messy business of murder so remarked on by Father Brown, nor the gothic villains of a Sherlock Holmes novel. Where in Dante's circles of hell will you find a man like Patrick? I think of Leah's hurt, of Izzy's soon-to-be-dashed hopefulness, and my flesh creeps to the extent that I do not go back to sleep.

I'm first up in the morning. I suspect Leah has been lying

awake as much as I have because she goes to the bathroom almost the moment I have finished there. This gives me time to clear the kitchen. When she comes into the room I have a table laid, croissants heated, and a cafetière of coffee ready.

'Did you sleep?'

She ignores that question so pointedly that I feel stupid for having asked it. I look at her face. Its naturally pallid colour has whitened. Her eyes are red and her nose seems to be pulled in as if pinched by an internal frost.

Without saying anything else I pass her a croissant and pour the coffee. She eats half of it, begins to sip.

'Is it alright?'

She ignores this too and I see a look of disdain cross her features. 'I didn't mean life,' I explain, 'just the coffee.'

No smile, not even the ghost of one. She's sunk further away from me but she is eating. I have another croissant keeping warm in the oven so I fetch and offer it to her without words. She takes it, equally wordless. I don't ask whether she wants more coffee. When I see her cup is empty I simply fill it up.

It doesn't take long to eat breakfast. I wash out the cafetière and refill it just for something to do. Her lethargy is infectious. I look at my watch. I should go down soon and open the shop.

Has she seen that glance at the time? 'I need something to do,' she suddenly says. 'Can I help you? Clean up a bit downstairs?' Her words sound sore again. I get the sense that she might not like the sound of her own voice.

I realise that she doesn't want to be on her own and the shop does need cleaning. 'I can close at lunchtime,' I say, then stumble quickly on in case she thinks I'm propositioning her. 'We can book a hotel in Ullapool, make plans.'

'Have you a car?' she asks suddenly.

'A small van. Why?'

'I probably need to go home. . .'

She talks slowly, unwillingly, and when she pauses I realise I feel markedly disappointed. I am a mystery to myself. I don't really want her staying here, do I? Let this pass from me.

'to get some money. . . so long as. . .'

She waits for such a time that I complete her sentence for her. 'So long as Patrick's not there.'

I thought she might be angry at my presumption, but she nods.

'You want me with you just in case?'

She nods again.

'Alright,' I say.

I go down and open the shop. I show her where the cleaning stuff is. All morning she works alongside me. We barely acknowledge each other, but I have to admit that the shop looks much better and I say so.

'Woman's touch.' She has trouble with the o sound. There is no laughter in her eyes when she makes this comment, no smile. She's filling in time too, absorbing and reabsorbing her wretchedness.

When we have a coffee break she tells me about her searches, her worry that Patrick might not be who he says he is. I nod and don't let on that I already know some of this, that I have followed her internet browsing.

Before we set off I ask her the way. She says she'll tell me where and when to turn.

What will we do if Patrick is there? What will I do? It's touching that she wants me with her, but I'm no use in a fight. My plan if trouble erupts (very rare in bookshops) has always been to go down with the first punch and stay there.

As I drive I feel her tension rising. Clearly Leah doesn't drive because she gives instructions at the wrong time.

It isn't far, but then I knew that. I nearly miss the entrance because it's so posh, a gravel drive between tall conifers. As we go down between the trees Leah grips my arm. The entrance is narrow. I hope we don't have to back out quickly. I'm not good at backing.

The drive suddenly opens out and there is this beautiful

house. In one glance I take in curves, chimneys, windows, red brick, red tiles and I recognise it. I know what I'm looking at. Can this really be where Leah lives? I need to concentrate, so I make myself stop looking and focus instead on the car that's parked right outside the front door.

Is he here?

'Mum's car,' Leah says.

I park the van behind a tall, thick conifer. 'In case he turns up,' I explain.

She gets out and tells me, 'I'll come straight out if he arrives.'

She goes into the house. That leaves me outside, listening for an approaching car, nervously waiting.

What I see distracts me. This house is wonderful. Greedily I drink in its character and think of the novels in my shop that come from the same period. This is Arts and Crafts at its very best. Some of my favourite book designs are from the same period. One I still have was even designed by Charles Rennie Mackintosh himself. Now I have time I take in roofs and windows, the sheer organic feel of the place. My eyes light on the chimneys, the changing gradient of the roofs, the lack anywhere of right-angled precision. It is to die for. I imagine the rooms inside and think of her sleeping in my poky bedroom, sitting in my square-as-boredom-itself sitting room. I wish I hadn't come, that I'd never seen this. Why on earth is a woman who lives in a house like this spending time with a poor specimen like me? I'm way, way out of her league.

The house is set in its own grounds. I don't want to put a price on it but this must be a millionaire's palace. Time passes. It's getting cold in the van. I start to day-dream. I imagine myself living here. I think of a library. It must have one. There must be other empty rooms. I imagine all the books you could store in such a house. I consider how much you could shrink away from the world. There would be no traffic or people noise, room to breathe deeply, and this is a place where I could feel intimately connected to the single period in history that I most admire.

My wait goes on. I think of Patrick seeing the house for the first time. If he really is Leah's half-brother, he has a chance of inheriting. *Neither shalt thou covet they neighbour's house, his field or his manservant, or his maidservant, his ox or his ass or anything that is his.* This is worth coveting. Who wouldn't covet such a property? I've been here so long I'm already picking out the detail. The door handles must be original. The bell is on an anachronistic cord pull system. The front door itself is solid oak.

Still she doesn't come out. I wonder if it's warmer outside the van. Should I turn the engine on just to get some heat into the car? Leah must love this house. Everyone who has ever seen it, never mind lived in it, would be bound to love it. This is another thing that Patrick has robbed her of. He has excluded her from this building. Is that why he did it, I find myself asking. I think of the misguided woman living with hope inside such a place. To have to leave somewhere like this, go so far away you can never get back...

Then Leah is coming out of the house. Her face is strained. I start to ask but she shakes her head, gets quickly into the car as if she wants to be gone.

She's very quiet, subdued, so sunk into herself she doesn't give me instructions. I have to feel my way back.

Then, on a straight section, I feel her grip my arm and duck down. A single car is coming towards us.

'It's him.'

I slow down. He's slowed down too because the road is narrow. He looks straight ahead as we pass so I can see him clearly.

Is this what evil looks like? He is ordinary, a strong young man but just normal. If you passed him in a crowd you might give him a glance but you wouldn't stare. He looks totally relaxed, untroubled.

What is he thinking, I wonder, as he drives towards that lovely house. That Leah will be there waiting for him, expectant, longing? Or that Leah will be gone and so out of his way? But why should he want that?

I'm overtaken by a spasm of hate. I find myself accelerating to the next farm drive, turning quickly and following him, keeping well back. I learn the registration number, cramming it into my brain by repeating it over and over. LV 63 RUJ. To make sure it stays there I make a story out of it. LV is an insurance company. 63 is the year my Dad was born. RUJ now stands for Royal Ulster Jellies.

Before Patrick reaches the house I slow down and, to Leah's relief, turn the van round again at another farm gate. I wonder if Leah understood what I was doing. A tiny part of me wants to impress her and anyway, her battle is becoming mine.

'His registration number,' I say. 'Now we can trace him.'

She says nothing and suddenly I feel a fool. I've as good as told Leah that I followed her searches.

We get back to my flat. I park the van and let Leah into the shop.

'LV63RUJ is his registration,' I tell her. 'It's worth a try.'

I realise I sound too eager. She just isn't interested. I look at her and see the sadness.

'Patrick was all Izzy would talk about.' Leah is in despair. She goes on. 'Even I don't matter to her. She gave me her credit card, said she'd use her debit when I was away. She didn't even ask where I was going or who I was going with, just handed the card over and told me the pin number. Then we were back to Patrick.'

Leah is talking slowly, sullenly. 'Izzy had no interest in my sudden disappearance. She asked me nothing about where I was last night.'

'You were gone a long time.'

'Listening,' she says. 'Listening to his praises.'

She starts to take it out on me. 'So don't tell me to go to the police. I can't. I really can't.'

How unfair, I think. I put my hands up as if surrendering. 'So he gets away with it?'

'What else can I bloody do?'

Her speech is getting stronger. She makes that comment with some emphasis. A thought occurs to me.

'Did you talk to your mother?' I ask.

She shakes her head. 'Only you.'

Is that a compliment or a burden?

A long pause follows. For the first time with her I feel the need to say something, to start some sort of conversation, but I don't know what to say so we sit in silence.

'He's called Uncle Joshua,' she suddenly says. 'I've never met him. He left the family before we were born. She's never told me why. I need to find him to understand what's happening here. Was he around when Izzy got pregnant? Did he meet her lover? What does he know about my grandparents? I'm sorry. It's such a long way, but I need to understand what's happened. I found his address in Izzy's book.

It's a long speech for Leah, full of pauses, slowly spoken as if she often has to work out how to say a word before she attempts it.

The slowness of her delivery gives me time to think. 'What if we go to Ullapool and he isn't there?' I ask.

'Then we come back.' She pauses. 'We come back and I give up.'

Silence fills the room. I'm angry too, but I need this to work.

She is thinking furiously. 'Patrick has the photo. He might be my half-brother, in which case he is a monster. I thought about this all last night. It's my word against his about the rape. If he isn't related to me then who is he, how has he got the information? How did he get the photograph?'

I'm nodding, trying to understand.

'I just think Uncle Joshua will know something.'

'But we should phone first shouldn't we, at least check he's there?'

She looks at me, almost glaring. 'What if he contacts Izzy before I can talk to him? I must leave her right out of this, at least until I know, until I'm certain.'

'So we turn up in Ullapool and hope he's at home?'

'You don't have to come.'

'I said I would.'

She looks at me then, a long look that I simply parry.

Her tone changes. 'I'd like to have you with me,' she says. 'It's probably my fault, but I have no one else I can ask.'

Chapter 10

Hotels, even the cheapest, cost a shed load of money.

'Look,' I say to Leah later that evening, as gently as possible, 'we do need to know that your Uncle's there and that he'll see us.'

She says nothing. She's slowing right down. It's as if she's been usurped by misery. Her head is down, but suddenly she raises it and looks at me. 'Who is he?' she whispers.

'Patrick?' I ask.

She nods. Another long pause and then, 'He told me his address. He wrote it down: 48 Waterloo Terrace. But I don't think he lives there. He's not on the electoral register. I checked. He's not on LinkedIn, or Twitter, or Facebook.'

'And his car isn't his,' I add. 'I checked the registration and it's a company car.'

'It's as if he doesn't exist. Can you live in the 21st century and leave no trace? Who the hell is he?'

Leah slumps again as if the question is too big for her.

'But he must be someone,' I say. 'Izzy made contact with him. We don't know how. You told me he has the same photo your Mum brought to the cafe. We need to understand that link. You don't want to ask your mother, so we need to go and see your Uncle Joshua. That's what you think, isn't it?'

No reaction, nothing, so I leave it. I daren't push my own views. I have to give her time.

That night we lie awake with a wall between us. I can tell she's not sleeping. It's in her eyes. I'm not sleeping either. In the middle of the night I tell myself it's hopeless. She's missed her chance. She should have gone straight to the police. She's not her mother's keeper. If he will do that to Leah, what is he capable of doing to the mother? And just how far is Leah prepared to go to protect her mother? She could involve her siblings but she won't. She doesn't trust them.

The image of that wonderful house swims like a goldfish round and round in my head. Patrick, I'll have to keep calling him that, must want it for himself. With Leah out of the way he has every chance of manipulating Izzy until he gets it.

Then I hear a noise in the house. It's faint at first, hardly there at all, but just occasionally it won't be suppressed. Leah is crying. Patrick has robbed her of energy, eviscerated her hope. She is saturated with what has happened to her. With me it is different. I am energised. I am steeped in hate.

But I am also afraid. I am afraid that Leah may take another way out. I have seen a rabbit caught in the headlights of a stoat's eyes. She is close to torpor. I need to get her moving. We need a plan.

***

'Tomorrow,' I tell Leah next morning. She's sitting red-eyed at breakfast. Her lovely face is now pasty. Because she's eating so little I've made her porridge, but she's not really touched it. Instead she stirs the spoon round and round. 'We'll go to Ullapool tomorrow. It's Friday so I'll only have to shut the shop for two days. But...' I pause here, 'can't we do something to check that he's still living at that address?'

She puts her spoon down. 'No,' she says. 'We just go. If you won't take me I'll catch the train from York.'

I stare at her.

She looks up. 'I've never met him. I don't know what he's like. I can't take the risk of him phoning Izzy before I've had a chance to meet him. We weigh him up first and then we ask our questions.'

'Okay,' I say. At least she's still talking.

She goes back to playing with her food.

'Today we book. Do you need to buy anything? It'll be really cold up there.'

She seems to hear that.

She takes out the credit card Izzy gave her. 'I can buy clothes. Now I can even pay for the hotel.'

She knows so little. How do I explain this without making her angry?

'It's your mother's credit card. Whatever you use the card to buy will appear on a statement they send to your mother. That way she'll know what you're doing, where you are, what you're buying. If she knows, Patrick will know. Besides, your spending patterns will be different from hers. The bank may even phone her to check before they authorize the payment.'

I know I'm taking charge and I don't want to, but if we are going we must go tomorrow, just to keep her moving.

I hand her the computer. 'Find us a hotel then. Look for late bargains. I'll open up the shop.'

Going down the stairs my mood swings. I tell myself I can always walk away. I'm a bookseller, not an action hero. This may well be beyond me. There is also a question in my head that I need to answer. Am I doing all this out of unselfishness? Am I willing to be so involved only because she's a human being in trouble?

Chapter 11

Yesterday Leah bought a padded jacket and a pair of fur-lined boots. She's wearing both. We're in my van which I've tidied but I can't disguise its functionality. We're on the A19 just south of Newcastle. My van is not the fastest vehicle on the road. Lorries overtakes us. I've got my foot hard down and just occasionally, going downhill, we reach the speed limit.

There is urgency. Once we know what we are up against we'll need to act. Leah is sitting very still. She stares ahead through rimed windows. My van is for local journeys only. I use it to clear houses and carry books. It's old and there's not even a radio to distract us. The windscreen wipers are poor. We started early. There are only 6 hours of daylight and I'm thoroughly unnerved by the idea of driving through Scotland in winter and in darkness.

We're booked into The Ferry Boat Hotel on the harbour front in Ullapool. It's a twin-bedded en-suite room. It's not what we wanted, but in winter some of the hotels are closed so the rest are busy, particularly at weekends. We booked for two nights. Leah wanted one night only, but I told her we couldn't drive up in one day, see her uncle and drive back the next. It'll be awkward sharing a room. We'll have to take turns to change in the en-suite and that'll be a fag because I'll have to remember to take everything in with me. I've never slept in the same room as a woman for a whole night and I feel a bit like the narrator in *Lolita*. These days particularly, that isn't a good feeling.

It's just after dawn. The rising sun suddenly gleams on the sea to our right. For a moment I'm exhilarated. I nudge Leah and point to it. She glances sideways, then goes back to staring ahead.

Patrick has killed any capacity of enjoyment in her, even

of a gleam on the winter sea. He's wrapped her whole sensory world in an opaque, plastic film. I want to tell her I'm sorry for my moment of forgetting. But I don't because what happened, happened to her. It didn't happen to me.

We take a break in the services overlooking the Forth Road Bridge. We've been going for four and a half hours. We both need a drink and I need a break from the road and gear changing. I can already feel my left calf stiffening.

The moment we get out of the van the east wind cuts into us. With heads down we rush for the automatic doors. Without waiting for Leah I join the Costa queue. When I see her coming out of the loos I expect her to join me, tell me what she wants, help me to carry, but instead she chooses a window table and sits staring across at the bridge. Exasperated, I buy two Americanos, two blueberry muffins, and a pack of small shortbreads.

She says nothing when I reach her, simply reaches for her coffee. I feel taken for granted, but I'm so thirsty I begin drinking. I too stare at the bridge, and I understand immediately why it is so loved.

'The coffee's good.'

She's back with me. Those are the first words she's said since we set off.

'I chose a good table,' she adds.

'It's beautiful, isn't it?' I wave a hand in the direction of the bridge. 'Have you seen it before?'

'Only in pictures.'

We watch as a train crosses.

'Built at the same time as your house,' I say.

I'm hoping for a conversation, but we relapse into silence. She's hungry again, gobbling down the muffin and reaching for the shortbreads.

'Do you want a panini?'

She shakes her head. 'We don't have time,' she says.

I fill up expensively and we head north on the A9 towards

Perth. In exposed places the wind buffets the van. We can see hills in front of us and most are white-capped. Against the russet browns of winter bracken and heather the white is attractive, but the road is already gathering slush. Soon the mountains close in on both sides and the afternoon is already fading. In places, the snow reaches down to the edge of the road. I can see where snow ploughs have been active. Spray from lorries drenches the window. The wipers only just cope and I worry we may not make it, but the sky is clearing.

By the time we pass Aviemore we are back into darkness and I realise the van has another problem. Its lights are less than brilliant. I never drive it at night. I'm tired now, but Ullapool is only 56 miles.

The road to Ullapool has less traffic but it's slow going. The darkness is endless and watching the side of the road becomes hypnotic. At one point Leah suddenly touches my arm. 'Slow down,' she says. 'Look.'

At first I can't make out what she is pointing at, then I do. On both sides of the road there are eyes. They shine in the feeble headlights as much as the cat's eyes in the middle of the road.

'What are they?'

'They must be deer,' I tell her. 'In winter they have to come down from the hills.'

As we watch, the eyes go out as the deer ignore us. They put their heads down and continue feeding.

We set off again. I notice the snow poles with rings to tell you the depth. The sky above our heads is now full of stars.

'It's nearly 7 o'clock,' Leah says. 'We'll leave my uncle until tomorrow.' Then she adds, 'Poor Martin, you must be so tired. I don't know how you've done it, driving us all this way.'

The hotel is easy to find. We park outside. As we get out we are aware of the heavy slab of water on the other side of the road. In the wind it is slapping against the shoreline. We can't see this, we can only hear it.

I get both cases and lock the car. Together we rush into the hotel.

We register at the bar. We check the room. It's not great. The two beds fill the room and the en-suite is tiny. Will there be enough room to shower and dress? I see Leah go to sit down on the bed. Her face is haunted. I sense that lethargy will take over if she sits for too long, so I intervene. 'Food,' I say. 'I'm starving and there wasn't much room left in the bar.' She nods and we head downstairs immediately.

The room is a fug of alcohol and food. Leah finds a table and I grab two menus. Then she surprises me. She takes over, asks me what I want. I watch her fight her way to the bar and see the drinkers on their stools make way for her. I watch as she points to the menu and uses her fingers, nodding in confirmation. When I see the barman read the order back I get concerned, but there's no need. He sends his notes to the kitchen and gives Leah a number stuck in a wooden stand. She brings that back and goes for the two glasses of wine.

'Not useless,' she says when she gets back.

And it's as if something has happened between us. Was it sharing a day's silence? The length of the journey? The deer's eyes in the darkness? This warmth and the incipient food? We are both leaning forward as if, at this moment anyway, we are content to be together.

Leah sips her wine and then says, 'You didn't have to do this.'

That gives me my chance. I'll ask it baldly. 'Why exactly are we here?'

She frowns and pauses for such a long time that I wonder if she knows. Then it's as if she decides she can trust me.

'There's something going on I don't understand, Martin. I made a terrible mistake. I thought Patrick was my half-brother. I thought everything was above board. I was even pleased for Izzy that she'd found her son.'

'Well, mostly pleased,' she adds.

'I know men can be creepy. He wasn't like that. He didn't seem underhand. Afterwards he actually said, 'I know that's what you wanted.' Can you believe it?'

She looks at me then. 'Martin, that's when I knew. I don't know if I can put into words what I feel. He was so certain, so absolutely convinced. God matters to him. He told me that, but for all the saints in heaven he walked away afterwards as if raping me had been part of God's will.'

She shuts her eyes tight. Is it to stop tears? I'll be so embarrassed if she starts crying here, in this crowded bar.

But she doesn't. She shakes her head, has a long slug of wine and continues. 'And I was wrong about him. I pride myself on being right about people. I watch others, measure each person I meet. He knew that, called me the watcher, which disarmed me so much that I stopped watching him. He read me and he betrayed me.'

'I feel such a fool,' she adds.

Now is the moment. Now is the time I can reach out and take her hand. You see, it's changing for me. It's no longer just about sex. I recognise the symptoms. I'm falling for this strange girl. Then I mentally kick myself. Is it her vulnerability I find so attractive? She has never seemed vulnerable before. Is that it, or has her house become my Pemberley?

So I keep my hands on the table and the moment passes. Another silence settles between us.

'I know I haven't answered your question,' she suddenly says. 'You see, I don't understand. Who is he?' Her voice is suddenly raised, has some force. 'I hate him for what he has done to me. I'm frightened by how much I hate him. I want to destroy him but I can't. Izzy is my friend as well as my mother. She's my best friend and I just can't do this to her. I'm stuck.'

She slams her fist down on the table as she says this, startling the waitress who is arriving with enormous plates of fish and chips.

We eat. We are both hungry. There will be no more

revelations for the moment. But when we are finished it's as if the food has given her energy.

'He calls himself Patrick. Officially he doesn't exist. He gives his own mother a false address. Is he a fake? Have we let a cuckoo into the nest? And the photo he sent her. It told us nothing about him. It was a passport photo. Then his clothes. He wears such old fashioned clothes. Who is he? More to the point, what is he about?'

'And you hope your uncle will throw light on this?'

'He might have met Izzy's lover. He might know who he was, what he looked like. He might know about my grandparents. I need to know everything he knows. You can see that.'

I nod.

'He's the only chance I've got.'

'You could tell your family what happened, appeal to them for help.'

And I see at once that everything between us is smashed again. She looks at me with utter contempt. Doesn't she like her family?

She doesn't want a pudding. She doesn't want another glass of wine.

I'm hungry. I order apple pie and custard. Leah grudgingly says she'll have a coffee.

I think, well that's over. I clearly said the wrong thing.

I eat my pudding in silence.

Leah has finished her coffee when she says, 'I'm sorry, Martin. You don't know my family. If you did…'

Chapter 12

It's about 5am. Martin is asleep, snoring quietly. I've slept a little. I was tired when we went to bed, tired and full of fish and chips, but now I'm wide awake.

My head is obsessed with what we are here for. My uncle is called Joshua and although I've always I known of him I've never met him. We get a Christmas card each year and that's it. His address is Ullapool but he lives outside the town in the middle of nowhere. Will he be in? Will he see me? Will he know any of the answers to my questions? I know it's stupid to speculate when there's nothing to go on. I need my sleep. I must look dreadful.

There's a street light right outside the window and the curtains are thin. I am so far from sleep that I distract myself by looking at Martin. He has thrown off the duvet and is lying on his side in his boxer shorts.

Why was I ever interested in him? He isn't beautiful. His face is plain, open but the opposite of rugged. His hair is in strange tufts and already receding. His body is slim but soft and white. His hands are slightly pudgy. My eyes travel along his legs. They are not the legs of a walker or a cyclist. I can see no definition to his muscles. He is a creature of the indoors. He belongs in his bookshop and I have dragged him here because he was the only person I knew who would come with me. I let my eyes travel along his exposed body once again, down to the boxer shorts, and I don't feel even a twinge of desire. Has Patrick done this to me? When I used to walk to the bookshop I was keyed up with longing. But then I was in control.

Was I slumming it with Martin in those days? I could never have taken him home with me. I mean, what would my siblings have thought?

But now I have no home. My wonderful house is closed to me so long as Patrick is there. If I walk away I will lose my mother, but haven't I already lost her? I'm the helpless smaller meadow pipit chick that is already on the edge of the nest. One more push and the cuckoo will have me out. Where will I live then, and what will I live on? Izzy pays for everything. I am not in Dad's will.

There are voices outside on the pavement. The town is stirring.

I look again at Martin. I still have Martin. Perhaps Martin is all I have.

***

I must have fallen asleep. When I wake up Martin has gone. It's 9.30. He's made his bed and I panic for a moment because I can't see his case. But it's there. He's got up, showered, dressed, and gone out without waking me. Has he gone for breakfast, fed up with waiting? Fed up with me? Has he just gone for a walk?

They serve breakfast until 10. I'll have to be quick. Without Martin here I can shower and then dress. I don't have to take my clothes in with me.

But when I come out of the shower, naked, having hung up the towel, I see Martin sitting on the bed. He's startled. He should look away but he doesn't, and I remember my striptease routine. Coolly I walk across to my case, get clean knickers out, turn my back and dress in front of him, ignoring him as if he isn't there. I sense he's watching me. Only when I have dried my hair do I turn and face him.

He looks awkward, then says, 'I don't expect you want to hear this right now, but you are very beautiful.'

Most of me doesn't want to hear that, but part of me does.

'And you are very kind for letting me sleep,' I tell him.

'I suspected you'd had a bad night. We can just catch

breakfast. Shall we go down?'

He's waited for me. He is a gentleman.

***

Soon we are back in the van. It's a dull day, so unlike yesterday. There are no views, no white-capped hills. The mountains are shrouded. The sea is leaden. The land is dull brown, and the only colour is the orange/yellow seaweed exposed by the low tide. We drive north, at first on reasonable roads and then on a single track road with passing places.

Everything is drenched. Sometimes the rain on the windscreen turns to sleet. Why does Uncle Joshua live so far from civilisation? What is he running away from?

Every now and then Martin stops to consult the map we've bought. Not much further, he tells me. He's looking for a sign. When he sees it he turns off the road and heads downhill on a track with grass growing in the middle. Now I'm worried. What will I find? What will Izzy's brother be like?

At the side of the track, runnels of water skip and gurgle their way down to the sea. The whole landscape works like a downpipe. Even the road itself is acting as a conduit for water.

A house emerges from the greyness. It's modern. It announces itself with two notices. One says,' Reiff Holiday Homes'. The other 'Camusghlaslan'. It's the name we are looking for.

There's no light in the windows, nothing to show that anyone is at home. My heart sinks.

Then Martin points. 'Look, smoke from the chimney. We're going to be alright.'

We get out. It worries me that no one has come to the door or peered out of the many windows. If you lived this far out, wouldn't you be alert to a strange van bumping its way down your track?

The rain hits us immediately. We scamper to the front door

and stand close together under the awning. There's no push button bell or knocker but there is a real bell, like the one we had at school. Martin rings it and we wait.

At first there's nothing, then a light is switched on and we hear footsteps. The door opens. A woman emerges. Her clothes give no clue to her age. Her face is wrinkled. She's small and lively. Her hair is a mess as if she's stopped caring about it. She's wearing a sloppy woollen jumper, jeans and slippers. She doesn't say hello. In fact, she doesn't say anything at all, just stares at us.

We can feel the rain on our backs and the warmth of the house on our faces. There's a smell of wood smoke from inside.

Then, 'Well, I'll give you full marks for being different. What happened to the suits and the tie?'

Her voice is sharp, defensive. I'm shaken. I was ready for an emotional reunion, not this.

'Hello,' Martin says. 'My name's Martin and this is Leah. You've not met either of us . . ..'

She interrupts. 'We're not coming back. There is no way we are ever coming back. I told the last pair he sent. So I suggest you get back into that van of yours and go.'

She looks at us with contempt and goes to close the door. This is not going well. We've come all this way.

'I'm sorry,' Martin says, 'but I don't understand. We know nothing about a previous visit. Leah is Joshua's niece. Her mother is called Isabel.'

The woman hesitates, peers at us nonplussed. 'So you're not from the Living Saints?'

'No.' Martin says this firmly. 'I've never heard of them.'

There is a silence inside the house as if someone is listening intently. The woman is scrutinising me and she seems doubtful.

I've let Martin do all the talking so far but it hasn't been enough, so I make this woman, this stranger, the second person in my adult life that I have ever talked to. 'My father was called Gary,' I say. 'He ran a grocery business. I have two brothers and a sister. My sister is called Julia and my brothers are called James and Daniel. Julia is the oldest and I fit in between James and Daniel.'

We hear footsteps. The woman stands to one side and a man appears.

I stare at him. He has something of Izzy about him. His cheek bones and his mouth are much the same. He has a similarly thin face. I keep staring. He is my mother's brother but he isn't like Patrick. At first I see no resemblance and I breathe more easily. Then I see it. He has Patrick's eyes. They are the same warm brown colour, an exact match only much older. The lids hang heavily, particularly on the right side. I stifle a shriek. If this is my Uncle Joshua, then Patrick really is my half-brother. I look again and wonder if I'm mistaken. Patrick's eyes are warm and confident. Uncle Joshua's eyes are full of hurt.

'The names are right, Hilary,' the man says. 'Come in out of the rain.'

He turns and goes into the house. The woman follows. It's a narrow entrance. I hesitate. Martin has seen this.

'What's wrong?' he whispers

His hand stretches out for mine. I don't want that, so before he makes contact I wrap both arms round myself.

'His eyes are just like Patrick's,' I whisper.

Their house is bigger than it seemed from the road. I follow them into the lounge and see an enormous picture window. Opposite that is a log-burning stove. There are old settees covered with throws, and books and magazines everywhere.

I make for the fire. Uncle Joshua comes towards me, takes a long look at me. 'I thought you were the one who doesn't talk,' he says abruptly. He's wary of me, uncertain. Hilary is looking at me too.

I can't get over his eyes. They are the same but different. He must think me rude the way I am staring at him. He looks me up and down. 'If you are who you say you are, how's my little sister, Isabel?'

I can't answer. Because of his eyes I want to shrink away. I want to be mute again.

Uncle Joshua leans back. 'Come here,' he says. 'Give your uncle a hug.'

He comes towards me and I can't help it. I stiffen, pull my elbows in, close my eyes. He stops, looks at me again. A shadow passes over his face. 'I thought you claimed you were family,' he says. 'Isn't that why you've come?'

Martin has stopped scanning the books. He comes to stand beside me. 'Leah's mother doesn't know we're here,' he says.

'And apart from being Martin, who are you?' Hilary asks. She's still suspicious. 'Are you friend, husband, or lover?'

I glance at Martin. The question has thrown him. There is a real answer and a wished-for answer, so I speak for him. 'Friend,' I say, not looking at Martin's reaction.

'I'm not a Living Saint,' Martin adds, 'whoever they may be.'

Uncle Joshua turns to Martin. 'Have they been bothering you?' he asks, sharply.

'No,' he replies. 'Who are they?'

Uncle Joshua shakes his head. 'They'd left me alone for years. But just recently they're back after me, hence that non-welcome you got from us.'

I feel ungrateful. I feel I'm not making the right impression, so I make myself walk to my uncle. 'I'll give you that hug now, if you still want one.'

I hug him quickly. His body doesn't feel like Patrick's. There's nothing creepy about him. When his arms come around me I find it's alright.

The room relaxes. Hilary offers coffee. We both say yes. They leave us together.

There's a pause. I look round the room. It has the feel of a place on the edge, a last retreat. I notice the windows overlook the sea. It must be quite a view if it ever stops raining.

'Alright?' Martin whispers.

'Yes.' I want to tell him how shocked I am, but there isn't time.

Uncle Joshua returns with a plate of biscuits. I'm still full of breakfast. He hands me a coffee, offers sugar.

Hilary comes in with the other mugs.

I sit down and take a sip. The chair makes me feel safer. 'I'm sorry I didn't hug you at once,' I say to Uncle Joshua, 'but you have his eyes.'

'Whose eyes?'

'Patrick, the man who assaulted me, the man who doesn't exist.' I find I'm crying. I don't mean to cry. I thought I was over that but the tears are back and I can't go on. I'm really embarrassed so I duck my head.

A hand gently touches my shoulder. I look up. It's Martin.

'Patrick claims to be Leah's half-brother. We need to ask you some questions.'

Sacridium 1

(Extract from the diary of Matthew Holmes, included here by kind permission of the Elders of the Church of the Living Saints)

A fortnight ago our beloved leader John Holmes passed to glory. Now I have inherited his mantle. I have become the leader of the Church of the Living Saints. The Elders have bestowed on me my father's title. I have become God's Man.

That means they have placed the Keys to the Kingdom into my hands. From now onwards I will choose who is worthy to be saved; saved from the agony of death and raptured straight to Heaven. That will happen on the Day of Judgement, the day when this world ends as one day soon it surely will. On that great day, when all around us the ungodly perish, it will be my destiny to stand at the side of God Almighty Himself and welcome my Living Saints into Paradise. I now understand the direct lineage between St Peter and ourselves. We are the true inheritors of the Gospels.

I am admitted into the final secrets. My earthly father's papers have been handed to me. I read them all. I read far into the night and I was surprised, shocked even. Some happenings, which I was an unwitting part of, were not as I thought them to be. This place has secrets, and not all our dealings with the world appear to have been as straightforward or as honourable as I had imagined. Is that because of my faulty understanding?

I have prepared myself for this moment. I have kept myself pure. Out there, beyond our enclave, temptation lies. I have never been out there. I went to our school. I worship only in our church. I have worked only at our headquarters. I have walked only in our gardens. I have never paid income tax. I have never voted. I have never eaten a crumb or drunk a single drop with anyone who was not one of the Saints. When I married I was a virgin. I was never unfaithful to my wife, and if God never gave us a son it is perhaps because they, the whole world-wide congregation of the Living Saints, they are now all my sons.

And I'll let you into one of the secrets of this place. We believe in evil. The Devil is out there, rampaging. He is the incumbent and we are the insurgents. The Devil has taken over the world. He is winning. Materialism thrives. Pornography is everywhere. Secularism has triumphed in the west. These have to be the last days as they were foretold.

We are God's freedom fighters. That's why I admire ISIS. They share our views on evil. They know the danger. Even communists understand that purity has its price. In the words of Saloth Sar,[1] to give him his real name, they know it is better to kill ten innocent people than to allow one guilty person to go unpunished. I have said it before and I say it again, the death or the life of individuals is unimportant. What matters is the struggle between God and the Devil.

God took my wife early but I am not alone. Katherine is often by my side. Katherine was my temporal father's gift to me. Out there they would call her a personal assistant. I have no doubt that she is beautiful in the eyes of God. Perhaps one day I will see that for myself. She is efficient. She is duly humble. She manages much of the office and the institution, bringing me papers to sign, making sure that my desk stays clear.

The only blemish I can find in her is that she has never married. It is every woman's duty to submit to a man and to produce children. But then I look at her and I suspect I see why she has never been chosen. She serves God well in all the other ways.

I wish that she could laugh sometime, even a smile might light up that face of hers. I have tried to amuse her, to lighten her load, but so far with no result. It is early days, I suppose.

---

1 Saloth Sar called himself Pol Pot.

It's already a whole fortnight since I was chosen. But I write this with trepidation. I find it hard to whisper it even to myself: I feel no different. I am the same person I always was. I have experienced no change, no sudden revelation. Leadership has brought only an increasing loneliness, almost an alienation. What did I expect? A voice in my head, a sudden influx of wisdom?

And whisper this even more quietly. I am not a well man.

Chapter 13

My hand is on Leah's shoulder. It is only the second time since the rape that I have dared to touch her. I want to leave my hand there. I want to go back and answer Hilary's question with a stronger word than friend. I want Leah to reach up and touch my hand, however lightly, however quickly, by way of acknowledgement.

We have always been alone before.

She sits quite still, both hands by her side. When she seems calmer I remove my hand from her shoulder and sit down next to her.

'I need to know more about Isabel's first baby.' she says.

'Julia?'

'There was another one before Julia, a boy called Patrick.'

Uncle Joshua's face answers her question before he speaks.

'Leah, are you sure?'

Our journey is a waste of time. He doesn't know.

'The moment we cremated Dad, Mum started to look for the baby she gave away,' Leah tells him. 'She found him. He's called Patrick.'

I watch Uncle Joshua. He shakes his head again, but there is something else, a look of pain. It's there for a second and I know Leah has seen it. Uncle Joshua winced as if, even if he didn't know about Patrick, he understood what might have happened..

'Tell me about Patrick,' he says. 'What's he like? How does he act?'

'He isn't one thing really or even one person,' Leah begins. 'That's what I don't understand about him.'

'Tell me.'

Leah describes the strangeness of him, his old man's clothes, the wholesome look, his not knowing how to act in the café, the buying one coffee, his not eating and not drinking with the family at first, the charm, his belief in God, the estate agent demeanour. I knew all that, but I didn't know about his visit on Christmas morning and not coming into the house. When Leah finishes she shakes her head. 'I saw all this,' she says, 'and I never added it up. Instead I trusted him.'

During this recitation I notice that Joshua and Hilary exchange looks, that Hilary comes closer to stand beside him.

Joshua makes Leah go over the scene in the café. This time she adds the details of his bagging a table and walking into someone's space to do so. Joshua makes her go over that part again. Another look passes between them.

Uncle Joshua frowns. 'The last time I spoke to your mother, Leah, was when I was eleven and she must have been nine. The last time I saw her was a year later. I remember staring up at the house I used to live in. She was in her bedroom looking out of the window. She saw me and I waved but she never waved back.'

Leah interrupts. 'Did the house have a high hedge and a red door. Did Izzy once have a dog?' There is an eagerness in the question that surprises her uncle.

'Yes,' he says. 'How do you know?'

She tells him about a visit she remembers when Izzy took her children to see her parents. Izzy's mother had pleaded with her father but he'd been adamant, pulled his wife back in and slammed the door.

'A high hedge, a red door and a dog barking.' Leah's voice has an odd sense of triumph in it. 'An old woman pleading and a man shouting, 'Do you want to be cast out?' I've never known if it was a memory or a dream until now.'

Joshua leans forward. 'How were they?' he asks. 'They must both be dead by now.' His voice is needy.

Leah shakes her head. 'That's all I know. It's a blur. I was very young.'

Uncle Joshua seems disappointed.

'What does it mean, being cast out?' Leah asks him.

Sacridium 2

(Extracts from the diary of Matthew Holmes)

My Saints are restless. I sense the need for a new direction, that if we aren't a mission we are nothing. If I am disappointed in God's silence then they, my followers, must not be disappointed in me. So, in the absence of a clear direction from above, I have found a new idea growing in my head, and who is to say that God did not plant it there?

I have become concerned about casting out. The power that all Elders have is to cast people out of the church. You are either with us or against us and, if you question us, if you set yourself against us, we cast you out from God's grace. We cast you out from worshipping with us, and from having any contact with the congregation. In this way we split families, tear parents from children, turn husbands and wives into strangers.

My idea is that we may in the past have cast out too many, become too exclusive, perhaps (dare I say it?) allowed ourselves to be too afraid of the Devil. Before I became leader, obedience was everything. Now, when I want to ask questions, I have to provide my own answers. As leader I have to learn to think and that is daunting.

Our task as Living Saints is to be worthy of being raptured when the time comes, but isn't it our task also to preserve our numbers for the rapturing? We are shepherds and these people are now my flock. Over the past years our numbers have dwindled. We do not allow contraception. Our families are large, yet the numbers in our congregations do not grow. Why is this?

Today I asked for a list of those we have cast out, those we have shut out from our fellowship and from our society. The list is long and so many others have left of their own will. I was struck by that. So I have instituted a new phase and as I preached these words I felt at last God's benediction. As I preached I felt the strength of his will in the room, a strength which I know was also felt by others. We need, I told my followers, to reach out to those we have excluded. We need to explore if there is any possibility of shriving them and bringing them back to fellowship. A sigh filled the room. They have all lost someone. They each have family members who have withdrawn or been cast out. I urged my followers to use all our power and our wealth to forgive these people, shrive them and welcome them back into the Living Saints. I set up a task force to accomplish this work. I paired off our young men destined to be leaders and promised timed exemptions from our rules, but only where there was a real possibility of success. 'Go forth,' I told them, 'strong in your faith, and use all means to bring back to the fold those who have been scattered.' How can we fail when God is for us? A woman called Isabel has already made contact.

Now, as I walk round, I feel an energy in the building, a hopefulness. Perhaps soon we will see other returners. The congregation will increase. We will see the splits healed. I talked this over with Katherine and was surprised by her reaction. For a moment her mask slipped. 'I like being exclusive,' she said, then apologised and wished me well with the enterprise. She is a funny woman, so complete in herself, so un-needy. I put my hand on her head to bless her and felt a momentary wince, before submission.

About the other matter. The doctor visited me and has referred me to a consultant. I'm not worried about my health. God would not make me His Man only to shorten my life. That is not His way. But I am worried about having to go to hospital. Next week, for the first time in my life, I will have to step outside these gates and go out into the world.

Chapter 14

'Casting out is the worst thing they can do to you. I was cast out,' Uncle Joshua tells us.

'So was I,' says Hilary.

'You were both Living Saints?'

'Yes, Leah. I was a Saint and so was your mother. Your grandfather was an Elder of the church, and from everything you have told us I believe Patrick is a Living Saint too.'

Martin interrupts. 'How can he be? Patrick is no saint.'

Hilary tells us that being a Saint has nothing to do with goodness. Now I'm confused. Don't churchgoers have to lead good lives? Patrick told me he believed in God and that God was the most important thing in his life, but after he raped me he wasn't even apologetic or embarrassed. Izzy never told us she went to church. I don't know who Hilary is. She seems older than Joshua. I want to ask her the question she asked Martin.

'I don't understand,' I say. Who are these Living Saints?.

Hilary takes a deep breath. 'They think they are God's chosen ones. They think they will be raptured straight to Heaven on the day of judgement. People get chosen in life for all sorts of reasons, like brains or beauty or the ability to run faster or further than anyone else. The Living Saints are chosen for two things only: their gullibility and their obedience. They make sheep look like rebellious mavericks. If God wants them, he's welcome. If he really is the guy who made all this wonderful variety, they must bore him rigid.'

'Hils!'

'I'm done,' she says, suddenly turning away and going to the window. 'Your turn.'

'It's like a warm bath,' Joshua says. 'If you want to understand it you need to know that. As a child I loved it and

I loved them.'

Watching Uncle Joshua I sense his distress. He seems bereaved, unhappy. Outside it's still raining and I wonder what happened that made him escape to this awful place.

He shakes his head, then surprises me with the way he begins his story. 'Have you ever wanted to belong? I mean, really belong to a group larger than your family, a group that knows your name, welcomes you, gives you what every child wants: a large family you meet almost every day?'

I nod and wonder again about blood and family, amazed that my uncle begins with my own temptation.

'You go to services and everyone greets you, makes a fuss of you. When it's your birthday they hold a party and you get lots of presents. You have to go to church every Sunday, but the service is full of lovely words, like special and chosen. It's a whole life. You belong to the congregation. They make you feel loved. Everyone greets everyone else. It's one hell of a safe space to be in. People round you smile at you. Of course, there's a lot about the Devil, but he gets other people. Hell is for other people. So long as you stay with the congregation you are beyond his power. When the time comes you will be raptured up to Heaven. You may not even have to grow old and die. After the service people mingle. The Elders seek you out, make a fuss of you. I loved it. Isabel loved it too. In many ways I still miss it but,' and he pauses, 'we have to grow up.'

Warmth and charm. Patrick had both. I think about the way he included all of us on that first meeting. The way he made me feel.

'It's funny what you notice when you're a kid,' Uncle Joshua continues. 'There was a young woman I knew as Mrs Evans. One Sunday she wasn't there and her husband was tight-lipped about it. Mrs Evans had always been particularly friendly to me so I looked out for her each Sunday but she never came back. Had she disappeared? Had she died? And she wasn't the only one. I took to scanning the congregation and it kept happening, not all the time but occasionally. It was mostly women who disappeared. I asked Dad about it and he wouldn't answer. I pestered Mum with questions and eventually she gave way and told me Mrs Evans had been cast out.'

That phrase again.

'Being Saints we didn't go out much. We weren't allowed to mix with the world. It was our house to other Saints' houses to the Living Saints church and the Living Saints school. That was the routine. That was our world. But, only a few weeks after Mrs Evans disappeared, we'd run out of bread so I was sent to the local shop. I was told to go straight there and come straight back, not talk to anyone.' He stopped. 'I was eleven going on twelve, I remember I'd just started secondary school when this happened. I got my loaf and went to pay. Mrs Evans was in front of me in the queue.'

'She looked ill. That's what I thought. I didn't know then what unhappiness can do to people. I asked her if she was feeling better. She looked at me and told me straight out that I'd be in trouble if anyone saw us. I think I said something like, 'I always talked to you before.' She told me that was then. I remember thinking, she wants to talk to me, so why's she gone all strange? 'What's changed?' I asked her. And there were those words again, 'I've been cast out.' You've got to remember I was a kid and no one had told me what that meant. 'Is that why you disappeared?' I asked her. She nodded. 'So when will you be coming back?' I asked.

He stopped in his story, looked up at Hilary. 'That's when she cried. Except it wasn't like crying. It was a howl and the whole queue turned and stared at us. 'Shh, Mrs Evans, it can't be that bad,' I told her. I remember she tried to get herself under control but couldn't and just ran out. I knew the rest of the women in the queue blamed me for making her cry, so I dumped the bread and scarpered.'

'That night I asked what being cast out meant. My dad

walloped me, told me never, ever to ask that again. I don't know what it is about being eleven or twelve but you want to kick a bit. You need to do a little asserting. He walloped me, then told me I was making him and my mum very unhappy. 'Not as unhappy as Mrs Evans,' I retorted.'

Uncle Joshua stopped again. 'You know, it's unbelievable what happened next. He said nothing to me at the time, just sent me to bed. Then my dad, my own father, reported me to the Elders for talking to Mrs Evans.'

Sacridium 3

(Extracts from the diary of Matthew Holmes)

The consultant sent me for a scan, then asked for biopsies. He was clearly being extra careful. It was the first time I had been out in the world and I was astonished. It was not as I imagined. People were kind, patients waited in orderly queues; I was seen on time. I am sure the Devil was out there but I saw no sign of him, only caring people rushed off their feet. Now I must wait for the results.

Meanwhile there are problems with my scheme. I thought that to put out the word, to heal the rift in families, to allow returning would achieve easy hits. I had not realised how far the world has lurched away from us. In many cases the breach is so substantial that it cannot be healed. The hope is draining away from my mission. My followers say, 'I contacted my brother, my son, my father. They wrote back with love but cannot manage without the devices we do not use. They want to surf the internet and use smart phones. They want to drink with friends who are not members. They want to eat at weddings outside the Living Saints. They do not want to return, unless. . .'

I hear the Devil in all this.

No, I tell them. There can be no changes to our rules. Saints do not compromise, because God Himself does not compromise.

They are disappointed and then they come with further questions. Can they have extended exemptions, they ask. We might persuade these others to return if we can be with them fully. Their questions make me afraid. A month only, I tell each of them who asks me, exemptions for a month only. You can eat with them. You can drink with them for a month. Then you must return fully, bringing them with you, or return alone. And if they come with you they must undergo a period of purification. When I say this I see the hope fall out of their faces and something lurches in the pit of my stomach. I fear that what I am about will fail and what was a matter of resignation on their part will turn into one of despair.

Only Katherine remains unchanged. She seems inured to all feeling. She is a wonder. I now know she absorbs information and never relinquishes it. When I ask for the notes on a member of the congregation, for instance for the account of their last Face to Face, something registers in her eyes. I suspect that she has read all the files, that she knows what are in fact the secrets of our confessionals. She always says the right thing. If I ask for her views on someone she shakes her head and says that it is not her place to offer an opinion. But I know she could. I caught her out one day. We have one of those rare individuals, so dull that he is blameless, so obedient that she could know nothing to his detriment. When I asked about him she said immediately, 'He's okay,' then became confused, didn't know what to do with herself. I also found her looking at one of my hospital letters, the ones that are private and confidential, even from her.

I hate the waiting. Is my God vengeful? Have I so displeased Him that He punishes me by making me fail in what is after all His venture? I can't really have cancer, can I?

Chapter 15

'The very next morning,' Uncle Joshua says, 'I was hauled up before a group of Elders.'

Hilary's hand is now on his shoulder. She says, 'Josh, you don't have to do this.'

'I think I do,' he says. He glances at me. 'Leah needs to understand.'

'I don't know whether it was then or later that I realised something about them,' Uncle Joshua continues. 'I was very young. I was terrified but I was also conscious of little things going on in the room, sly glances to a particular man. They asked me what Mrs Evans had said when I met her in the shop, asked me three times in different ways and I told them three times, word for word. It was odd. They didn't ask if she had told me why she had been cast out but I knew that was what they were after. It was what they wanted to know but they wouldn't ask it, as if they too were scared of something. They began to relax, were actually smiling at me and I thought we were done, so I asked the question they wouldn't.'

'And much good it did you,' says Hilary.

'I just asked it straight out, 'Why was Mrs Evans cast out?' My question shocked them. They actually sent me out of the room, told me to wait outside. I leant against the wall and stared at the white paint and the terracotta flagged floors. I was to get used to staring at blank walls. It was ages before they asked me to come back in.'

'Mrs Evans,' they told me, 'has chosen not to be part of this congregation any more. She is no longer a Living Saint. She will burn in Hell for what she has done. That is all you need to know. That is all you ever need to know. And remember, the one attribute God values above every other is obedience.' That was it and it was a kind of threat. They were warning me off.'

‘What had she done?’ I ask. ‘Did you ever find out?’

Uncle Joshua looks at me. ‘She’d dared to complain about being molested by one of the Elders. He used to grope her and sometimes he kissed her, forcing his tongue into her mouth. But the Living Saints have a rule. There have to be two witnesses to any wrong-doing. If you persist with your complaint when you are the only witness, they think you are attacking the church and need to be expelled.’

‘And the Elders are always men,’ Hilary adds.

Suddenly I understand. If Patrick belongs to the Living Saints, and if I seek to destroy him by telling them about the rape, they will ask me who the other witness is. I am Mrs Evans. I am in the same position as she was and Patrick can, within the rules and practice of the church he loves so much, do anything he likes to me. And perhaps it’s even worse for me. I am the odd girl, the one who doesn’t speak.

I know he hasn’t finished. ‘Go on, Uncle Joshua, tell the rest of your story.’

‘There’s much about my younger self that I don’t really understand. Why did it matter so much to me? I was not the first child to look at their parent and suddenly see them as faintly ridiculous. Taking your parents’ most cherished belief and shaking it is almost a rite of passage. It’s what kids do.’

The rain is heavier. We can hear it drumming on the roof.

‘I simply carried on asking questions,’ Uncle Joshua continues, ‘and I asked them out loud. I asked them in class. At first they invited me to go to what they called Face to Face sessions. The idea of these is that you are face to face with a God who knows all your secrets. It’s like a Catholic confession only much more brutal, and there is no silence of the confessional and no forgiveness. Anything you tell them about yourself is taken down and may be used against you. Outside the cult it would be called blackmail. Inside the cult it’s seen as a form of pastoral care. Stalin was raised in an extreme Orthodox church. I always suspected that he learnt much of what he did in the purges from the way he was treated as a small boy.' He suddenly grinned at us. 'I'm going off track, sorry.'

'I noticed at once that it was the same Elders who were there to hear my Face to Face confession. The room was white. There were no pictures, just a ring of chairs for the Elders and a stranger, someone I'd never seen before, who took notes. I remember I looked at his notebook and thought, you'll get nothing from me.' He broke off. 'It was as if I already knew I was determined to leave them, as if they had touched something stubborn right at the heart of me.'

'It began with smiles and niceness. They're good at niceness, at making contact, at seeming. Their opening gambit was about putting the unpleasantness behind me, bringing me back to God. They wanted to help me, if I would let them.'

'I'll always remember their first question. Was there anything I wanted to tell them, anything I might be ashamed of.'

'I was nearly twelve, going through puberty. Of course there were things I was ashamed of. I shook my head. 'Do you say your prayers every night?' I told them, 'Yes'. It had only been a few weeks since I stopped. 'And when you get into bed do you keep your hands well away from your private parts?'

This is unbelievable. We stare at each other. Uncle Joshua stops.

'That was the question. I promise you, that is exactly what they asked me. And I saw the danger. If I refused to answer that was an admission of guilt. If I answered and said no, they would know it wasn't true. I could think quickly then. I found a way out. 'Why would I want to touch my private parts?' I asked them. 'I don't understand,' I told them. 'I don't understand why you are asking me that.'

'I remember they looked at each other and then one of them shrugged and they let that matter go. But for what they called my wilful disobedience I was isolated for a week in one of their safe houses.'

He breaks off from his narrative. 'By the way, I suspect the green door Isabel went through when she was looking for Patrick belongs to one of their safe houses. They have lots of them. They use them to house families and for punishments. In my case I was locked up. Meals were brought in and empty plates taken away. Elders seemed to take turns to come in and warn me about Hell. They told me that was where I was heading if I abandoned the Living Saints. There was no work set, nothing but the Bible for me to read. I was expected to stare at four walls and ask for forgiveness. They were trying to break me, but with each action they took I knew them better and I knew I was right to want no part of their church. I began to think if they were the people I would meet in Heaven, then Hell might be the better option. One day they forgot to lock the door so I simply walked out and went home.'

I guess the next bit, tell Uncle Joshua my guess, 'And Grandad wouldn't let you in.'

Uncle Joshua looks at me with respect.

'Right, niece. You're absolutely right. The door was locked. When I rang the bell my dad came to the door and wordlessly handed me a piece of paper. It had an address on it.'

'I took the paper and walked away. I remember Isabel was staring out of the top window, her face pressed against the glass. I looked at her and waved. Waving back might have got her into trouble.'

'Whose address was it?' I ask, riding the pace of the story, wanting to know it all.

'Mrs Evans.'

And of course it would be.

It was worth coming all this way. I'm getting the Living Saints' measure. I stand up and walk round. 'It's what they would do.' I turn to Martin. 'Don't you see? They knew her, knew she was decent, knew she would take Joshua in. They also knew they could be held responsible for a twelve year old roaming the streets, so they used her humanity, that same humanity they utterly lack, to make sure Joshua was looked after. If anything had happened to him it would have reflected badly on them.'

It all fits. 'Patrick knows me in the same way they knew Mrs Evans,' I continue. 'He knows I love Izzy, so he thinks he can assault me because I don't speak and because I won't want to ruin my mother's happiness. It's the same thing.'

'Yes,' Uncle Joshua says. 'Exactly the same.'

He is nearly done. 'One more thing. Years later I found that they paid for her to look after me.'

I go to embrace my uncle. 'Thank you for telling me that. I'm sorry for your hurt.'

He hugs me back and then Hilary hugs both of us. For a few moments we rock together. I feel again as if I belong. I hold onto both of them for a long time because I know I'm crying.

'Do you want lunch, Martin?' Hilary asks when we separate. Is that to allow me time to pull myself together?

He doesn't immediately answer. I glance his way and notice how pale and pained he looks. Hilary has noticed it too. She tidies coffee cups away. Uncle Joshua picks up the biscuits and they leave us together.

'What is it?' I ask.

'I don't know if I can do this,' he says. 'It's not just Patrick now, is it? We are up against a whole cult. As I was listening I thought, where are the thunderbolts? What they do is so irrational, so unconnected to the very texts they base their faith on. Their treatment of that poor boy....'

I think he's stopped but he hasn't. 'It's cost your uncle his life. They are utterly ruthless. What did it cost Mrs Evans? Just who and what are you fighting?'

I hear the pronouns: the '*I*' of I don't know if I can do this, the '*we*' of we are up against this, then the '*you*' of what are you fighting. Most of all I hear the '*they*' of they are utterly ruthless. Martin's right. The picture has moved, expanded, and the horror has increased. I am not alone. I fit into a pattern.

Sacridium 4

(Extracts from the diary of Matthew Holmes)

I may have discovered a weakness in Katherine, a chink in her armour. It was when Patrick came to see me. Since he made contact with Isabel he no longer shaves every day. He has dispensations about the clothes he wears. He believes he can bring Isabel back to the fold. He reports also that the family is wealthy, that they have a wonderful house which the Living Saints could make use of. When Katherine shows him in I sense that she is not so inviolate, that she finds him charming. He is laughing and for him she smiles, a smile she doesn't want me to see.

'Thank you, Katherine,' I say.

She turns archly and leaves us together.

I look into Patrick's face and see ambition there as well as devotion. But if Isabel re-joins the Saints, then my scheme will be judged a success. Numbers will have risen. So if this thing can be accomplished by extending temporary exemptions, if we can secure her back in the fold and at the same time enrich our organisation, then we need to do this quickly.

He tells me Isabel is enraptured with him and he, who is too much alone since his foster parents died, needs a family. It is a match made with God's approval. I see only the happiness it will bring to each of them.

He explains about the daughter, Leah. It will not be as easy to bring her into the fold. He describes her as wary. He tells me that mother and daughter are very close.

I allow him to eat and drink with the family. He is humbly grateful. I see salvation in him so I put my hands on his shoulders. 'You are trusted,' I tell him. 'Trust yourself also in this.'

I will watch him like a hawk. In a few weeks' time I will take his Face to Face. That will be his test.

I grant him exemptions. I tell him to do whatever is necessary to make time alone with Isabel so that he can bring her back to her rightful place. He kneels in front of me. That night I pray that he be given the wisdom to bring this about and quickly.

You see, I find myself in a hurry. I now know I have pancreatic cancer and that it may already be too late for me. I want to say the Lord giveth and the Lord taketh away, but the words no longer run smoothly through my mind. I have told no one about my illness.

Chapter 16

Hilary is back. 'I can offer bread, cheese, pickle and apples. It's not much, but we didn't know you were coming.'

We accept. I offer to help. Joshua lays a table. I'm still wondering who Hilary is. She seems older than my uncle, but it's difficult to be sure. She doesn't wear a wedding ring. They exchange glances, exchange pain. Now they are sharing getting our lunch.

We talk about Scotland, about living so far away. Uncle Joshua asks me about my siblings, about Izzy, about Gary. It's a niece uncle conversation, excluding the others. It's Martin who drags us back.

'And what about Mr Evans?' Martin suddenly asks. 'What did he have to say when his wife was cast out?'

I see them exchange glances. This time it is Hilary who answers. 'We need to come clean with you. My married name was Evans. I am the Mrs Evans who cared for Joshua. My ex stayed with the church. Our three children stayed there too.'

I take this in slowly. Hilary Evans looked after Uncle Joshua and now she lives with him. I want to know why they are together, but I don't have the right to ask. Instead I stick with the story. 'So you were the victim and you lost your family.'

'Yes,' Hilary says.

'Never allowed to meet with them?' I ask.

'Never met with them,' Hilary says. 'Of course I fought for access, took them to court and won my case. When the court found in my favour the Living Saints promised to allow access. I waited but it never happened. My own children wrote me letters saying they wanted nothing more to do with me.'

It gets worse. I've read most of the New Testament. I thought it was imbued with the spirit of forgiveness. I don't understand what I'm hearing. If they believe in God, how can they act like this?

'So what did you do?' I am incensed on her behalf, and on my own, of course.

She'd gone back to the Living Saints once Joshua left home because she was lonely. Her husband had sent her a message saying that he was willing to re-marry her if she returned. That came as a surprise to her because she didn't know she'd been divorced. She'd stayed a Christian. Most outcasts do. Believing herself still to be married she'd had no male friends, hoping that one day her husband or one of her children would seek her out. It was the hope that had kept her going.

At first she went back she wasn't allowed to see her children. She could only see them when certain formalities had taken place. 'You know,' she told me, 'they wouldn't let my husband make love to me until these formalities had happened.'

'I didn't know that,' Uncle Joshua says. 'You never told me that.'

They brought her in front of a group of Elders, including the man who had abused her. They told her this was a Face to Face. If she satisfied them her children were waiting to greet her, and her husband could once again take up his rights as a married man.

Martin is listening intently, 'And did all these Elders happen to be men?'

Hilary Evans nods. 'Of course. Men always dominate in cults like this. They claim authority from biblical times and there is no abuse of women that isn't sanctified somewhere in their holy texts …'

I want to understand what we are up against, so I break in with, 'In this Face to Face, did they ask if you held to your previous accusations?'

She looks at me, and from that look I know I'm right.

'So the price of going back was to lie,' I suggest. 'Once you lied they would let your children see you?'

'Yes. You seem to have the measure.' She looks at me, then

quietly says, 'So I lied.'

She sees me react.

'Leah, I'm not proud of what I did. I'm not proud of the lie. It was repulsive to see that man who had molested me smile the smile of power, the smile of the winner. I remember the way his colleagues turned to him.'

'And were your children waiting for you?'

She shakes her head. 'I didn't see them for another month, until I had proved my subservience to my husband. They kept me in a safe house, made me do menial tasks. They even made me clean toilets with a tooth brush.'

Now I know I can't keep my secret. I have to warn Izzy. If they treated Hilary like this, how will they treat Izzy? If Patrick should welcome her back to the fold, what will he ask of her? What kind of life will she lead? It's like a warm bath, Joshua says. I know my mother. She always was too susceptible, too subservient. It's only lunchtime. If we set off now, can we get home tonight?

'A month?' Martin queries.

'A very long month.'

'And then?'

'And then I met my children. . .'

I'm in a hurry. I want to go now so I risk completing her sentence . . .'and found you didn't like them?'

Hilary turns on me sharply. 'How did you know that?'

'I guessed,' I say, but she is still staring at me.

She ignores that. 'They were so cowed, so brainwashed. I saw nothing of myself in them. This will pass, I told myself. They are shy and one day they will open up to me.'

I want to add, 'They never did,' but Hilary says it first and I am suddenly tired of my own cleverness. Instead I ask the question that only Hilary can answer.

'And are you free of it now?'

'I miss my children as they were, not as they are now. I miss them every day. When they cast me out I should have taken them with me. But yes,' she says, and breathes out deeply. 'It's taken years. I've found a good man.' She ruffles my uncle's hair. 'I've kicked God and all his works deep into the Atlantic. When I left the second time I was determined not to waste any more of my life.'

'Patrick raped me,' I announce. They've told their heart stories. I must tell mine.

Hilary comes over and puts her arms round me.

Uncle Joshua puts his head in his hands. 'You're never free,' he says. 'Even here, all these years later.'

'He is almost certainly my half-brother and he raped me.'

The words bounce off the walls. 'Okay,' says Hilary. 'He's had your body, don't let him have your mind. Don't let him mess with your head.'

'My mum's in danger.'

Uncle Joshua completes the sentence. 'And you can only rescue Isabel at the price of breaking her heart.'

'Yes. That's about it.'

Sacridium 5

(Extracts from the diary of Matthew Holmes)

Now that my cancer is confirmed, problems crowd me. I must appoint a successor, but how much time do I have? I don't mean living time, I mean time when I can still think and act, when this body will still let me be God's Man. The consultant gave me possibly two months. Of course he hedged his bet, quoted statistics, but a month at most is what I am acting on. Who shall I choose?

I have no son, only daughters, so there is nothing easy about the choice. We need continuity and we need someone with many years in front of them to follow my short stewardship, which has not been glorious. A few have returned, but only a very few. When I look at the list I know they are people who couldn't find their niche out there in the world and had nothing to hold them there. Most are a certain needy type. Some are in want of financial assistance so our funds are more stretched than ever. Many of our Saints are old so we will dwindle further. World-wide more leave than stay. The birth rate is also falling. I wonder if 'outside' is having more of an influence than we know.

We need vigour. We need a genuine evangelist, someone who can mesmerise and bring back the lost. Isabel has visited us. Patrick brought her to a gathering and introduced her. I myself saw her shiver with the warmth of her welcome. The congregation recognises Patrick as one of them. He has lived all his life at the heart of the Living Saints. And when I watched them watching him, I wondered if I might skip a generation with my choice. Tonight I will hear his confession. We will go Face to Face and if he impresses me, well then. . ..

I must prepare, and this time I will resist Katherine's kind offer to type the document for me as she usually does. Patrick knows all the old questions. I must find new ones. I read Patrick's record. The handwriting slows me down but I find nothing to worry me. He seems uninterested in sex. He has not yet married. He says the most perfect things. Those who have shrived him are enraptured. Is it the cancer that makes me ask if this is all too good to be true?

Chapter 17

It's stopped raining. The clouds that have hugged the mountains all morning are rising. There's already a glint of light on the water.

'So what are you going to do?' Hilary asks me.

'I have to tell Isabel. She has to know what Patrick is like. She's going to be hurt either way. It is only a matter of timing. And…'

'And what?'

'I just can't let him get away with this.'

'I took them on,' Uncle Joshua interjects. 'Hils took them on. We both lost. You can't win against God. They are ruthless. You will find there are no limits to the way they will fight back. Don't do it. You seem to have a nice young man. Live your own life. Stay with us for a few days so we can get to know you. Let Isabel take her chances. She knows them. She's an adult.'

He sees I am unmoved so he tries again.

'If you must do this, remember they are certain. This direct line to God makes them act decisively. In their purified minds they can justify anything at all and that includes murder. Hilary's story and my story tell you how ruthless they are. But at least they let us go. We didn't really take them on in the way you plan to. Don't be fooled by their gospel or their sanctity. If you attack them directly they will defend themselves. They will do anything to stop you.'

'Uncle, if I walk away, who does he rape next? What happens to Izzy?'

Hilary joins in. 'I see you're a brave girl and I know you're a clever one. I suspect you are determined. My advice is the same as Joshua's. Don't. They are fireproof. You can't tackle them with logic. You can't complain without another witness.

If you try they'll ask questions, real searching questions, and twist every word you say to suit themselves.'

I smile then. 'As far as they are concerned everyone knows me as the girl without a voice. They think I'm mute. I don't intend to say anything to any of them. But I do intend to destroy him. Just don't ask me how.'

***

Yes, at first, when drinking my coffee that morning, I looked at the books on the shelves. But I've listened too, taken it all in. I'm still tired after nine hours of driving yesterday. As the horror has mounted I've done what I always do: fall back on books and the words of the wise. T*he time is out of joint. Oh curséd spite that ever I was born. . .* I stop there. The idea of putting this right is completely impossible. I want my dusty books and shelves. I want to catalogue and price. I want to take in a pilc of no longer wanted texts and search for the rarity. This isn't, this doesn't have to be, my problem.

I look across at Leah. She's not words, she's not print on a page. She's flesh and blood and skin and feelings.

I can't cope with any of this. I drift away back into books. Kurt Vonnegut's *Mother Night*. How did he describe it, this ability to ignore inconvenient truths and contradictions?

I have never seen a more sublime demonstration of the totalitarian mind, a mind which might be linked unto a system of gears where teeth have been filed off at random.

Then I wonder if I'm doing the same thing. I remember my dad saying to me, 'Not everything's in a book.' Even that memory is stopping me dealing with what's happening in front of me. You see, I'm not angry any more, I'm afraid. We're not just up against an evil individual.

Hilary offers Leah a tissue and Uncle Joshua is touching my arm.

'Martin, have a glass of wine. It's not every day we have

visitors and we never have family.'

'Thanks,' I say. I look over at Leah. What I want to shout out is what I've already said to her, *I really don't know if I can do this.* The words are on the tip of my tongue.

This room is full of pain. Joshua lost his family. Hilary lost her children. Leah is a rape victim. Crushed and defeated, Joshua and Hilary have ended up here in this remote part of Scotland. Despite the difference in age they have clung together and they seem happy, seem okay.

Leah is anything but okay. She looks at her watch and I understand that she wants to be gone. If she has to break this bombshell to her mother she wants to get on with it. Only politeness is holding her here. But it's already too late to set off now. She must know that we need a full day for such a long journey.

That's when it happens. The rain is long over. Cloud has been clearing. Blue sky has spread around the house, but only now does the view through the window expand in the last rays of the winter sun. The landscape it reveals is largely flat, glazed by the rain and dotted with small lochans. From this plateau fantastic mountain shapes rise up. One has multiple ridges, another is worn and crenelated. The strangest of them all is like a ruined Indian temple or an old-fashioned sugar loaf.

'Look,' says Uncle Joshua. He points to each mountain in turn and names it. 'Quinag, Suilven, Canisp, Stac Pollaidh, Col Mor, Cul Beg, Ben More Coigach.' It's like an incantation, a litany. Each is distinct in the washed air, most are snow-capped. We stare at the sudden beauty of them, but even as they are revealed, the sun dips below the horizon. This first sharpens and then extinguishes these wonderful shapes, so that the moment they are gone they feel like apparitions.

When the show is over Joshua turns to us. 'The trouble with having once belonged is that you miss the feeling, however much you hate the institution. Hilary and I have travelled to escape, always moving on until we found this place. Now these mountains hold us here. They partly fill our God-shaped hole.'

She is holding his hand. When she sees Leah watching her she pats it twice and then lets go. 'Two orphans,' she says. 'We ran away together because we had no one else. We travelled, frightened that the Living Saints would come after us. They have long arms and traced us even here. We are a threat to them. We know how they work. They hate publicity. They fear what we could say about them. Leah and Martin, I want you to know that we resisted our relationship for a long time and then we both thought, why not?'

Why not indeed.

This short northern winter day is already over. Leah and I finish our wine and exchange phone numbers with Uncle Joshua. We promise to return before too long and then we are back in the van, heading along the grassed track on our way back to Ullapool.

Sacridium 6

(Extracts from the diary of Matthew Holmes)

Katherine has made everything ready. I know she expected to be here, to make notes, because when I told her that wouldn't be necessary it was like suddenly seeing into her mind. That's the second time today that I have disappointed her. And she did an odd thing after that, when she next came into the room. She who is always so upright and proper in my presence actually leant against the filing cabinet with her hands behind her as she talked to me.

Patrick comes straight in. He is on time. I am dosed up, ready for him. I indicate the chair on the other side of the table, where the reading light is shining brightly. He sits with his hands down by his side. I sit opposite him, position my notebook and pen in front of me, then place my elbows on the table. Patrick looks round and seems puzzled. Every Face to Face is scribed.

'No,' I explain to him. 'There will be no record of this conversation on the files. I will take notes only if I need to. This is between you and me and God. As God's Man I give myself that dispensation.

We begin with a prayer. 'Almighty God,' I pray, 'who sees into the hearts of all thy servants, who understands our weaknesses and from whom nothing can be hidden, I ask your blessing on Patrick. I ask that you guide him to confess any sins he may have with a full and frank heart, knowing that your forgiveness awaits all your Living Saints who open themselves to your mercy in sure and certain hope that we will be worthy of a place at your right hand. Amen.'

He bows his head during the prayer and brings his hands together. His Amen is heartfelt.

I raise my head. I expect him to keep his eyes lowered but he is looking straight at me. His brown eyes meet my gaze and don't flinch, so that I feel it is I who am being challenged. I look down to remind myself of my first question, but he is talking before I have a chance to.

'I'm jealous,' he suddenly announces.

'And how does this jealousy manifest itself?'

A smile spreads across his face. 'You will see God before I do,' he says, as if this is a fact, a simple truth. 'You have been deemed worthy to go through your own crucifixion. You will meet him face to face, purged by the pain of your cancer.'

I swallow hard. 'How do you know about my illness?' I ask.

He hesitates. I note the way he touches the side of his nose. Then he spreads his hands and bows his head. 'It is immodest,' he says. 'I know it is immodest, but part of me read your illness in your face. The rest of it, I won't say God told me, but it came to me in prayer.'

I look at him. This is the boy we brought up, the boy I used to beat the Devil out of.

'I was praying for you.' He twists away. 'I'm sorry. Only when I spoke those words did I realise how they would sound. I don't want you to think for an instant that you, of all people, need my prayers. I just sensed the burden you carried, so I prayed for you.'

'And God told you I was dying?'

'Yes.' He holds my eyes with a half-smile and there is nothing mendacious in that look. It is neither unduly humble nor brazen. What it is, is certain. What it seems like is chosen. And how else could he know?

If he were a liar he would now lead the conversation away, but he doesn't. He repeats his assertion. 'I was so jealous when God told me,' he adds.

Even though my successor is choosing himself, I find myself on high alert. I know that all religions encourage excess and we have to be on our guard. God has never spoken directly to me.

I have occasionally felt the warm glow of his approbation, but words with specific information, never! I have grown used to a God who is oblique, and yet to the young man sitting in front of me He is a conversationalist. Even the prophet Mohammed heard Gabriel talking to him only in the chiming of bells.

What do I really know about Patrick, I ask myself. I know he was a difficult child who missed his mother at first but settled down well. I know he was the cleverest boy we have ever had in our school. I know his holiness has set him apart. He prays more than others. He fasts much longer. I know he is modest and that his fellow Saints hold him in high esteem. And he is bringing Isabel back to us. He is my only real success. Do I make him God's Man? I should pray about this, but God has never spoken directly to me. Now who is jealous?

Patrick's excess of fervour might be a problem. We are a charity and we have to satisfy the Charities Commission. That is important to us. We need that favoured financial position, especially because we are not as well off as we once were. We have to live alongside the world even as we keep ourselves apart. I have read my Bible. I love and live by St Paul, but the man who never met Jesus is the one who laid down the rules we live by. *And last of all he was seen of me also, as of one born out of due time.* What does *last* mean? Is it just a statement that places Paul in the same line as the disciples? Or is Paul saying that he is the last for all time, that there will be no more direct contact, that the age of revelation is over and finished for good?

But if God didn't tell Patrick, how the hell does he know?

The consultant knows. My doctor knows. Both are bound by the Hippocratic oath. Katherine put the appointments in my diary. She will have seen the word oncology, but I have never told her which cancer and how long I have left. The letters from the consultant have always been stamped private and confidential. I have opened each one and not shared the content. I have kept them safe in my room, but Katherine may still have read them. Or have Macmillan nurses contacted when I asked them not to? Have they talked to Katherine? Has Patrick been in my room, seen my medicines, looked them up and knows they are for pancreatic cancer? Does he also know it kills quickly? We don't have the internet. My room is locked at all times because it contains the records of previous shrivings. No one but Katherine has the key.

I think furiously. I know I must not rule out divine intervention.

Either God told him, or Patrick and Katherine are spying on me. It's time to speak.

'Patrick, you were always special. I have seen God's purpose in you. Isabel conceives a child out of wedlock and leaves that child with us. I see a message in that. I find meaning in that. God can use two sinners to create the goodness I see in front of me.'

He is immune to flattery. He doesn't blush or smile. He listens intently.

'I am dying and it will not be long,' I tell him. 'I must consider who will be my successor.' I planned this question for later but the sequence has been lost. 'Who should I choose?'

I planned this question because even if he expects it he cannot let me know that. A prepared answer will give him away. An actor who knows his script will hesitate before he starts to speak but his answer will not be plucked from the air. It will have the sequence the playwright has devised. By whatever he says I will know him.

His answer is immediate and startles me. 'Not me.' he says. 'I beg you not to choose me.'

Now I am wrong-footed. I had him down as ambitious. I stare at him.

'Of course, you weren't even considering me,' he says. 'Why should you? I'm far too young. I'm unmarried. I beg a thousand pardons for my answer, but this is not a normal Face to Face. That must be what has thrown me.'

I'll push this further. 'Why not you? God talks to you. You are known for your piety.'

If he is an actor he is a great one. He looks to one side, furrows his brow, seems to interrogate the wall. Then he turns back, shakes his head and very softly says, 'No.'

'There must be no scandal attached to God's Man. Is there, could there be any scandal about you?'

He thinks first, then says, 'I enjoyed eating with my mother and Leah. Her Christmas cake was delicious with a really thick layer of marzipan. Is that a scandal? I liked the change of clothes. I was going to confess both of those things.'

I say nothing. I let my silence interrogate him. He thinks for a long time. I watch his eyes. I look for the way the face echoes the mind and I see nothing to worry me.

Finally he shakes his head. 'No, there is no scandal about me.'

'You should marry,' I tell him.

Again he surprises me. 'I have someone in mind, but I would want your blessing before I ask her. Because of who it is I will need your blessing.'

He is well liked. I have seen the looks pretty girls give him. 'And who is your chosen bride?'

'Your personal assistant. I'd like to marry Katherine.'

Chapter 18

By the time we reach the main road it's fully dark. Leah is desperate that we go home now, drive through the night if necessary.

'It's late. I'm tired,' I tell her.

'Then is there a train?'

'Not from Ullapool.'

She tries everything. 'What if we check out and get part way?'

'Where do we stay? It's midwinter here. It's Saturday night. I'm just not up to driving through the night.'

Reluctantly she agrees.

'What if Izzy is already in Patrick's power?'

'I know that's what you're afraid of,' I tell her.

'What if he raped me so I had to go away, so that he has her to himself? Time matters. As far as Patrick's concerned, Izzy's a push over.'

'Then phone her.'

She shakes her head. 'It needs to be face to face. There'll be two shocks if I phone her: what I have to say and the fact that I speak.

'What harm can a day do?' I ask. She has to be reasonable about this. 'If we leave at 6am we can be back at your house by four o'clock tomorrow afternoon.'

Leah relapses into silence. I concentrate on the road. It's easier driving narrow lanes at night because headlights are such a give-away.

At dinner, in the crowded bar, I notice Leah relaxing. We've been eating in silence, but she suddenly looks across at me and says, 'Martin, I realise I ask too much of you, but I want you to know I am grateful.'

She joins me in having a pudding and another glass of

wine so I take a risk, ask a question that's been nagging at me. 'When I mentioned your family yesterday, you got cross with me. Will you tell me about them?'

She talks for more than an hour. By the time she stops the tables have been cleared away and a traditional Scottish band has begun playing: a drum, two fiddles and a clarinet. But I don't hear them. I'm on the moor, standing by the side of the sinkhole, and at last I understand why Leah won't contact her family, why she stopped talking. Was it an honour or an act of complete desperation that made her begin to talk again, and to me?

I set the alarm for 5.30am. I am ready to get up then but Leah relents. 'You need breakfast,' she says to me in the darkness. Three hours will make no difference. I'm not being fair.'

We are first down for breakfast and I order a full Scottish, which is a mistake because it takes time. Leah is finished with her croissant before my piled-up plate arrives. I expect exasperation and get ready to eat it quickly, but her mood is altered. I wonder, when she filches a piece of bacon from my plate, if she isn't putting off telling her mother.

I pay for the hotel and we strap ourselves in for the long journey. It's near dawn but not fully light. The road takes us along the loch side before we head back across the moors to Inverness.

Silence allows the mind to ponder options. We will get there. I will drop Leah off at home and she will tell her mother. I imagine the scene. There will be tears, perhaps tantrums, but it has to be done. I imagine a reconciliation, a long hug. Then it strikes me: I will have no further role in her story after that. I will leave them together. I will drive back to my flat. I will return to my previous life and it is perfectly possible that I will never see her again.

Is that what I want? Yesterday I wanted to shout, 'I don't know if I can do this.' Now, suddenly, I don't know if I want my old life back either.

I turn to look at Leah, her eyes intent on the road, her face fixed.

'Look out,' she yells.

Three deer are charging across the road. I miss the first two but not the third. It thuds into the front of the van before I can bring it to a halt. The impact spins us. We are lucky the road is clear, because if something else had been coming we'd have hit it head on. I jab at the hazard warning lights. Even though I've stalled, the engine is still working. Quickly, I steer round the animal and park.

Leah is there before me. The deer is lying in the road. Its back must be broken but it's still alive. Its head lifts up. It's clearly terrified of us and doesn't understand why it has stopped running. We watch as it stretches its neck, sticks out its tongue, willing itself to do what its body did so effortlessly only a few minutes before but no longer can. Rich red blood seeps from its hindquarters.

'Do something,' Leah shouts at me. 'Do something.'

What? There's nothing to be done.

I grab my phone but there's no signal. The animal's front hooves are now scraping at the tarmac, trying to get a purchase. It's still not fully light. We are in danger. If only I hadn't glanced across I might have missed it.

I turn to Leah. 'There's nothing I can do.'

I look down the road. We are on a straight stretch. The deer came out of the trees, very close to the road, so it wasn't my fault. There's a terrible silence except for the scraping noise. I can't bear what I've done. I can't bear to see it suffer. I run to the side of the road, dig out a round rock from its grass hollow, and then I approach the deer. It's female, has a thin fine neck and large bewildered eyes. I must do this in one go. Holding the rock as high as possible I stand on the neck, pinning it to the ground, then smash the rock down on the deer's head. The forelegs twitch but the neck is still. Just to be sure I pick up the stone and smash the head again.

All movement has stopped. I turn to Leah. 'I'm sorry,' I say. 'It was all I could think of.'

I throw the stone away, notice the blood on my hands.

Leah shudders but is very calm. I now have time to look at the van. The front corner is smashed. The side light is hanging down but the wheel hub is clear. I try the engine, gingerly moving the van forward. It's driveable, but we'll have no light on that side. When we go fast it'll rattle, but it might get us home.

I turn back to the animal. The deer is lying in the road. In the half-light it will be a danger to other traffic. I know what we have to do.

'Leah,' I say, 'I'm sorry, but we have to move it. I think I'll need your help.'

I wonder if she has this in her, but she has. She's silent, then she nods. Will the shock of all this send her back to speechlessness? We take a back leg each and tug. It's much lighter than I thought. The animal moves along the tarmac, rubbing its fur the wrong way, leaving a trail of blood. We pull it clear and abandon it at the side of the road.

'Come on,' I say, seeing Leah still gazing at the smashed head. 'We need to set off again. We've a long way to go.'

She doesn't move. She's staring at the animal. I risk putting an arm on her shoulder. She doesn't throw it off but seems to wake up in an instant from whatever trance she's been in. Then she walks to the car and silently gets in.

I set off. 'It's all we could do,' I insist. 'No one else is at risk.' I keep my eyes on the road in case of more deer. For a long time we drive in silence. We reach the A9 and set off south. Now I'm reconciled to slipping back into my old life. I'll have to get the van mended. Is it time to buy something a little more up to date? Can I afford it? After what has happened it'll be a relief to be back in my flat. I'll have a take-away, put on some music.

'Stop the car,' Leah says.

I see the layby and shoot into it. Leah opens the door and is copiously sick, retching through the open door without getting out. I stay looking straight ahead. Only when she is finished do I reach for the glove compartment and take out a part empty bottle of water.

I offer it to her. 'To wash your mouth out.'

She does so, spitting out of the door.

'Okay?' I ask. 'Shall we go on?'

She nods and I head out, back into traffic.

Indian, I think. I'll have an Indian take-away, with chapatti and a naan bread.

The light widens. The mountains recede. We are south of Perth and heading for Edinburgh before Leah speaks again.

'Can we stop,' she says, 'when there's a chance?'

'Are you feeling sick?'

'No, just thirsty.' She pauses. 'And you need a break.'

'Of course,' I say. Nine miles further on there's a service station. I pull off.

She has two coffees in silence, downing one after the other, then eats a panini. I watch. Colour is back in her face. She looks better for the food.

'This morning I was looking forward to being home.' She says it like an announcement. 'The closer we get, the more frightened I am.'

'You have to tell her,' I say.

A look of annoyance flits across her face. She kills it, ignores my interruption. 'I was also looking forward to being on my own again. I'm not used to sharing my time, except with Izzy.'

This is my chance to say I was thinking the same thing.

'You are a surprising man,' she says, looking straight in front of her. 'Back there I froze and you acted.' She shakes her head.

I cannot account for or describe the effect her words have on me.

Sacridium 7

(Extracts from the diary of Matthew Holmes)

Patrick is asking to marry Katherine. I stare at him. He can have his pick of our young women and yet he has chosen a plain woman who is much older than he is.

Katherine makes the appointments, Katherine manages my prescriptions, and Katherine has access to the internet. I imagine she could easily discover which cancer my particular medicines treat. God did not tell Patrick I was dying. Katherine did. God does not speak to Patrick any more than he speaks to me. But Patrick knows I can never challenge his assertion. He's clever, but now I know him for what he really is.

I stay in my role. I bow my head. 'Good choice,' I tell him. 'You will find her a loyal and true wife. I give my consent.'

Patrick bows in return. 'Then I will ask her to marry me.'

I know him and suddenly I understand much more than that. Perhaps, after all, he has the attributes we need in the next God's Man. He has the appearance of holiness but he is not holy. He is an effective operator without the handicap of being principled. He understands how to gain and keep power. He has allied himself to Katherine, the only person, apart from myself, who knows the truth about our organisation. And Katherine will have demanded a high price for her support. When I think about it they are well matched. They will act together and keep control of the worldwide body that is the Living Saints. In marrying her he will set himself apart, and by disappointing all the young women he will not set up jealousies.

And the fact that he is a barefaced and convincing liar I now see might make him a perfect God's Man.

'You, Patrick,' I say to him, 'are quite remarkable. I'm proud to have had a small part in your upbringing.'

Does he know I know? He bows his head again. But I will not let him off so easily.

'I can recommend that you are my successor, but to prove yourself to your flock you must bring your mother, Isabel, fully back into the fold.'

Is that enough of a challenge? I wonder how effective he really is. Without dynamic leadership the Living Saints will dwindle to nothing in the next decade. Knowing him as I now do, I need to make his accession harder. So I toughen the challenge by adding, 'and you must bring her daughter, all the money and the wonderful house with you. We need this as proof that God really does work through you.' Is this me talking or, after all these years, have I finally let the Devil speak with my voice?

Was that a shadow that passed across his face? I was looking for it but I cannot be certain. He is quite wonderful.

I add, by way of further explanation, 'There are many Elders who want to be God's Man. Only if you manage all three of these tasks will you win their approbation.'

I want to add that I know he already has the power to slap them down, that he has probably read their Face to Face reports and is word perfect in all their weaknesses. Is it my cancer that adds, 'May God continue to guide and bless you.'

Chapter 19

It's after 8pm when Martin turns the van into my drive. I've been counting down as we have got nearer, thinking of the words I'll use to tell Izzy, what I'll say, the precise way I'll go about breaking her heart.

But when we turn into the drive and see the house, it's dark and silent. I know even before Martin switches off the engine that Izzy isn't here.

'Wait there,' I tell him. 'I'll just make sure.'

I walk towards the door. I remind myself that I don't talk, that I am back in my silent zone. The door is locked. I have my own key so I go inside, switch on the lights and listen. The silence is total. I walk through to the kitchen and there, on the kitchen table, is a note from Izzy. It's too long to read at a glance, so I take it with me to the door and signal Martin to come in. We read it together.

Dear Leah,

I hope you enjoyed your holiday. I don't know when I will be back. I've gone to spend some time with my son at his church. I went to visit the other day and they gave me such a warm welcome. Some of the older members of the congregation remembered me from nearly fifty years ago.
When I was young I used to really believe in God and I'd like to take this chance to see if I can believe again. Our needs change as we grow older. My husband is dead and my other children, even including you, are living such busy lives now. I do not look forward to being always on my own.
Patrick is such a loving son to me. I can't tell you how much he is loved here. Even those who were born long after I left

the church make such a fuss of me because I'm his mother. I've not only found a son, but I have found a possible home and a cause.

Of course I love you all, my other children, and I long to welcome you here. Leah, I know you share my love for Patrick and you would always be welcome to join us. I will send Patrick one day to pick you up and bring you to where I am now living.

We do not use mobile phones, so please write to me.

Your loving mother

Isabel.

She's gone. Patrick has already snatched her up. Even two nights has been too long to be away. I hand the note to Martin who is staring at the house. I watch him tear his eyes away from stained glass, oak panels and all the beauty of this place. He reads the note twice, then hands it back.

'No address.'

'No.'

'So you can't contact her and, monstrously, you are to wait until Patrick comes for you. Leah, you can't do that.'

'How else can I contact Izzy? How else can I ruin him? Oh Martin, I should never have gone away.' That sentence comes out as a wail.

'Leah,' he says to me firmly, 'you couldn't have stayed here after what happened. You are not to blame.'

He has a point.

Do I despise Izzy for her weakness? I try to work out what she is thinking. *I do not look forward to being always on my own.* Uncle Joshua talked about the warm bath of belonging.

Martin re-reads the note. 'She's made her choice and she sounds happy,' Martin says. He looks at me. 'You can always walk away.'

When I don't reply he stares around him. 'This is perhaps the most beautiful house I have ever been in. How can she bear to leave it?'

'How long for?' I ask him.

'I'm sorry,' Martin says, 'I don't understand.'

'How long will she be happy for?' He can't answer my question so I carry on. 'I think I know what Izzy wants, but what does Patrick stand to get out of all this? He is probably her son. He must want to know who he is and where he came from, but what then? He has his life to lead. Will he love her for ever?'

Martin shakes his head. 'I don't know.'

'That's what I don't understand.'

I look at Martin. This morning I was looking forward to getting away from him. Now I find I'm on my own again and I need him. What if Patrick comes here, picks me up and takes me somewhere else entirely? What court would believe that I willingly put myself back in the hands of my rapist? I'll need to leave this house again, ask Martin if I can stay in his flat for a while longer.

In the event I don't have to. 'Come on, Leah,' he suddenly says. 'I need to get you to my place. You can't stay here. If there's anything you need, get it now. We can presume Patrick is coming back to check on you and we don't want him to know you've been here.'

'Sit down,' I tell him. 'I won't be long.'

'I'll stand,' he says. 'I'm dog tired. If I sit down I'll only fall asleep.'

Fifteen minutes later we are back in the van. We stop once on the way to the bookshop to get a take-away. When Martin returns to the van with a bag full of food and hands it over it smells wonderful. I feel as if I've been let off what I came back to do, but I know it'll be much more difficult now and that the issue has only been postponed.

After we've eaten I want to begin planning, but Martin is too tired.

'Tomorrow,' he says. 'Tomorrow.'

Sometime in the middle of the night I wake suddenly. An image of the deer desperately trying to get up has come into my head. I see its tongue sticking out to one side of its mouth and the eyes staring. It is and it isn't the deer. I'm sure it has Izzy's features. It's as if she's calling to me. It takes a long time to go back to sleep.

***

Martin is up before I am. He's laid the table and is making toast. I see he's been re-reading Izzy's note. Suddenly that feels like an intrusion.

When the toast is ready and he's poured my coffee he begins.

'You have to join the cult.'

I stop eating, stare at him.

'If you want to rescue your mother, you have to meet her. The only way to do that is to ask to join the cult,' he explains.

'But Patrick won't let me join.'

'I think he might.'

He continues. 'You see, I keep wondering what Patrick's up to. Even if Izzy really is his mother, why is he spending so much time with her? Why does it matter so much to him that she joins the Saints? It's more like a love affair than a mother/son relationship.'

I'm interested. I keep silent.

'Two solutions suggest themselves.'

Does Martin ever listen to himself?

'First, that he wants something. I suggest that might be the house and the money.'

'Second, that there might be some kind of push to regain members. Remember Hilary's non-greeting. The Saints had been sending people to see them even in that remote area of Scotland.'

'Everything was left to Izzy,' I tell him. 'She can make a new will. She is quite free to give it all away in her lifetime.' If she does, it will leave me without money and without a home.

Martin does a kind of gulp, then says, 'Look, I'm not being funny when I say this, but why did he assault you? Yes, there's the obvious reason. But he knows you and Izzy are inseparable. He took a risk. Was it to get you to go away so he has time to work on her?'

I am about to drink but I put the mug down.

'*A home and a cause*,' Martin reminds me. 'I think I might have been wrong. I now wonder if Patrick had any intention of picking you up. If I was Patrick I wouldn't risk going anywhere near you until I'd got your mum to sign everything over.'

I look at him with new respect. 'Julia,' I say. 'In spite of everything, we have to talk to Julia. Julia is my dad's executor. If it hasn't gone through probate, Izzy can't sign anything over, can she?'

Martin stares at me. 'Your family? You want to involve them, after what they did to you? Remember,' he adds, 'Julia doesn't know you can talk.'

'You'll have to tell her what's happening. You'll have to phone her.'

'But who do I tell them I am?'

I don't understand the question.

'Even if I agree to make this crazy phone call, even if I wind myself up so that I am capable of talking to your siblings, why should they listen…' He stares at me as if he wants me to understand without him having to spell it out.

I'm thinking that once Julia knows, it will be her problem, part of her battle for control of the family. I'm wondering whether I can let that happen. Until now I haven't understood how much I see this as my fight. I still don't understand what Martin isn't saying. He looks at me miserably.

‘Hilary’s question,’ he finally says. ‘She will want to know who I am, or rather what I am to you.’

I don’t want this now. There is a real battle to be fought, and I want to concentrate on strategy. Surely this can wait.

‘Then tell them.’ He looks relieved. But, perhaps because I don’t understand this talking business, my tongue is saying the next bit before my brain has worked out that it mustn’t be said. ‘Tell them whatever you want to tell them about us.’

It’s said and I know at once I’ve hurt him. When I was mute I couldn’t do this to people. And he’s right. Julia will want to know exactly that.

We can’t start with a phone call. I’ll have to write to her. We need her here. It’ll take time, but we have to.

I tell him that but he’s still looking hurt. How do I apologise? What are the best words to use? Suddenly I know what the word crestfallen really means. One minute he’s helping me, involved, explaining things with his head up and his eyes bright. Now it’s as if a crazed osteopath has done something catastrophic to his spine. And it hits me again that he might have developed feelings for me, that he might even love me.

I’m all ready for action but Martin, because it can’t be about him, because it isn’t about his family, is now concentrating on me.

And I need him alongside me. I need his voice to speak for me. I understand him better now. No one else is as completely on my side.

And because I need him I lean towards him, kiss him on his forehead. ‘You’ve been so good to me over this,’ I say. ‘When she comes, why don’t you tell her you’re the best friend I’ve ever had?’

It’s not what he wants to hear, but it will have to do for now.

Sacridium 8

(Extracts from the diary of Matthew Holmes)

On good days I try to make myself imagine what I no longer believe, that there is a God.

I have given my life to Him. I have fasted for Him. I have spent whole nights on my knees for Him. I have resisted the temptations of the world so that I am worthy of His approbation. In His name I have split families, withdrawn His favours from those who would not follow His rules, even locked them up. For years, for long years, I have done all this. And He must have watched and waited. When I prayed to be worthy of leading His church, did He even then plan to make me His Man only to mock me and kill me with cancer?

The agony of that knowledge is intense. By making me God's Man He took away from me all who could console me, left me alone with unanswered prayers, alone with that growing understanding that the only answers I have ever received have come from people.

I think I can cope with His absence. If there is no God, I am just another human being who has wasted his life for a lie.

But if He exists, if He is there, then mocking me was not enough to satisfy what I can only call His sadism. I think of what He did to Job, then self-pity floods me. I force myself to say it out loud. If He exists and controls everything, then He turned part of my own body against me, triggered my pancreas to mutate and kill me.

This means that exactly at the moment I no longer believe, exactly when I am free to walk away and enjoy the things I have denied myself all my life, He has snatched that freedom from me. He has robbed me of will-power so I do not have the energy even to walk out of this building. I am going downhill so rapidly, I do not think I even have two months left.

But there is a confusion in my thought, as if I am already dying. Belief and reason have always been opposites. Even as I deny His existence I do so partly because I do not believe that He would act like this. I know that thought is nonsensical. I know it is illogical. But thinking and believing are like looking down a row of mirrors when all you see are further reflections of yourself.

So, just in case He is there after all, just in case He is the bastard I now take Him to be, I am determined to have my revenge. I will give him Patrick, the least suitable person to run His church. Perhaps He will like Patrick, perhaps they are even kindred spirits. Patrick is my act of revenge on all those who encouraged me to waste my life.

But first he has to marry Katherine and fulfil my challenge. He can't know how little time I have left. The hospital told me face to face. It has never been written down. Even Katherine cannot know for certain how advanced my cancer is, so in my dying days I will watch what they both do now. I will watch them both for my own amusement.

But to those I have harmed by following the wrong God, or the right God wrongly, I am truly sorry.

Chapter 20

When I've written the letter to Julia I ask Martin where the post box is and he offers to show me. Then just before I post the letter he grabs my wrist.

'You do know that this is your last chance to walk away. Are you still determined?'

We stand there in the high street, surrounded by a slow crawl of cars and people. I feel exposed out here. I've only talked within rooms or the car until now.

'I'm worried for Izzy,' I tell him. 'We know what the Living Saints are like. We can guess what Patrick is. If you're right, when he's gained his brownie points by taking Izzy back, when he has her money and the house, because I too suspect that's what he's really after, what future does she have?'

'One of her own making,' he counters. 'You're not responsible for her. She's an adult.'

Why is he saying this, I wonder. Why is he being so tough on her?

'And my family. What about their inheritance?'

'They don't inherit until your mother dies. It's her money until then.'

I choose to stay silent. I'm still determined to destroy Patrick. I need to post this letter now. I want it to go today so Julia has it tomorrow..

He doesn't let go, as I expected. 'I'm frightened for you,' he says. 'It's all or nothing, isn't it? Your mother has clearly joined the enemy. You have to go to them and you don't even know where they are. Even if you find them and turn up there, Patrick may guess what you're up to. Why should he let you see her?'

I look at Martin, look him straight in the eye. It was his idea. This is exasperating. We are both holding the letter.

'You hate him, I know that. You want to destroy him, and to do that you need another witness, but no one else was there. What are you really thinking? Remember what we heard about the two witness rule. If you're right and your mother is besotted with Patrick you'll probably have to shred his reputation before she'll come away with you. I had an idea about that. Do you want to hear it?'

I nod my head. He lets go of the letter. I don't immediately post it.

A mum walks by, talking to her child in the push chair. We wait until they've gone.

'I suspect you are not the only woman Patrick has assaulted. To each act there will be only the victim as witness. That's not enough. But if you could find two witnesses to similar acts, then the Elders would have to listen.'

Clever man.

'But there's a serious snag. You really have to think about this, Leah, before you post the letter. You have to think about your potential witnesses. If they side with you and give evidence against Patrick, they have so much to lose. Think of what happened to Hilary. You have to ask, what's in it for them? Why should they take the risk?'

He's right. I hadn't thought of that.

He goes on, building his case. 'Your mother's letter says he's loved, that they make a fuss of her because of him. That's a problem for you. It increases the risk for anybody helping you.'

Now Martin's looking smug. I want to shout that Patrick's an evil bastard, but Martin is there before me.

'I sell non-fiction too. Evil bastards often thrive.'

He sees me hesitate.

'I know your anger. I know your love for your mother. I hated hearing what they did to Hilary. You can waste a life hating. I'm not trying to stop you, I'm just saying we need to be clever about this.'

He's right, and he clearly isn't finished.

'I don't want you going home and waiting for Patrick to pick you up. That's too much of a risk.'

I'm thinking hard. This is a new Martin standing in front of me.

'But unless I wait for him, how do we make contact?'

'The green door. Over there, the green door. We start there. We go to them.'

'We?'

'Of course.'

I must have smiled. 'Why we?' I ask. 'I thought you had reservations.'

He answers slowly. 'I think it's because of those reservations. It strikes me that the person you need with you is someone who has already worked out some of the consequences and most of the ways in which you can fail.'

We have reached a decision. I gesture to him and we post the letter together, then turn and walk back to the bookshop.

***

Later I need to know if he has answers as well as questions. 'So if I find other women he's abused, how do we persuade them to testify?'

'Use God.'

'How?'

'We need every Bible reference we can find about the need to bear witness. I'll do it. I'll look them up.'

That long journey. All this must have been going round and round in his head.

And he has more to say. 'We record your conversation with them.'

'Is it alright to do that?'

'Alright in which sense?' Martin doesn't wait for an answer. 'We've agreed Patrick is an evil bastard. I may be only a bookseller, but I think you have to fight evil with everything you have. I think that need, whether you believe in God or not, is absolute. I think it becomes a human duty.'

I've been staring at him for some time. Given how I have hurt him, it's remarkable how much he's willing to help me.

'How do we record?'

'They say they don't use modern technology at all. If that's really true, they won't be able to defend against it. Take in a small microphone.'

'They might search me.'

'But Uncle Joshua told us the whole thing is male led. Perhaps you could hide the microphone in your toilet bag. They won't search that. Maybe you can bug an important room.'

I look at him again. 'Why are you stuck running a bookshop?' I ask.

He frowns. 'I've never thought of it as being stuck. I love books. I love my life in the flat above the shop. I love. . .'

He stops himself in time, covers up by counting on his fingers. 'I'm my own boss. I work all day every day with books. One day I'll make a great bibliographic discovery. I have the shortest possible commute. In the evenings I have my music.'

A contented life, and then I came along.

He looks at me. 'I'll think of this as a kind of reverse holiday, a holiday from lethargy.'

He's trying to smile. 'I'm very grateful,' I tell him, and I really am.

'I need to open the shop,' Martin says. 'I need to sell some books, make some money to pay for the damage to the van.'

***

Julia comes to the bookshop two days later. Leah's letter has fetched her within forty-eight hours. She's alone and I'm relieved. I've dreaded the whole family turning up at the same time. It is my chance to play the part Leah has assigned for me. I don't want to let her down. Julia is taller than I expect and rings the bell forcefully. I'm nervous but determined. I see her as the bullying child of Leah's story. She can't know that I know that about her. Perhaps that will give me an edge.

I open the door to her and say, 'Hello, you must be Julia.'

She scarcely gives me a glance. Instead she looks for Leah. When she sees her standing behind me she says, 'This had better not be a waste of my time.'

I watch Leah shrivel under her sister's glare, so I go and stand beside her. I have to join the macho male world. I have to stand up to her and try to be impressive.

She turns her glare on me.

'And who the hell are you?'

Her perfume is overwhelming and her glare intimidating, but the thing about being a great reader is that you have a thousand role models when it comes to dealing with the Julias of this world. I think of George Campbell in *Whisky Galore* and Augustus Fink-Nottle transformed by drink. Lines from Volpone merge with the steeliness of Prince Hal.

'I may not look the part,' I say. 'I admit that my appearance is uninspiring. It's the hair and the imminent baldness. But I am both your sister's friend and the man who has the greatest chance of preserving your inheritance.'

'Scam,' she says. 'You're a scam and Leah fell for you.' She walks into my space and stares into my eyes. 'I'm not having this. I am the executor and our inheritance will stay quite safe without your help.'

It is perhaps from films rather than from books that you learn the use of ignoring the preposterous and sticking to the point.

'One of the executors,' I remind her. 'Half the total number. Have you completed probate?'

'None of your business.'

'Quite right,' I agree. 'It is none of my business. It's not even much of Leah's business.'

She stares at me.

'Yes, as you see, I know the contents of the will and I think you might just need a little help from the two of us.'

In her own way Julia is magnificent. I don't know if she has ever done drama, but she goes into a convincing impersonation of an estate agent weighing up a property. I watch her eyes take in the drab appearance of my shop, the old labels stuck on with yellowed tape, the worn stair carpet, the pile of books by the counter, ready to topple. She looks, she assesses, then she dismisses me. The fact that she does this wordlessly is most impressive. I feel Leah's disappointment. This isn't what we wanted.

'Your mother may even now be giving away everything you hope for,' I say.

Her voice is incredulous. 'She wouldn't dream of it.'

'No, but Patrick might well do the dreaming for her.'

I see that this has gone home.

'And she is not only an executor of the will but its sole beneficiary, isn't she? So there's really nothing you can do.'

'I'll put a stop to this nonsense.' Julia is almost at the door.

'Your mother's disappeared,' I explain. 'If we are to stop this nonsense - your words - we first have to find her and make absolutely sure she hasn't already done the deed.'

Julia is now in the doorway, looking from Leah to me and back again. Leah is nodding, keeping to her silent role.

'Probate will need my signature,' Julia says. 'I'm sure of that.'

'Then you haven't yet signed. Good.'

She's looking at me curiously. 'We haven't finished the sale of the company. There are no final amounts.'

'Good again. We have a bit of time.' I use that pronoun deliberately.

Julia's hating this, hating the fact that I know or guess more than she does, hating the fact that I have made her talk to us. Leah, on the other hand, is now more relaxed, but not tempted to speak.

‘And once probate is completed the money is released and your mother can do exactly what she wants with it,’ I explain.

Julia is silent, so I spell it out, press home my advantage.

‘That’s true, isn’t it? The moment probate is settled she can give her whole fortune away at once, on just her signature, can’t she?’

Julia nods. ‘I think so.’

‘And you would have no redress?’

Julia shakes her head. ‘It’s hers for her lifetime. But that was not what Dad intended.’

‘Look, we only know so much, but what we know worries us. Come upstairs to the flat. Leah will make coffee and I’ll tell you what we know after seeing your Uncle Joshua. The really important thing we need you to find out is whether your mother can give part or all of her inheritance away before probate. We suspect she can. I even worry that she already has.’

Julia leads the way up the stairs. Leah squeezes my hand, then follows. It’s a quick stealthy movement but it means I’m doing alright.

Part Three

In my letter I wrote that you must have nothing to do with loose livers. I was not, of course, referring to pagans who lead loose lives or are gamblers or swindlers or idolaters. To avoid them you would have to get right out of the world. I now write that you must not have anything to do with any so called Christian who leads a loose life, or is grasping or idolatrous, a slanderer, a drunkard, or a swindler. You should not eat with any such person.

St Paul 1 Corinthians 5 9–11.

Chapter 21

With Julia involved, a sense of urgency develops. We've checked the house and Izzy hasn't returned. We both know the next move. Leah needs to talk to Izzy and find evidence against Patrick. To do either of those things she must join the cult and I know, for all her bravado, that she is scared.

As soon as we know it is safe, Leah has to knock on the green door and ask to join the Saints. But before she does that we must be certain that Patrick isn't living there. So we take turns to observe.

It is just possible, if you crane your neck, to watch the green door from my bookshop, but we soon abandon the idea because it's uncomfortable. So we become regular visitors to Costa and monopolise the table in the window.

These are largely silent vigils. Leah, who now chats to me in the privacy of the flat, doesn't like to talk outside it. So we sit and read. I'm plying her with spy novels so that she can learn the role. John Le Carré has always been my favourite. I wanted to start her with *Call For The Dead* because it's so brilliantly plotted, but it has no scenes of observation, no passages of sustained terror, so I give her *Tinker Tailor Soldier Spy*, tell her to disregard Smiley and concentrate on Peter Guillam, particularly on his visit to the fifth floor.

At first, watching takes priority, and her eyes flick up often from the page she's reading to observe comings and goings across the road. Then I sense the book pulling her in, absorbing her fully. I know from her comments when we are alone that she's back in attack mode.

'At least I know my enemy,' she says. 'I know exactly who I'm fighting.'

A day later she tells me, 'I think I've been a bit of an actress all my life. I think I can do this.'

'Are you afraid?' I ask her.

'No,' she lies, 'not any more. I want to get on with it. I keep worrying about Izzy.'

Two mornings watching and no sign of Patrick. Men and women seem to use the house as a meeting place. Tesco delivers. The post lady brings nothing but junk. They don't recycle on a Thursday.

'Look,' Leah says that evening, 'why don't I just knock on the door, ask to join?'

'Cameras,' I remind her, 'ways to record.'

Her impatience erupts. 'Your department,' she tells me. 'Get on with it.'

So I'm left with turning my idea into a reality.

'And I'm going to need those quotations,' she reminds me.

'Truth is everywhere in the Bible,' I tell her. That night I use the internet and scribble down lines for her to learn. My favourite is one from John's Gospel: John 8:31-32 . . . *So Jesus said to the Jews who had believed in him, 'If you abide in my word, you are truly my disciples, and you will know the truth, and the truth will set you free.'*

'I've written it down for you,' I say, and hand it over. Then I find myself adding, 'Buddha said something similar four hundred years earlier. He said, *'The truth will set you free but first it may make you miserable.''*

She looks at me in disgust. My talking in quotations annoys her. She is terribly strung up, hating this period of waiting, worried about her mother.

'Why must you always. . .' she starts when the phone rings.

I pick up. It's Julia. I mouth the name to Leah who quickly nods.

'It's started already,' Julia tells me. 'Someone claiming my mother's authority is making moves to sell the company.'

I ask for details and she explodes at me. 'I don't know any details.' She makes it quite clear that if she did she wouldn't be phoning me. She'd be sorting it herself.

'How can I help?' I ask.

She wants to bring James in on it, wants to bring him to meet us tomorrow. At first I don't realise that she's actually asking me, seeking my permission.

'Hold on.' I smother the mouthpiece with my hand and ask Leah. She nods again.

'Okay,' I tell Julia. Then I add, 'Leah's nodded so it's okay.' I must remember my role. I'm only the spokesperson. I ask Julia if she can ask James about miniature cameras and recording devices, explain why.

She gives me a time. I check it with Leah, tell Julia, then she rings off.

'Was she really asking our permission?'

'I think so.'

'That won't last,' Leah says.

***

A day later, James follows Julia into my now crowded flat carrying a black leather bag with BOSS ORANGE on the flap. We are introduced. I find I'm instantly aware of him and wary because he takes me beyond my brief from Leah. He asks lots of questions and I keep expecting him to realize that Leah must have started talking. How else would we have amassed all this information and done all this planning? But he seems oblivious, even going up to Leah and embracing her, telling her he is sorry she was assaulted.

Julia has clearly briefed him and brought him up to date.

Leah warned me that he and Julia are rivals, but for the moment he seems strangely deferential to his older sister. I get the impression of someone on his best behaviour.

I like his hair. I like the way he uses it. I like the length which is just too short for a pony tail but too long to be controlled by gel. I recognise in him someone who wishes to seem different.

‘When you find Mum,’ he says to Leah, ‘will you let her know what Patrick did to you?’

She nods.

‘You do realise that she may not believe you?’

Leah shakes her head.

James is really gentle with her. ‘I think,’ he says, ‘that you should consider the possibility.’

Leah shakes her head again. I can see the force of what James is saying, but he doesn’t push it.

‘And you’re determined to go into the cult?’

She nods again. James switches to me.

‘Perhaps I can help with gizmos.’ He searches his bag and holds up what looks like a just-hatched small black snake. This, he explains, is a lapel camera; equally it can be used in a bag. He hands it to Leah who threads it through her jumper.

Then he turns to me. ‘Martin, you will need to monitor and record on your computer. You can do that from anywhere round the world. You don’t even need to be monitoring the signals in order to record. I can set it up so it’s activity activated.’ He slows down. ‘Leah, I imagine you’ll write your questions. If anyone replies you need to activate the camera/mike.’ He’s still being very gentle with her. ‘Look, I’ll show you.’

He does what all IT competent people always do. He takes over my computer and it quickly becomes his. He opens menus, clicks on items at speed, and installs new software so fast that I have no chance of being able to replicate the sequences. He clearly hates my machine for being slow. He taps his fingers as small circles whir round on the screen. Julia watches the operation intently. I’m sure she wishes us to think that she understands everything James is doing, but I suspect it’s an act.

After fifteen minutes the computer screen goes blank. ‘Now just squeeze the camera, Leah. You can squeeze it anywhere. It’s touch sensitive.’

Leah does as she’s told. My lounge appears on the screen

in black and white with the kind of grainy image that we are used to from journalists' sting operations.

James turns the sound up. As he does so Leah clamps a hand over her mouth. The others think she's done that in amazement. I suspect she was about to say something and is determined not to. The room stills and we are all listening to Leah's breathing.

James is sitting there with the air of a conjurer. Leah reaches down to her jumper and switches the camera off.

'Important to do that,' James says. 'First, to save the battery. You only have a few hours. Second, so that Martin doesn't monitor any part of your life you may not want him to know about.'

Julia has had enough of being quiet.

'The money,' she says. 'That's what really matters.'

'The important thing,' James suggests, rather than states with certainty, 'is who has the original will? It's usually lodged with a solicitor.'

'Not me,' Julia confesses. 'Mine's a copy.'

'But do you know which solicitor drew it up?'

'Yes,' Julia confirms.

'Local?'

'Yes.'

'Well, let's go.'

They leave, promising to be back soon. The moment they are out of the front door Leah starts.

'James hugged me,' she says, 'as if he cares.'

'They are not as you described them.'

'They are not as I've ever known them,' Leah confirms, then adds, 'Extraordinary. I suppose we have Patrick to thank for that.'

'They're worried.'

Leah's mind is well in front of mine. 'Trying to sell the company. It's really happening, isn't it? It's why we're now working together. What's Patrick playing at? Does he think he can get away with all this?'

'He must.'

'Dead right,' she says. 'Izzy has forgotten us, or she's being hoodwinked. But why does he think he can do this? What does he know about the law that we don't?'

She's pacing, further wearing the already worn carpet. Then she stops.

'I mean, what are we up against here? I guess the Living Saints have lawyers. I guess they've advised Patrick that this matter will never come to court. It may already be too late.'

'Then we have to ruin him, not just in the cult but in the courts. We need that evidence, Leah.'

Leah sits down, the fight in her suddenly quietened. 'He's a monster, but what has he said to Izzy? I need to go soon, don't I? I need to make contact first thing tomorrow.'

When James and Julia return they bring bad news. 'Unbelievable,' Julia says. 'You need the original will to act and my mother has it, which means Patrick has it. She spun them the line that it was just a matter of collecting it on my behalf, because I lived so far away. The firm actually handed it over. They're now terribly apologetic. I've roasted them, threatened them with the courts.'

'This happened partly,' James adds, 'because Patrick spoke on behalf of Julia, told them what a high powered job she does and how difficult it was for her to get away. He also pointed out that as Isabel was the sole beneficiary of Gary's will it made no material difference if Julia was there or not.'

I sorted my aunt's will. I try to remember the forms. 'But the money will have to come to the solicitors, won't it?' I ask, 'And it can only be released with your signature?'

Julia corrects him. 'To their solicitors. The firm was reluctant to tell me this until I proved exactly who I was. The money will now come into another solicitors entirely. That gives Patrick total control.'

James adds, 'They think it's a family matter. They see no

cause for action on their part. All Patrick has to do is wait.'

Leah has seized a piece of paper. She scribbles on it, *So why is he in such a hurry?*

I'm not sure I understand. Leah scribbles some more. She must be dying just to say it, I think.

It's a risk. We could go to court, create a stink?

'Leah's right,' Julia says. 'Why is he in such a hurry? Why can't he wait? Clever girl,' she adds.

'Before Mum changes her mind?' James suggests.

Leah scribbles. *She's besotted – talks of nothing else.*

'The will can go through. Everything goes to Mum. Whatever my suspicions I would have to sign,' Julia says. 'Even now that's the case, so why is he doing everything in such a rush?'

James is searching his bag again. 'These may help find us an answer.' He unwraps what look like large smarties.

'Bugs,' he explains. 'If Patrick has a room, we need to plant one there. They stick to anything metal. When I say we,' he explains, 'I mean Leah.'

He hands them to her and she takes them, weighs them in her hand. They both know Leah is closest to her mother, that her muteness is suddenly an asset, that it has to be Leah who joins the cult.

'Computer, Martin,' James demands, and I hand it over again. Another blur of menus and choices, download and install times, then James points out three new icons on the screen.

'These will light up when the bugs pick up anything. Do you want me to link them to speech-recognition software? It'll turn spoken words into text, making it quicker to monitor.'

I nod.

'I only hope this antiquated piece of junk can cope with its new workload.'

'James!' says Julia. 'And you were being so well behaved.'

The next morning Leah and I go to the café. When a group of young women enter the green door opposite, Leah gets up and crosses the street. We've agreed that she will knock, ask about joining, learn the process. She will, of course, tell them who she is. There's no point in not doing that. The way to her mother has to be through Patrick.

I watch her cross the road and even I have to concentrate on keeping her in sight. She has a knack of seeming invisible as she walks. She attracts no glances. I think I understand why. When I said there were many ways of not belonging, I meant only in dress, in superficial matters. I've always known that there are really only two groups of outsiders: extroverts and introverts. Extroverts like James love attention. These people have a choice. They could easily belong, pass as normal, but crave attention and so need to stand out. Introverts like Leah, and perhaps also like me, are people who could never pass as normal but hope to get through life quietly, unnoticed, on the margins.

As Leah approaches the door she doesn't turn to see if I'm watching. She is completely in role. I see her drop her head the moment she has knocked. We have talked about that too. To gain access she needs to act as if she is and always will be submissive.

Then the door opens. She holds up her mobile phone. We wrote the words last night. The message says, *Izzy is my mother, Patrick my brother. I want to join the Living Saints, if God will have me.*

I wrote those last five words. Very few people in my experience question what they are hoping to hear. I'm confident they will let her in.

There is a hurried conversation between two young women and then Leah is welcomed and steps inside. The door closes and I'm on my own again.

What do I feel?

Ever since the rape Leah has been with me. We've spent ten days together. I have never lived so close to another human being for such a long time, in fact ever since I left home to go to University. It feels strange, abnormal, as if being on my own is no longer as sweet as it once was, as if my careful construction of an independent life no longer satisfies me.

Have they phoned Patrick? Is he on his way, even now, to pick her up?

She has stepped away from me and I can't communicate with her, only monitor what she chooses to let me know via the camera.

She is the one in charge. Perhaps she always was.

***

An hour passes. Then two. I'm trying to concentrate, trying to price the new stock and put books on the shelves. Two customers come in and say they're glad I'm still open. I tell them I've things in my life that have pulled me away. I reassure both of them that I have no intention of shutting up shop. And all this time I feel disconnected. I'm functioning okay but I'm in two places at the same time. A kind of automated me is in the shop while the real, vital part of me is outside Costa, forcing people to walk round me as I hog the pavement, my eyes on the green door. I hope that Leah will emerge soon, but I fear that Patrick will come running in and that will be that.

The longer time drags, the greater that fear.

I watch the shop door. I see shadows as people walk towards it and I hope one of them is Leah. My body judders each time the shop bell sounds. And this is only the beginning.

Surely if Patrick does turn up Leah will activate the camera? We haven't arranged that, but I hope that's what she'll do and the computer screen is still blank.

Then she is suddenly in front of me. It takes all my self-control not to hug her.

'Tomorrow,' she tells me. 'Tomorrow at 11 o'clock they will admit me to the Living Saints for what they call induction. I am to take a case packed with everything I need. I will need to bring enough for several days in the first instance. If I'm successful, they say, I might be away for ever.'

We stand apart in the shop. If we were friends I think we would hug, high five, touch. But because we have been lovers, and because of Patrick, all that is forbidden.

'Did it go well?' I ask her.

'I confused the girls,' she tells me. 'I don't think this has ever happened before. They panicked a bit, then made a phone call. After that it was plain sailing.'

'So what happens next?'

For a terrible moment I think she's going to shake her head. I keep reminding myself that I mustn't presume anything between us, that a joint enterprise is simply that. Familiarity breeds all sorts of different reactions and contempt is equally as possible as love.

She stands there and I see her as vulnerable. From what little I know of her she has never been loved for herself. Might she not be intoxicated by the warm bath effect Uncle Joshua warned us about?

The shop bell goes. A customer says, 'Hello,' and begins his slow peregrination round the shelves. Leah gives me no more than a little grin as if she is pleased with herself, then she is past the sign that says private and climbing the stairs away from me. I can't follow her. I need to stay with the shop. Some lines from Donne come unbidden into my head:

From dull privations and lean emptiness / You ruined me and I am re-begot / Of absence, darkness, death / Things which are not.

The customer picks out Gavin Ewart's collected poems. I know he won't buy that. It's been on the shelves for ages and is priced at £30.

Hands that wiped arses, hold glasses. / Lips that fellated are intoxicated.

I see him peruse, shudder, and return it to the shelf.

My two selves have come back together. There is again only one of me. She will tell me everything that happened in there or she won't. Either way I will know. I go back to my pile of books. The customer moves on to the biography section, picks out *Double Act, a life of Tom Stoppard.* Then there are slow footsteps on the stairs. I'm ready for anything, for Leah having packed her cases because she's moving out, for Leah dressed up against the cold spring and going for a first walk on her own. I turn slowly towards the sound and see her at the foot of the stairs, holding a cup of coffee. Wordless, she hands it to me.

'Thanks,' I say.

Wordless, but not gesture free. As she turns to go back upstairs she touches my elbow. It's so gentle I'm not sure what to make of it. It could have been accidental but I don't think it was. Then this strange insistent dance begins inside me once more, and all the words from my second-hand life crowd back into my head. *Oh then I see Queen Mab has been with you.* And Michael Frayn's great line: *It's not the despair. I can cope with the despair. It's the hope.*

***

The next day I watch Leah cross the road. She is carrying a suitcase. Goodbyes are horrible when you can't say what you want to say. Yes, she pecked me briefly on the cheek, clutched my elbow. Now she is walking away from me again. I watch her go up to the door, put her case down, and knock. There is no look back to me. Again, she bows her head as she waits.

This time the door opens wide and it's Patrick. I recognise him from the car. I see him embrace her in the way I no longer can because of him. Then the door closes on both of them and I am terribly afraid.

Chapter 22

I knock on the green door. I'm in role. I bow my head. I have brought a case with everything I'll need. I keep telling myself that this is a Christian community, that no harm will come to me. Once they know what Patrick is like they are certain to reject him. Then Izzy and I will be free to leave at any time.

Footsteps are coming towards the door. Then Patrick himself is standing in front of me. This was always a possibility and I am prepared. I keep my head bowed.

'Hello sister,' he greets me. 'Welcome to the Living Saints.' Then his arms are round me and I want to scream, but I don't. Whatever happens now, I will ruin him. I step back out of his embrace and, keeping my head down, I touch my breast bone in supplication and turn on the camera. If we are alone in this house, if Patrick has designs on me, I now have the means to destroy him. I am one witness. The camera is the other.

I have stepped back and he stands looking at me, straight into my eyes. Does he wonder why I am here? Has he guessed? I want to look back at him. I want to register defiance, but I must stay as I am. I am the supplicant. I reprise the role of the naïve girl he raped. I slowly drop my eyes.

'I am overjoyed,' he says, with what I can only describe as a smirk, 'that you have sought us out.'

I had forgotten quite how tall he is, how powerful. But his looks are different and so is his speech. He is shaven. He is wearing trousers with a crease and turn ups, a blue shirt and v-neck sweater. He is once again out of date with the modern world. He is as I first saw him. But his speech now has authority. I hear in it the trick of control.

'God must have smiled on our last meeting,' he says.

That almost breaks my pose. My head wants to rocket upwards, remind him exactly what happened, and ask him what this holy shit is that he's putting into his voice.

He steps forward and places his hand on my head. It's like an invasion. It feels creepy and I want to scream. The nearness means I can now smell him. It takes all my self-control just to stand still.

'Bless you for understanding. May God bless you and keep you.'

He doesn't lift his hand off my head immediately. Instead he lets it slide across and down the back of my head as if he is stroking me, as if he is testing me.

Then he has removed his hand and he's looking at me again. This time I keep my head up, if only so the camera can see him more clearly.

Moments seem to pass. Am I prepared for the possibility of another assault? His physical presence in the room is huge. I can feel him deciding what he will do. Then he suddenly claps his hands, other people appear, and I can breathe. The women I met on my first visit are there. I recognise Martha and Rebecca among them. They welcome me warmly and then stand back.

I have returned to the comfort of being mute. I am free to observe without being expected to talk. Patrick tells me these women will be my sponsors.

They are like creatures of the late fifties. Their skirts are below the knee and cling only at the waist. Their blouses have buttons, high neck lines and collars. Their faces are natural without make up. Their hair is undyed. No one is blonde. Will they expect me to dress like them?

I notice how they are with Patrick. When I first met them they seemed not to know what to do with my request to join. They looked at me suspiciously. Now they are standing back waiting for Patrick. This is, I realise, the quaintest thing about the group, this deference to the man. I give them each a bow and that lets me touch my breastbone and turn off the camera. If Martin has watched my arrival, the presence of these others will reassure him and I need to save the batteries. I have no idea how long my mission will take.

There is another silence. Then Patrick says to the women, 'Take care of her. Explain our ways, go through the process.' He turns to me and adds, 'I must go, but I'll see you later. I'll take you to meet our mother.' Then he is gone.

The others relax as soon as he steps out of the room. I find myself in the middle of a storm of conversation as they all talk at once.

'I love your mum. It's so nice she's back.'

'Fancy Patrick being your brother.'

'You don't look like him at all.'

'Different dads I expect. Well, these things happen I suppose, or they did in those days.'

Their conversation washes around me. Its unspoken assumption is that we are all now in the same group. Part of me warms to this sense of belonging, part of me is already building walls. I know I should seem grateful so I smile and nod. Then I get out my pad of paper and write, *How is my mum?*

The question enthuses them.

'So happy to be back.'

'Oh gosh, I mean, it's as if she's been back for years.'

'You'll see her eventually.'

Eventually? I write.

'Well, we were surprised when Patrick said that about meeting her later.'

'Normally you would have to wait much longer.'

'It's because of who you are, I expect.'

'And who he is.'

Rebecca takes over. 'Perhaps we should start,' she says.

The others nod.

Rebecca leans forward and looks into my eyes in the way no stranger ever does. She stares at me for a long time as she takes my left hand in both of hers. I feel I am being examined.

Silence. I maintain eye contact. I tell myself that eyes are not windows into the mind. No one can read your thoughts. I try to hold her look without staring. Through my peripheral vision I see that the others have joined hands. We are linked. The moment lengthens.

'What we offer you,' Rebecca eventually explains, 'is nothing less than the everlasting and personal love of the Lord Jesus.' She pauses. 'I have looked into your eyes and into your mind, Leah, and I feel your loneliness. I feel your emptiness. I also feel that you are not yet receptive to the great present which is offered to you: eternal love, eternal redemption. Open your mind. Do not reject us or push us away.'

All this time my hand is being gently squeezed, the way Izzy used to squeeze it when I was a little girl and something had upset me.

It feels weird, warm and creepy but I mustn't show that. I want to run away, but I know I have to relax and let this happen. Unless I get inside the headquarters I can't reach Izzy and I can't destroy Patrick.

We stay like this for some time, then the circle relaxes. The girls drop hands and I have to stop myself from showing how relieved I am.

'Are you without sin?' Martha asks.

No, I want to write, I had sex with a man who wasn't my husband. His name was Patrick. Instead I write, *Of course not.*

They frown. They ask me what my sins have been.

You want a list?

They actually do want a list. And I suddenly realise how little I have prepared for this. What is a sin? What isn't? I have to buckle down. I have to concentrate. What was it Martin said about people never questioning what they want to hear?

I write slowly. They lean forward to read my scribble. Writing is better than talking. It gives you time to think. I write, *My greatest sin is being godless. My life without faith feels pointless. I've been to other churches and they seem only to play at faith. I want to give myself to God, utterly. I want to live in his love.* I haven't written so much for years and my hand is already tiring, but the sisterhood is nodding.

'We'll help you to do just that,' Martha assures me, and pats me on the knee.

***

I don't complain when my lunch is brought to me in a separate room and I eat it in isolation with only the Bible for company. I welcome this break. The Bible knowledge I do have comes from school. I remember quite a lot about Jesus. But he doesn't seem to feature much with the Living Saints. I thought I remembered parables, miracles and compassion, but when Jesus does come into their increasingly neurotic narrative it is only as judge and disciplinarian. Everything they've taught me so far comes from the Old Testament or from St Paul, bypassing the gospels almost completely. Weird.

I am no longer frightened. So long as I'm with these religious groupies I feel almost at home in this house with the green door. I'm back to playing two parts. To the Living Saints I must seem the mute, submissive disciple. But, if I am to survive and succeed in my mission, I must remain the sceptical observer. To me this kind of schizophrenia is quite normal. I've been this way with my family ever since I stopped talking. I was always this way at school. I am even like this with Izzy.

Then, in a rush, I realise that with Martin I have sometimes been whole and undivided, that Martin is the only person in my life with whom I can just be me.

I save the thought for later. I need to concentrate on the now.

There is a service at 6.30pm in the church at Headquarters. They want me to go and anyway, they tell me, that's where I will be staying.

'You'll like the preacher,' Rebecca assures me.

Martha drives the car. I try to follow the route but it's too dark. Although I think I recognise some buildings, I'm not sure exactly where we are going.

It doesn't take long to get there. I'd guess at forty minutes, but I forgot to time it. When we arrive I stand and look at the building in front of me. I can do this safely. They would expect me to be in awe of this plain, spot-lit, white painted building. My perusal gives me time to turn the camera on, to film the main door and the surroundings.

If they lock me up here, will Martin recognise the building? Will he be able to rescue me?

The moment we walk through the entrance I am aware that it is a fortress. One gate leads into a short corridor which leads to a heavy double door. The moment we go through, it is closed behind us. I already feel trapped. The floors are tiled and the place echoes. Its noises have a metallic quality. There is something else too, a vibe I can't place. I want to stand and listen, but they rush me through to the church.

When we walk in I try not to gasp. It has no windows. It is an entirely enclosed space. Martha and Rebecca bring me in and I stand in what I can only describe as God's bunker. It is church-shaped with a high nave, two aisles and an altar. But instead of windows there are expanses of white paint. It is also quite small, almost intimate. I ask myself why there are so few Living Saints, especially if anyone can walk in off the streets and ask to join like I did.

As the service progresses I mimic whatever Rebecca and Martha do, but in silence. During the Bible readings they are kind enough to find the place for me. I follow the words on the page, head bowed over the book, concentrating furiously. Only when hymns are being sung do I have time to look around.

The space is about two thirds full. I think of the congregation at Dad's funeral, people brought together because a man had died. This group to either side and in front of me is much less varied than the mixture of those who knew Dad and those who worked with him. There is more uniformity of dress and much less variation in type. This congregation shares a certain look and it comes over as smugness. I think of the young Joshua and the young Isabel who each in their own way rejected this, and I can see that this uniformity is both warm and smothering. So why has Izzy come back? *I do not want to be always alone.* The hymn finishes. The congregation sits and Patrick comes forward to the rostrum.

'You'll like the preacher,' they told me.

This is a bunker packed with assumptions.

I watch my half-brother. As he raises his head I notice a spotlight gradually add a kind of radiance to his human form. His look is serene. Another spotlight shining from behind him gives him a halo. In front of me my rapist is being canonised.

'It is,' he begins, 'the simple things that always shock us the most.'

He rotates his head, drawing in his followers. I recognise the performer in him, the man who came to us with such false humility, who made a fuss of me; the man who calmly pulled his pants up and zipped his trousers after he'd finished with me. I recognise my enemy.

'We have in this world a thing of real power, the most powerful thing we could ever have been given. Of course, I'm not talking about nuclear power, I'm not talking nanotechnology, whatever that may be. . .' He pauses and they duly laugh, then he starts again with raised volume and greater urgency. 'I'm not even talking about the forces of nature like great tempests, hurricanes and volcanoes.' Another pause. He slowly rotates his gaze again, this time to include the whole congregation, to give them guessing time, to pull them in, to make them complicit. Then he lowers his voice. 'And this thing of power isn't hidden,' he tells us. 'You don't have to mine down into the bowels of the earth to find it. There is no need to cross deserts or be blown across oceans. And no laboratory has ever devised anything with quite the force that lies in a simple, readily available book.' He pauses again, smiles. Then, '*You* all know what I am talking about.' The word *you* is emphasised. '*You* know because you live with this thing daily. Its power lights you up, its glory inflames you. You know I am talking about the word of God.'

Relief and recognition. They understand. Rebecca smiles down at me and I smile back at her. Martha pats my knee. 'It can be yours too,' she whispers. I smile back and cross my fingers. It seems the appropriate response, to act like the child they want me to be.

Patrick has gathered them in and is moving on, gaining speed. 'So what shocks me so much? What shocks us all when everything I have said is such simple truth? You know the answer to this too. What shocks us is how much the word of God is ignored.'

'Not by us,' Patrick is quick to add on a rising note. 'I truly believe not by any one of us.'

'I want you to think,' he tells them, 'of the billions of people on this earth. Think of the continents, think of every land mass that is raised above the oceans. Think houses, villages, towns and cities. The word of God is available to each and every one of them. You've got that picture. Now come back nearer home. Every British child is given the Bible when they are at school. Every hotel room has a Bible. Whatever your language, there is a Bible in that language.' He suddenly taps the microphone and the noise level jumps. 'There are no excuses for ignoring God's word,' he shouts. 'Everything you need to know to be happy and to lead a good life is in here,' and he thrusts a Bible aloft as if it is the cup of cups, as if it is a trophy he has personally won.

'This book has the answers to the questions they continually ask. It's time tested. It has never failed a man who truly believes. So why is it spurned? Why is it ignored, this thing that was paid for with God's own blood, this vital container of truth brought to us by the agony in the garden?'

I find I'm having to fight to remain the sceptical observer. The effect of his performance in this confined, windowless space is extraordinary. His voice seduces, involves, reassures. And the most remarkable trick is its sincerity. I glance at Martha and Rebecca. They seem transported, but for Patrick it is time to break his own illusion. His voice drops an octave, becomes raw as he cries out. 'So why are there so few of us? Dear God, why so few?'

And by way of answer to Patrick's agonised question I hear a murmur, at first scarcely audible, as if several people choose this moment to whisper to their neighbour. Then the murmur grows, is in danger of being decipherable, when Patrick surfs its growing crest with words of his own. 'Because it is so difficult. Because what God asks of each one of those billions of people is so hard and it takes a special kind of perseverance and obedience to follow his rules.' He holds out his arms, palms upwards, and almost laughs as he says, 'The kind of perseverance and obedience that you all have in spades.'

He leaves no gap. 'We believe every word of this wonderful book. And we suffer for it in exactly the way Jesus suffered. When we go into the world we are scorned. They laugh at the way we dress. They permit the unworthy to denigrate us. They tell fantastic stories about us. They continually lie about us. And that's what I want to concentrate on next.'

This time the pause is so long it feels uncomfortable, even personal. He has lowered his voice, is tapping the edge of the pulpit in time to his words. 'And amongst its precepts we learn that there is no more damaging a thing that the Devil can do than encourage false witness against the righteous. Envy of the truly holy man can lead deranged and damaged individuals to invent stories…'

Suddenly I realise what he is doing. He wonders why I am here. He fears that I might be a danger to him. He guesses at the damage I might do, so he is neutralising me. They are about to be warned not to believe whatever I say about the rape.

'… and sexual smears are always the most damaging of all because they are incapable of proof. That is why we have the two witness rule. We need to beware all bearers of false witness. These evil individuals can split us apart, can destroy the union of our great cause. God has mighty punishments in store for such people.'

He has them. He knows he has them. They are shaking their heads. Indeed, he is confident enough at that moment to ignore them and look straight at me. He thinks he has me exactly where he wants me. His look says, if that's your game, there is no possible way you can win. The whole point of his sermon has nothing to do with God and everything to do with neutralising me.

He is doing this because he knows I could be dangerous to him. But if I'm a danger, why has he let me in? Does he think I'm only the silent, stupid girl who developed a crush on him? Did he see through that and is welcoming me because here he can observe and control me? He could have arranged to fail me in the house with the green door and sent me packing. I mean, I hardly distinguished myself today. So if I am a danger, why has he allowed me to come here where I can do him most harm?

He knows the rules. He has just re-stated them. Unintentionally he might just have let me know that there are others in this congregation who could bear witness against him. Was he warning them as well as warning me? During the next hymn I scan the congregation more exactly. I am certain that Izzy isn't here. She is the one person I can and must tell about the rape. I won't be deterred from that.

When we file out at the end of the service, Patrick is at the door. A plain looking woman with a rather stern face, partly hidden under an abundance of black hair, stands beside him and close to him. She is dressed like the others but she carries herself with a certain authority. I've no idea who she is. I join the line and notice how tactile my brother is with females of a certain age. The young women are embraced as if through the physical touch of them he can bind them into God's love. He grasps shoulders. He holds wrists and they are not offended. This is a closed world just like my special school was. Behaviours are tolerated here that would not be tolerated outside. Such behaviours have become part of the fabric of the building like they did for us. This is a world I know only too well.

When I reach Patrick I bow and draw back. I am among the last out, but my sponsors are right behind me. This is my public meeting with my brother. I find myself wondering what he will do. The woman with raven hair is examining me in a less than friendly way. Patrick hasn't yet noticed me.

When he finally sees me he turns to the woman beside him. 'Ah, Katherine,' he says. 'This is Leah, my long lost sister. Leah, this is Katherine, my fiancée.'

Life is full of shocks. But I find I can match him. I too can hide my feelings and play a part for the benefit of this small audience. Is that in the shared genes?

I walk forward to Katherine. I put a beam on my face. I hold out my hands so she knows what I am going to do and I embrace her, rest my head on her shoulder in exactly the way I embraced him before it happened. I hope he notices. But Katherine is not an actress. She visibly flinches. I feel her whole body go tense and I suspect that she doesn't enjoy the physical. So why is she marrying Patrick? More to the point, why is Patrick marrying her? I step back, reach out for her left hand and look for a ring that isn't there. Don't they do rings? This situation needs words. I get out my pad and write, *I'm so pleased for you both.* I tear the note off the pad and hand it to Katherine, who passes it quickly to Patrick. I notice she is much older than he is and I wonder why he has chosen her.

I hope I have been subtle enough. I don't want to put him

on his guard.

Patrick asks me to wait while he embraces my sponsors.

Then, with a different tone in his voice, 'Will you please come with me, Leah? There's someone else I want you to meet.'

Now I'm intrigued, but why the hurry?

I bow and follow him. Katherine watches us as we walk off together. I can feel her eyes fixed on me as if she is trying to work me out. Patrick leads the way across the courtyard into a building that is a warren of corridors. It gives me time to make sure the camera is in position. I don't switch it on. I have to preserve the battery and anyway, I sense no danger, only an anxiety on his part. Who does he want me to meet now?

We have reached a door. In front of it Patrick pauses before he knocks.

A voice answers. Patrick signals me to wait, steps into the room. I listen carefully but can only make out part of the conversation.

'Sir, I have brought my sister to see you.'

'. . .thank you. . . too ill . . .not fair on her.'

'Sir, she has joined the Living Saints. I have brought her back.'

The voice that responds sounds like Dad when he was dying. I think it says, 'point noted,' but I can't be sure.

Patrick soon backs out of the room and closes the door quietly, then puts his arm on my shoulder to usher me away. My flesh creeps. I stay in role. I recognise that Patrick has relaxed.

'That was God's Man,' he explains. 'He is our leader. I wanted you to meet him, Leah, but he says he is too ill. I'm sorry about that for your sake. He is a truly holy man.' His hand clutches at my shoulder. I feel his thumb beginning to caress my shoulder blade.

I free myself, take out my pad and write, *Can I see Izzy now?*

He reads it and nods. 'Of course. I'll take you to her.'

We go outside and across a courtyard. As I follow Patrick I think about what I've just heard. Is Patrick's hurry linked to the fact that God's Man is ill? 'She has joined,' Patrick told him, which isn't true. 'Point noted,' the voice behind the door replied. I store this thought and Patrick's lie for later. I am about to meet my mother, to rob her of her newfound happiness. I steel myself to do the deed.

We enter another building. This time I make mental notes of where I am going. If Patrick stays with us and I can't talk privately to Izzy, I may need to make my own way here and find her. The building is confusing. I note pictures and texts, where the fire extinguishers hang. I try to fix each turn and what comes next. Then we are standing outside another door. It has no number and no name. All the doors look the same. But then, I realise, numbers and labels are for outsiders. No outsiders ever come in here, so there is no need for labels.

Patrick knocks on the door and ushers me in. For a second I feel sorry for Julia's wish to be Head of the Family. Patrick is being proprietorial towards our mother. He has walked straight in and put his arm round her as if she is his property, as if he is about to introduce us. Then I look at Izzy and see how changed she is. Her clothes, which always had a certain style about them, have become plainer. She is wearing no make-up. She looks older. Her hair is reverting to white.

'Doesn't she look well?' Patrick is saying. 'Being in the community really suits her.'

I come forward to hug her. This has been the longest separation we have ever had. I reach my arms round her and find she is stepping back from me. Bewildered, I look to Patrick.

'She's back in the community already,' he explains. The anxious tone has been stripped from his voice. He has reverted to his sanctimonious mode. He spells it out as if I am a child. 'Our mother is following the terms of separation.'

I find my pad and write, *And I?*

'You are novitiate. You are not yet part of the community. Our mother cannot eat with you, she cannot drink with you and she must not yet touch you.'

I want to snap out of role. I want to shout, *But you told God's Man that I had already joined.* I don't. Instead, I bow my head and so we preserve our new identities.

'I'm so sorry, Leah,' Izzy says. 'Take the hug in my thoughts.'

Her subservience riles me. I stay with my head down, but risk another question for Patrick. *You touch me,* I write. *Martha put her hand on my knee.*

'We have special dispensations.' His face is set but the smile in his voice never wavers.

Then surely Mum can have one to hug her own daughter?

He shakes his head. 'Your mother was cast out. Time has to go by before she can be considered for dispensations.'

I'm getting nowhere and I mustn't blow my cover. I bow my head and write, *But she can talk to me?*

'Only if I, or someone of my rank, is present.'

I sit down. Izzy sits too. She tells me everything that Patrick could possibly expect of her. I listen to her talking of the warmth, of how much she has missed all this, of how wilful she must have been as a young girl ever to think of leaving. As Izzy talks, Patrick moves away and sits, leaning against the wall. His eyes begin to close, but when Izzy stops talking and asks me questions he comes over to supervise my answers. I've suddenly had enough.

I write, *I'm tired and have a long day tomorrow. Before that they've set me lots of homework. Will you excuse me?*

I see no point in stringing out this stilted meeting.

Patrick shows me to my room which is on the first floor of the same building. I follow him, learning the landmarks as I go. My case is just inside the door. A Bible is also there, carefully placed on the bed with the passages marked for me to study. There is a programme for tomorrow. I notice that Patrick makes no effort to follow me inside, but almost dramatically turns and walks away.

The moment he's gone I check the door. I haven't been locked in. I close it again quickly. Now there's nothing for it but to settle down and read the marked passages. I'm not used to study. My mind won't settle. I keep wondering how much Patrick has damaged my mission. There may be witnesses out there, but will they risk talking to me? They have been promised that God himself will punish them.

I must rescue Izzy. To do that I need to see her, talk to her on her own, explode her new certainties with my double bombshell of news. I must risk a night walk through this labyrinth. What will happen if I am caught? Can I find the way?

I work until the whole building goes quiet. Then I arrange my bed to look as if I am still inside it and switch my own light off. I make myself wait in darkness for a further half hour before I open my door and head downstairs. I have no torch and I cannot risk switching lights on. Luckily there is a moon and my eyes are already accustomed to the minimal light. I turn first right, then go left. I remember Izzy's was the third door. If I am caught I don't know what I will do. I have no pad with me to write on. It's in my room. I wonder whether to go back for it but decide not to. I count the doors and the posters. Every now and then I stop suddenly and listen but there are no noises at all. In this way I reach Izzy's room and turn the handle. The door is unlocked. I push it open and step inside.

Immediately I close the door behind me and stand inside in the darkness until my heart slows. I can hear Izzy's night time breathing. It's a familiar sound and makes me feel safe, so I approach the bed.

When I was a little girl and couldn't sleep I used to climb out of my bed and go to find Mum. Then I would stand at the side of her bed and wait for her to wake. I knew I wasn't allowed to wake her so I developed the knack of leaning over her and staring at her from close range. This usually did the trick.

I try that now and her eyes open.

She is disorientated and I am about to make that worse. She hasn't heard me speak since I was nine. That will be her first shock.

She's waking from a deep sleep. I give her time.

Then very softly and gently I say, 'Izzy, wake up. I need to talk to you.'

Her eyes go huge. I wonder if she thinks she's dreaming.

I smile at her. 'It's me,' I say to her. 'It's Leah.'

I try to speak very clearly but Izzy only looks confused, as if she just can't grasp what's happening.

'You're speaking. . ..'

'Yes, Izzy. For a long time I think I chose not to, but now I have to. And I need you to listen.'

'Leah?'

Of course, it's dark and she's only just woken from a deep sleep. I'm going too fast.

I see a glass of water by her bed, encourage her to sit up and take a drink.

She drinks and feels for the bedside table with the glass. I take it from her.

'Now, let's start again,' I say. 'I'm your daughter, Leah. I've started talking again and I need to talk to you.' She's coming to and is alert enough, so I dive in. 'I have to talk to you while Patrick isn't here. I have to talk to you about Patrick.'

'You mustn't,' she says. 'I haven't had dispensation. Tomorrow I have a Face to Face.'

She begins to put her hands over her ears so I pull them away. I try to build up to what I have to say.

'I've been to see your brother, Joshua. I know what happened to him and I know what happened to you all those years ago. I know about The Living Saints and being cast out. I know you had your baby in one of their houses and that you left your little boy with them.'

She's startled, unsure, caught in the headlights.

'Do you remember the day you took us all to see your mum, and Grandad wouldn't let us in.'

'You remember that?'

I nod. 'I've never forgotten.'

She's with me and I need to keep her like that. To reassure her I add, 'Patrick said you couldn't talk to me without supervision. I'm not asking you to talk, just to listen. You don't have to say anything. I'm sure that's allowed.'

I'm still holding her hands and she's no longer pulling away from me, so I change my grip to an affectionate hold.

'And I'm afraid that what I'm going to say will upset you. I never wanted to tell you this but I must. I know you love Patrick. I wish you could go on loving him. I actually fled the house to avoid telling you that Patrick is not as you think he is.'

She winces with her whole face, quickly slips her hand out of my grip and both hands move back towards her ears. Before they can get there I have to say the three short words I've been dreading.

'He raped me.' There. I've done it.

Now her hands have fallen to the bed cover.

I repeat the words, adding others.' When you were out he came into my bedroom. I went to hug him because he is my brother and the next thing I knew he was raping me.'

'He can't have.'

I go over it again. I tell her every detail, what he did and what he said. I describe the shock of it, the not understanding, my incredulity at his swift and terrible invasion of me.

Izzy recovers enough to shake her head. 'But he's not like that, not at all like that,' she says.

'Why would I make that up?'

'He's my son.'

'I think he must be. I've met your brother. Patrick has Uncle Joshua's eyes.'

She nods. Then she cries.

I climb onto the bed at her side and hold her to me, rocking her gently.

'I didn't want to tell you, Izzy. You have to believe that. I took myself out of the house. I went away so as not to tell you. I know you love him.'

'Why...?' she starts to ask, but I'm in a hurry. I'm in danger and I have to be out of here quickly, so I interrupt her.

'I think he wants me out of the way,' I explain. 'I think he's after the money. Did he make sure you collected the original will? I know he went with you to the solicitors. Have you already given him the money?'

She shakes her head. 'Not that...'

Every moment I'm in her room is a danger, so I interrupt again. 'Good,' I say. 'At least that's one problem we won't have.

She throws her hands up in the air. 'Shut up,' she says. 'Stop talking and just listen.'

She's sitting up in bed flapping her arms at me. 'Not that, Leah. Not that at all.' Her look is fierce. 'Why are you lying?' She almost shouts this at me. 'Why have you made all this up? Why are you telling me this nonsense about him raping you when you know it isn't true?'

I remember James's warning, but it's too late. I look at my mother. I read desperation in her face, but she is also determined.

'I'm not lying, Izzy. I've told you exactly what happened. If he can do that to me, what can he do to you?'

Even in the dark I can see how fixed and dead her eyes are.

'You're jealous of him, aren't you?' she says. 'That's what this is all about.'

At that I let go of her and climb off the bed. Patrick's had opportunity. He warned his whole congregation about what I might be going to say. He can't have warned her too, can he? I don't have time to argue my case. I need to know where the family stands. 'Have you already given him the money?' I ask.

She looks at me. 'We must all pay our dues to God. That's a matter between me and my conscience.'

Patrick's language. He has her all sewn up. I should never have gone away. I should never have come back. What am I doing here? It's all too late.

Now Izzy is sitting up and looking straight at me. 'I gave him away once. That was the most painful thing I've ever done. I can't abandon him again.'

'You gave him to the Living Saints, didn't you? You left him with these people?'

She nods.

'Well, look what they've done to him. Look what he's become.'

'Leah, you've never felt a mother's love.'

'He's a monster. You can't see it, but that's what he is. He raped his half-sister. He acts a part, Izzy. He isn't real!'

What else can I add? That is the only pitch I can make and I've said it all. But I see at once, even in this half-light, that it won't be enough. I've forced Izzy to make a choice and it's clear which way she will go. I wonder if I ever had a chance, if she ever really loved any of us.

Izzy's fully alert now. 'And you,' she challenges, 'are you real? All these years you've been able to speak and you hid that from us. I know I can't trust you.'

Game set and match to Patrick. I stand up and walk away.

'Good night, Mum.' I find I can't call her Izzy.

'We all keep secrets,' I remind her. 'You kept a secret once. His name was Patrick. That didn't make you a liar.'

***

I close the door behind me and begin to make my way back along the corridor. The moon has gone down or is now behind a cloud. It is nearly pitch black in the building and there are no shapes to navigate by. I turn right and run my hand along the wall. I count two further doors before I feel for a space where the corridor should be. Distances are longer in the dark and I'm getting confused. I wonder what I will do if I can't find my way back. But then my fingers grasp at air and I go round the corner I thought I might never reach.

Here there is just a little more light so I can speed up. I'm looking for the stairs and I've forgotten if they are on the left or the right. I spent all my time planning the journey to Mum's room, not the journey back. I can't see posters but I do bang my hand against the fire extinguisher. It wobbles but doesn't fall. As I work my way along I'm glad I didn't tell her about the others being involved. She won't suspect that I'm working with James and Julia. She knows nothing about Martin. Whatever she tells Patrick about my night-time visit, she can't tell him what she herself doesn't know. What has just happened makes me more determined to find proof of Patrick's assaults, however difficult that will now be. I need to rub her nose in the monstrous behaviour of her son.

A space on the right opens up and there are the stairs. I grip the banister with relief. I'm nearly back to my room. The moon is brighter and I can see my corridor quite clearly. It's bright enough to show me the floor, the left-hand wall and the edge of my door. I'm walking towards it and thinking of sleep when I see something move ahead of me. It's difficult to make out in this poor light, but someone is stepping out of my room and quietly closing the door. Whoever it is stands still and listens for a moment. This gives me enough time to shrink back into the darkness. As the figure passes me I recognise the shape, recognise the long dark hair. It's Katherine. She's been in my room. I wait until she's downstairs, then make my way back to my bed.

I have to do it. I have to risk the light. I count to sixty slowly and then switch it on. I must know why she was here. As far as I can see, nothing has changed. The bed, my case, the Bible with its marked pages, my notes, are all exactly as I left them. Why was she here? What did she come for?

Has she been in my case, found the camera and the electronics? A quick search tells me they are still there and exactly where I put them. Then what? What was she looking for? What did she come to do?

***

I know about the limited battery life. I know Leah won't take risks by filming what she doesn't need. But what if she's filmed nothing? What if they've found the camera and confiscated it? I can't sleep because I'm frightened for her, so I go to the computer. I risk re-running the film she recorded. It's all short clips of Patrick, except for the entrance to the white-painted building. That was shot when she arrived. She hasn't shot another sequence like it so she must still be there. It's longer than it needs to be. When I watched it with James I didn't realise that. James warned her about filming when she didn't have to, so why waste film on this when she's recorded nothing else? Then I realise that she's filmed the entrance and the surroundings. I become convinced that she's telling me where she is, as if she hopes I'll recognise something nearby. I play it again. There are shops to one side but nothing out of the ordinary, only a Macdonald's and a Costcutter. The quality is poor and it's dark. If only there was a street sign or a shop that wasn't part of a chain.

I pause the sequence and stare at the building. My mind wanders to the people inside. I think of Izzy, in love with her own son. I think of Leah, determined to get her revenge on Patrick, needing to ruin him. And I think of Patrick himself. If I were Patrick and I were after the money, I'd keep Leah away from my mother until the deed was done. I'd also keep her separate from other cult members for as long as possible. But he hasn't done either. He's welcomed her in, introduced her to others. I know that from Leah's first piece of filming. She's met other people and he's left her with them. Why?

The darkness puts no limits on my fears. I find myself wondering if I'm being too rational about this, even wondering if Patrick is psychotic. Armed with charisma and the word of God, psychotics can be devastating. Does Patrick believe both in what he preaches and in his own right to break religious law? I think of ISIS, of the self-appointed Caliph who, in the name of his compassionate God, beheads male prisoners and turns female captives into his own sex slaves.

It's 3am and I don't know if I'm weaving one of those fantastic scenarios that need darkness to support them and will vanish with daylight. The last thought I have before I fall asleep is that the Living Saints are used to people simply disappearing.

Chapter 23

It's morning inside the cult. In spite of having so little sleep I wake early. Grey light fills the room. Because the windows face east, a rising sun soon gives sharp edges to walls and corners. Even before I dress I look for traces of Katherine. I re-open the case. As far as I can tell, everything is as it was. Katherine didn't turn the light off when she came out, so she mustn't have turned the light on, I reason. So she couldn't have come to take something from the room unless the item was big and obvious. But she was carrying nothing of any size with her.

If she didn't take anything, perhaps she came to check on me, check I was still in my room. In which case she will have approached the bed and found me absent. But then she just turned and left. She didn't put the light on just to make sure, which seems odd. And why did she pause and listen after closing my door?

I rehearse what I know. She then left in a hurry. She passed me quickly as if she didn't want to be seen. But as far as she knew I was in bed, asleep, so she wasn't being quick on my account. Perhaps she didn't want someone else to see her. Patrick?

I need to be clever about this. There is an answer to this riddle. I try to remember Katherine's face when we first met. She was standing behind Patrick, watching his triumph. Her look was fixed, not pleased for him but indulgent. How well does she know him, I wonder. And even as I ask the question, my brain makes its own suggestion. Perhaps she knows him like I do, knows what he's capable of, knows he's not straightforward.

I sense I'm getting close so I keep going. I try to count the recent happenings that may have caused her to walk round last night. There's my presence, but she must have known I was coming. Patrick must have told her. Has something happened between her and Patrick? If it has, I have no way of guessing at that. Or was it the sermon? She was there, in the congregation. It was strange, wasn't it, that sudden jump from a world view to the danger of false witness, of sexual false witness in particular. Did that alert her? Did she begin to wonder why Patrick suddenly put that into his sermon, and does she mistrust him enough to need to spy on me?

Spy on me. Perhaps she didn't need to put the light on because she wasn't wanting to check if I was there. It never crossed her mind that I wouldn't be. Nor was she searching my room. She wasn't looking for anything. No, she was bringing something, bringing something she could place quickly before leaving again. And she listened outside the door because she wanted to be sure she hadn't woken me in the process.

I guess what that something might be. I've brought three of them with me.

Now where did she fix it? It has to be a little way from the bed because she never noticed I wasn't there. The room is equipped for study. There's a light to read by close to the chair. I was using it last night. It has a metal stem.

And there, low down, I find the bug she brought. Because she mustn't know that I know, I leave it exactly where it is.

But why plant a bug in the room of a mute girl? It's not for me is it? What else? Who else? Exactly what does Katherine suspect is going on?

My mind whirs with the weirdness of it all. They ban mobile phones for members of the congregation, but indulge in electronic surveillance. Perhaps my mother's room is also bugged. Perhaps they will soon play back every word of our conversation. In that case Katherine will know that Patrick raped me and that I can talk. My mother has a Face to Face today. If they don't know from the surveillance, they may know from her confession. Electronic surveillance? Is that how they maintain control? Does surveillance mean they know before each Face to Face exactly which sins the individual might be concealing? Is that how the pure in mind check up on purity?

There's a knock on my door. My breakfast is brought to me because I can't eat with the others. A morning of being tested beckons. As I eat I re-read what I studied last night. I check my watch. Five minutes to go before my first session. I must be on time. I take the camera with me. I know it's difficult, but evidence matters more than ever. I need it to convince my mum. I won't look for statements or confessions. Patrick has seen to that. I'll ask questions and note the things I've always looked for: those little tell-tale signs on people's faces. If I'm right about Patrick, there will be some evidence in this building. I need to find it before they simply unmask me and ask me to leave, or worse.

***

After all the intrigue of the night before, the building is calm and reflective in the morning. Its white walls and ash grey skirting boards set off the plain, wooden floors. People moving through the place treat it with respect. They whisper if they need to talk, so there is a library hush that permeates the very fabric.

The texts on the wall recommend *love* and *obedience*, puffing out their messages like a kind of spiritual air freshener. A poster saying, *God knows your innermost secrets* makes me want to shout, 'So does Katherine.' But I am in enough potential trouble, so I revert to the role of the disciple and bow my head whenever I pass someone in the corridor.

I find the classroom and it's empty, so I go out again and check that it is the fourth door on the right after the Madonna. It is, so I go back in and wait.

The waiting gives me time to check the quotations once again. I have learnt each of them by heart. Today I know the names of the disciples. Today I know that St Paul used to be called Saul of Tarsus and that he began by persecuting Christians. His is the story I am hanging onto. I've never persecuted anyone and if he can be accepted, so can I.

My sponsors bustle in. This time we start with prayers, kneeling on the hard floor. When we get up Martha sees me rubbing my knees. 'You'll get used to it,' she assures me.

They go through my homework and to each question I write down the answer.

They relax as I prove my scholarship. They no longer exchange puzzled looks and I find myself warming to their naive sense of duty. I am back to being two people. Ever since the rape I have tried to protect my mother, thought of her constantly, put her happiness before my own need for justice. Last night my mother rejected me. Is that why the easy affection of these girls is becoming infectious? But when we move on to the different roles of men and women I am appalled.

They are eager to tell me how lucky women are in the community, lucky because they are subservient. In the same way that we all have to obey God, women have the privilege of obeying men. Women don't have to make hard choices, and because of that they are spared from sin. The role of women is simply to obey, while men take the risk of leading. Men face up to the possibility that in making decisions they may annoy God himself. Because of these different roles, women are relieved of the onerous task of being Elders. Instead their duty is to provide succour. They must serve the needs of men, and it is only through serving men's needs that they can reach out to God Himself.

They smile as they say this and my face smiles with them.

It is easy just to listen and nod, but I must get on with what I came here to do. I need to word my question well. I can only ask it once, so I try to put it into their language. *These wonderful men may have needs. What do they do about those needs if they are not married?* I write the words so that only I can see them. Then, turning the pad round, I watch their faces as they read.

I see embarrassment. None of my sponsors wears a wedding ring. I see fascination. I do not see guilt. No one reddens up or draws in a lip or starts to cry. There is nothing to indicate that Patrick has done to them what he did to me.

'We believe very strongly that sex must only happen within marriage,' Rebecca intones.

Good, that's what I hoped you would say.

'We are God-fearing,' Martha adds. 'I suspect you find that difficult to understand. We fear God's wrath. We hope to avoid his punishments. None of the Living Saints would dare break his commandment about the sanctity of marriage.'

I haven't touched the camera all morning. There's been nothing to film.

Chapter 24

James hasn't gone back to university. Instead he's basing himself at the family house. He comes to the bookshop the day after Leah met Patrick behind the green door and offers me advice, even suggesting I open a café. But when I make him a coffee he immediately pulls a face and tells me to ditch the café idea. Instead he offers to set me up with a website and a link to eBay. That way, he tells me, with his help I can become the nation's second-hand bookshop of choice.

'Did Leah go?' he eventually asks.

'Patrick was waiting for her,' I explain.

'And has she sent us anything?'

'Not really. She turns the camera on when she's alone with Patrick. She did film the Headquarters' entrance, so I know she's gone there. There's been nothing else.'

'Leah's tough,' he comments, 'and clever.'

'Yes,' I say. Single words are all I can manage. I keep thinking of the way James treated his younger sister, threatening to drop her into the sinkhole all those years ago. I can't forgive him for that.

'I never realised she was clever until she bamboozled Julia.'

I say nothing. Having Leah's brother in the house when Leah is there at the same time is one thing; having him to myself is something else.

James abandons his coffee and begins to look round the shop, sweeping his hair back as he cranes his neck to see the higher shelves. He moves in the slow dance I have long associated with those who feel sorry for me. They realise within a few moments that they won't buy anything, but are determined not to be rude about it, so they circle the shelves when I wish they would simply go.

'How did you two meet?' he finally asks.

'Leah came into my shop.'

'I didn't know she read.'

'There's lots you don't know about her.'

He seems to weigh that up. 'Fair comment,' he grunts. The need for further explanation weighs on him. 'There were four of us,' he eventually adds. 'Leah was the quiet one, the one who kept herself to herself.'

He begins to irritate me. 'Was she always quiet?' I ask.

He sees straight through that. 'You know, don't you?'

I nod.

'It was a long time ago,' he begins.

I must look sceptical.

'Is that why she stopped talking?' James asks.

I shrug. I don't have permission to take up her cause. I mustn't explain what I only dimly understand.

He changes the subject.

'I hope I'm not taking up too much of your time. What I really came for was to see if there's been any news. Do you mind if I just check your computer?'

'Be my guest.'

He takes the machine over and interrogates it, then gives up within minutes. 'You're right,' he admits. 'There are only a few short clips, nothing we can use. I just hope the gizmos keep on working.'

He hands back the machine, snorts as if all this is a little beneath him, then says, 'See you tomorrow. Remember you said you'd phone me when she comes back.'

I want to ask whether he would care about any of this if the money wasn't at risk, but I don't. The shop bell jangles and I have the place to myself.

I miss her terribly. I hate the thought of her being in that place and vulnerable. I think of the way she was after it happened and I wonder if she ever thinks of me.

***

When the others leave, Katherine herself brings me my lunch. Before she has time to go, I thrust a written question at her.

Are you allowed to talk to me?

'Yes,' she says, and I see in her eyes that the question has affronted her. Perhaps she has a status I haven't guessed at. Is that because she is Patrick's fiancée?

Please talk to me about my brother.

She hesitates, so I write, *Please tell me how you fell in love.*

Her face is different. I have looked at faces all my life. I am an expert on faces. My sponsors' faces are open, almost childlike. Katherine's face is closed and wary.

Maliciously I write, *You are going to obey him for the rest of your life, so you must love him.*

She smiles, only it isn't a smile.

'I don't know what they have been telling you,' she says. 'It isn't really that black and white.'

The love or the obeying?

I need to be careful. Do I really want to be this self-revealing? The word dumb is also used to mean stupid. Will my muteness mask my intelligence as far as she is concerned? I sense this place doesn't exactly value intelligence.

'I don't know you well enough,' Katherine says. 'Perhaps when I'm your sister-in-law. Enjoy your lunch.'

She leaves and I process what her face has just told me. My best guess is that it isn't love and she won't obey. I read real frustration in that look, and when the kind smile came just before she left it was a learnt, unfeeling affair, as meaningless as *How are you today?* or *Enjoy your evening.*

I eat quickly. My head is back in the conversation with my mother. For years she did more or less as Dad told her. Is she still as malleable? I remember the way she refused to hug me yesterday evening, how she looked to Patrick for answers. And what did Patrick mean when he said she had been cast out? I just don't understand it. Did they cast her out when she got pregnant or did her father betray her in the same way he betrayed her brother, Joshua?

I think of Izzy, the woman I knew who liked clothes and loved James best of all her children, loved him enough to always excuse and forgive him, the woman who was my best friend for years. There is so much going for her in her own house where she has many rooms that are hers to command. Is she content to just have a bedsit room here? Does she really believe in God again and in this extreme community, with its demeaning attitudes towards women?

I look at my programme. The next item in my indoctrination is headed Separation, then I have some free time. I think I'll knock on my mother's door later, see if she will let me in, see if there is anything I can say to make her change her mind. Because if I can't, I don't know what I'm doing here. I no longer think I can find evidence against Patrick. In my special school we all knew which adults to avoid because they were a bit free with their hands, a bit creepy. If Patrick was like that my sponsors would know, but my question this morning didn't raise even a flicker of recognition.

While I'm waiting I hear footsteps. I think I recognise them so I open the door. My mother is walking along the corridor. She is alone so I step outside. She's walking slowly, head down. Her hands are clasped demurely in front of her. Her lips move as if she is praying, but her face is haunted.

There is no one about so I step out in front of her.

When she sees me the haunted look becomes one of terror. She grabs me. 'I want you to go,' she says. 'I didn't tell them about you. They asked and I didn't tell them.'

I can't risk being seen talking. This is a public corridor. Any moment now my sponsors will return. I do the things a daughter is meant to do. I put my arm round her. I kiss her and lay my face against her cheek. 'We all love you,' I whisper. 'You don't have to be alone.'

Then I quickly let her go, remembering that she is meant to have no unsupervised contact with me. Perhaps she is softening towards me, but it is too soon to suggest she abandons Patrick and flees this place with me.

I watch her walk away. She turns at the foot of the stairs and looks at me as if she isn't sure who I am any more.

This place which is always quiet dips into total silence, gives me a chance to listen to it. It is as if two orchestras are playing quite different pieces of music at opposite ends of the building, each at the extreme range of my hearing. On one side I hear the sounds of quiet contemplation, the notes of the monastic order like a choral work of extreme reverence freed from the pressures of time. On the other side is a quite different tune, something discordant and controlling.

I have time to myself. I need a change from small rooms.

***

Julia drops in later on the same mission, gets straight to the point.

'Just passing, Martin. Any news?'

I shake my head. 'Nothing,' I tell her.

She is the opposite of her brother's indolence. The shop which seemed a perfectly adequate size when James was here is suddenly too small as she paces round it. 'I should have gone myself,' she says, 'just marched up to the door and demanded to see my mother.'

'Wait and see what Leah comes back with,' I suggest.

'I mean, how can she ask the right questions? She knows so little about the world. She doesn't even talk. I should have gone myself.'

I follow her rampage through the shop without getting up. Suddenly she sees a book and picks it up, examines the back of the dust jacket, flicks through it, checks the price, snorts and transfers it to her left hand. I don't think I've ever seen such a quick appraisal. She resumes her stalking.

'Everything is usually left up to me.'

She hurls this comment when she next passes.

'Well, isn't it quite nice that someone else is taking the burden?' I ask her retreating back.

She turns, pivoting on one heel and the toe of her other foot. 'No,' she says. 'I always like to know where I'm up to. I hate waiting. She hasn't communicated?'

'James checked,' I reassure her.

'There's another one.'

I find it intriguing that Julia shares her views with me.

'James is just lazy. I don't know what Roz sees in him. She's a bright cookie and yet she's linking herself with my lumpen brother.'

I watch her take a few more turns round the shop. Her mobile pings. She lifts it, swipes and snorts, then returns it to her pocket.

'I actually need to be elsewhere,' she tells me. 'I don't have time for this.'

I tell her I have no idea how long we will have to wait.

'That's alright for you,' she counters. 'Your days are the same as each other. You can swan off to Scotland for a week and it won't affect your business.'

'Then go home,' I suggest. 'I'll email you with our conclusions.'

Now she really is upset.

'But it needs me to be here.' She doesn't explain what it is. 'It's always needed me.'

She's heading out of the shop when I ask her if she wants to buy the book she's still carrying.

Chapter 25

There will be another service at 6pm. Before that I have two hours to myself. If there is evidence to be found it won't come from my sponsors. I know that now. But what about from others? Who does the catering? Who are the office staff? What might a caretaker know? I decide to go for a walk. I need to fix the layout of the building. Is there only one exit? If I'm to achieve anything by being here, I must take risks. I need to explore.

I wave to the listening device as I leave my room. The three I brought with me are in my pocket. If anything happens to me, does Martin know where I am?

At first I aim for the church. My reason can be that I have come here to pray. I will play the part of an enraptured acolyte, wanting to explore my new surroundings. As I make my way along the corridor I listen to the building again, hear the same tunes playing against each other.

The church is empty and in darkness. Having no windows it is wholly dependent on artificial light. This thwarts me for a moment as I wonder where the light switches are and whether I would attract attention to myself by switching them on. I decide against it. I walk into the darkness and sit in the front row, close to where I sat the other night. I don't think anyone can see me so I don't pretend to pray. I sit there and listen to the building. Stone and metal. Only hard notes. Without light it feels even more like a bunker. There's something else too. I try my trick of fading into the building itself, of pretending I am part of the structure. It's then I realise I am not alone.

Someone else has chosen to come here and sit in this darkness. I can hear their breathing. It's long and slow. There are gaps between the breaths, which is why I didn't pick it up before.

Okay, I think. I'm doing what others do. I'm fitting in. If whoever this person is was not disturbed by my coming in, sitting here in the darkness must be commonplace.

Then a voice startles me.

'You must be Leah.'

I hold my breath. It's not a voice I know. Male. Older than Patrick.

'I know everyone's footsteps, but I don't recognise yours. That's why I know it must be you.'

I stay absolutely silent. I should run, but I'm too curious.

'You've been very quick finding this place. I give you full marks for that.'

The voice is coming from my right, from the point of the most intense darkness. Definitely male, very certain of itself, almost intimate.

'I come here often. I come here when I don't want to be watched anymore.'

I stay silent, of course. I don't move.

'They tell me you can't speak, but you can listen. Perhaps I can help you. Perhaps I have what you want.'

The darkness suddenly flickers. I left the door open and someone has walked past outside. The voice stops, waits, clearly doesn't want to be discovered.

'Information,' it whispers, so that I can hardly hear the word. 'Isn't that what you are here for?'

Am I perhaps not the only dissident in this organisation? I am about to get up and move towards the voice when I hear Martin's warning that we never question what we want to hear. So I stay put.

I'm stuck. I can't ask questions because that will blow my cover. I can't write questions on my pad because it's too dark. Information is what I came for. Is this a trap?

'Trust nobody. Quite right.'

I hear a chair scrape, that sharp noise wood makes when rubbing against stone. Then someone is moving in the darkness.

Stick or twist?

I don't think he's moving towards me. Has he given up, decided to leave me on my own? His footsteps are definitely receding, I'm sure of that. I'm losing my chance. Then the darkness quivers, but not like it did before. The door is shut, and what was only the edge of darkness becomes the thing itself.

I stop breathing. I hold my breath for a long time and it's then that I hear him. This unknown person is still in the church. He seems to have taken his shoes off and is moving towards me. Whoever it is knows this building much better than I do. Now I have no choice in the matter. Now I can only sit and wait.

He's moving slowly, carefully. Is he carrying his shoes? Fingers reach for me. I can feel them coming. They touch my shoulder and then grasp it. Whoever this is sits next to me.

I wait for whatever will happen next. I calculate where the door must be. If necessary I can run down the wide aisle. Some light must be visible through the edges of the door. I can always push him over and dash for it.

He must sense this. 'Please stay,' he says. 'I won't keep you long. I want to confess. I've wanted to confess for a long time, but not to them, so I've been waiting for a stranger and I've chosen you. I have sins that haunt me. Will you do me the honour of hearing my confession?'

His breath is fragrant with old age. He lets go of my shoulder.

'Her name was Hilary.'

Now I know who he is.

***

Late that evening James and Julia come back, this time together.

'Any news?'

I shake my head.

'I hate waiting. I hate not knowing,' Julia splutters.

'She'll be preserving the battery,' James says, 'in which case she's probably found nothing we can use. Unless the gizmo has stopped working.

Julia sums it up. 'So we are no further forward and three precious days have gone by. Mum is still in there. We don't know if Leah's even met her. The money's at greater risk and we have no evidence of Patrick molesting anyone except Leah.'

'She's doing her best,' James says, and I suddenly like him, before he adds, 'But is her best good enough?'

Julia snorts. 'So we fall back on the law. It looks as if we'll have to go to court. How I hate paying lawyers.'

Silence.

'Perhaps,' James quietly suggests, 'he doesn't shit where he drinks.'

Julia looks disgusted.

I want to laugh, then I understand. 'The ball-bearing factory.'

'Yes,' says James, 'the other possible place. Perhaps he daren't within the Living Saints, too much to lose. But at work that may be quite another matter.'

James looks hard at Julia.

'No, I don't have the time. Absolutely not.'

James suggests Roz.

'She's the right age. She's the right gender,' comments Julia.

'The evidence is the thing. We need that evidence.' James gets out his mobile phone and dials. 'Roz, we need you,' he says, then he's away down the stairs and we don't hear any more of the call.

That leaves me with Julia and a silence.

'How are you coping?' she suddenly asks. 'I don't know about your relationship. And I don't want to know,' she quickly adds, 'but this must be tough on you.'

I want to tell her about my sleepless night, but I don't. Anyway, there's no need to answer. Her concern is merely a pretext for talking about her own sleeplessness, about her fears of losing all that money.

James comes back up. 'Roz'll do it, but we need to get her into the factory if she is to ask questions. Sis, any ideas?'

'A Health and Safety Executive Inspection. They're always unannounced. I can set her up with the right credentials. Let's just hope they've not been inspected recently.'

'Perfect, Julia,' James says. 'It means she can go round wherever she wants and just talk to anyone she chooses.'

Sister and brother high five each other, go off together.

For want of anything else to fill this horrible waiting I look for a map of all Macdonald's outlets and all Costcutters. Perhaps if I cross reference I can find where Leah is. I'd like to know.

***

We are sitting in total darkness. This is the man who abused Hilary, who used to grope and kiss her, putting his hand on her knee, forcing his tongue into her mouth. This is the man who split Hilary from her family, and years later forced her to say that her truthful accusations had been lies. I remember her words: 'He smiled the smile of the victor.'

I know what he will do.

I get ready.

'I have always felt guilty,' he begins. 'I need you to know that. I offer no excuse. She was so beautiful, so kind to me.'

His voice is insidious. His face is very near mine. I can feel his words as well as hear them. I asked my sponsors about young men. Might they have said something different if I had asked about the old?

'I'm not what you would call a good-looking man. Once they look at me, women are not attracted. I never married.

Hilary used to feel sorry for me. I encouraged that. She used to come and sit next to me. Can you imagine the torment to a man like me of having a girl like that sitting in the next seat, as you are now?'

I have no weapon except the pen I write with. If I make a dash for where I think the door is, I will be running blind.

'To know that her thighs are within an inch of yours, almost flesh against flesh. I could feel the heat of her. She wore stockings, not tights. I'd noticed that about her.'

He waits for a reaction and I give none.

Emboldened by my silence he continues. 'So I'd reach out and place my hand on her knee. Like this…'

I feel his old hand alight firmly on my knee. His fingers stretch to find the edge of my skirt.

I must change the script. As calmly as I can I reach out and stroke the back of his hand. He gasps and relaxes. Then I place my left hand on his, gently at first, and hear his sigh of satisfaction. When I'm in exactly the right position I push down, trapping on my knee all but his little finger. Using as much force as I can muster I yank it upwards and backwards.

Something snaps.

He screams out in pain and surprise. 'You little bitch,' he yells. 'You little bitch.'

I stand up, turn round and move towards where I think the door is. He doesn't follow me. I can hear him sobbing and I'm pleased. He's had that coming for a long, long time.

Then the door opens. Has his scream been heard? The lights are switched on and for a moment I'm dazzled by their brightness.

Patrick is standing in the doorway. He comes towards me. He knows it wasn't me who screamed. He goes past to the still sobbing man and I see that he immediately understands what's happened. He looks at my assailant with contempt, then leaves him there and comes back to me.

'Are you alright?' he asks, taking both my hands in his.

Out of the frying pan. I nod, try to free myself. What is it about male hands?

'Are you sure?'

His grip is strong, almost threatening, as if he is warning me never to try that with him. I start to move away, and it's then that I see Katherine standing in the doorway, staring at the pair of us.

***

I try the Leeds area first. I thought Leah's film was of a cityscape. The Google map shows there are actually not that many Costcutters in Leeds itself; there are more on the outskirts. The layout of the Macdonald's map is the same. My trouble is I only have one search engine. It's wearisome work comparing the two maps. I find I have to go for my A to Z and mark each of them on the overall city map inside the front cover. I need a red pen to do that. The map is heavily black, and pencil just doesn't stand out. I've put all the Costcutters in and have started on the Macdonald's outlets when I realise that one possibility is in the Kirkstall area. I make myself carry on and complete the exercise. The only other possibility is in Bramhall. I note both postcodes down, then load Google Earth. This takes a long time, so long I wonder if I can do it faster using the A to Z, but the logistics are too complicated.

It's not Kirkstall. Next I look at Bramhall and I can see the two stores side by side. When I rotate the view a white building swings onto the screen. I'm sure it's the same one. I look up the right page of the A to Z and mark the spot. Knowing where she is might help me sleep.

Before I go to bed I check for other film sequences or recordings. Nothing. It's been forty hours since Leah stepped in through the green door. I hope she's alright.

Chapter 26

The next morning the atmosphere in the building has changed. I sense that at once. I'm told they're moving me and I wonder why. I am to pack my case and take it to reception. I decide to do as I'm told.

When I report, the receptionist hardly glances at me, but instead speaks quietly into her phone. After a few minutes, no less a personage than the stern Katherine appears.

'Hello, Leah,' she greets me. 'Please come this way.'

I follow her along another white painted corridor. I wonder where we're going. I feel for the camera and, because I'm afraid, I switch it on. She's walking fiercely, and I have to lengthen my stride to keep up. Dragging my case makes this difficult, so I pick it up. She doesn't turn round or offer to help.

Katherine stops, opens a door and invites me into a room. Even before I walk in I know who else will be there, and he is. The bugs are in the case. This is the perfect spot to place one.

I put my case down. Patrick can't attack me in front of Katherine, can he? I get out my pad and write.

Yesterday I was given a full programme for today.

'It's been postponed.' Katherine says this in a tight-lipped way.

I suspect they know I can talk, but there's no way I'm going to give in and say anything.

Have you a new programme for me?

'Not yet,' says Katherine.

'Yes,' says Patrick.

I study their faces. I see Katherine bite her lip and defer to him.

'There has been a change because your sponsors, in spite of the excellent progress you made yesterday, think you need time for reflection.' Patrick speaks with the sweet reasonableness of a holy man. 'They have challenged the speed of your assimilation without enough time for solitary prayer.'

Now I know he's lying and I wonder what has really happened. They are not standing close together. Katherine looks furious. What did she read into the way we stood together in the church last night?

Patrick continues. 'It is often best, when trying to reach God and seek his forgiveness, to be free from all distractions. In the old days hermits lived entirely alone, and our Lord went forty days and nights in the wilderness with no human contact.' He pauses. 'We have a number of other properties.'

Do they know I can talk? Do they know what I said to Izzy? Was her room bugged? I hope Martin is getting this. Is he watching his screen? Where are they going to incarcerate me?

'We are going to send you to 48 Waterloo Terrace. There you will be alone. You will find everything for your bodily needs. There you can spend time alone with God. Then, when you feel you are ready, we will shrive you in a Face to Face. If you come through all that unscathed, we will immediately admit you to Sainthood.'

I'm being locked up and the bribe is an even faster route to full assimilation. I remember how they locked up Joshua. They don't know about Martin. They don't know about Julia and James. They can't know I am recording everything they say. Perhaps they think no one will notice if I vanish from the world. But if I am to live my cover, what choice do I have?

I bow my head. I get out my pad of paper and turn away from them to conceal it while I write slowly, *You do me great honour.*

When I have finished I fold the paper in two. They are standing a little apart, so with another bow I hand it to Katherine.

She opens the note and I see it written on her face. She knows about the rape. Does she think I led Patrick on and have now come back for more of the same? There's real tension between them. It takes an effort for her to stay in role and say to me, 'I'm sure this is God's will.'

I stand obedient, rooted to the spot, until she turns and gives the paper to Patrick. I pick up my case as if I am being compliant, as if I am going to go wherever they send me. But, while they are distracted, I get a good two-handed grip on the handle. I swing the case round and round, turning like a hammer thrower, and finally hurl it at them with all the force I have. Then I run.

I head back down the corridor, head to my mother's room. It has to be now. I saw so much in their faces. They know about us. If they listened to the conversation I had with Izzy they will know she lied to them in her Face to Face. If she has already made over the money then she is also in great danger. I have no idea how I will rescue her, but I must try.

My calculation is that they won't follow me immediately because they can't afford to be seen chasing me through the building, but they may try to stop us leaving. I go up the stairs two at a time and burst into my mother's room.

It's empty. Perhaps this is also a trap, but I risk a quick look round. It's set up for the next occupant. There's no sign that my mother has ever been here. Of course, they would move her, wouldn't they? They would take her to one of their safe houses, use the same excuse they tried on me. They've locked her up. I spin quickly round so the camera gets a full view. Is Martin watching this?

Then I go back into the corridor. I need to flee the building, but Katherine is waiting on the stairs to stop me. I crash through a swing door and see more rooms and another door. Where is Patrick waiting? Where does this corridor end? They know the layout of the building much better than I do.

I find unguarded stairs and hurtle down them. I've lost all sense of direction now. I try to remember where reception is and run that way. I know I've guessed right when I see Patrick waiting for me, so I turn round and sprint down yet another corridor. This time Patrick is following me, taking long purposeful strides. His face is set with a kind of glee, so I must be in a private zone where no one will see him hunting me. I increase my speed and see a blank wall ahead. It's a dead end and Patrick is close behind me. He stretches out a hand to catch me.

I've run out of choices. Patrick has chased me into a cul-de-sac. He must think he has me trapped, but there is a single door on the right-hand side. If it's not locked, perhaps I can escape out of a window or at least find somewhere to hide. It's my last chance. I make a dash for it and grab the handle. The door opens, so I dive through, slam it shut behind me, and lean against it. Breathing heavily, I hold onto the handle. Patrick's footsteps falter. I look for a key but there isn't one. If he tries the door, I know I won't be able to hold it shut.

But he doesn't. I know he's waiting out there because I haven't heard him going away. Why doesn't he attempt to follow me in?

I am in a room I recognise as a sickroom. At its heart is one of those part beds, part trolleys that you find in hospitals. Dad died in such a bed. He was hooked up to similar drips. I see in front of me other harbingers of serious illness: the monitors and mini trolleys, the pads and sick bags. These are gathered like albino ravens foretelling an approaching death.

The trolley bed is in the centre, but the room wasn't designed as a bedroom. I see at once that this is a plush space. A large oak desk with an inlaid leather jotter has been turned ignominiously against the wall. Perhaps it once dominated. Paintings on religious themes are spread across two walls. To one side there is a great brass eagle with a Bible on its back. One whole wall is lined with bookshelves, another is filled top to bottom with files, as if the space, without the bed, is part library and part study.

Like the chapel this room has no windows to bring light

in or for me to escape through. It too has the feel of a bunker.

But, whatever its real purpose, it is now a sickroom. Whatever its previous function, it now waits for a death.

I step away from the door to find somewhere to hide. Why am I no longer being pursued? Why hasn't Patrick followed me in here? Surely it will only be a matter of time before he tries the door. I shrink into a corner and wait for the inevitable.

But no one follows me in, so eventually I walk towards the bed to see who's lying there.

I discover a man with the same look my father had the last time I saw him alive. His form is shrunken, there is a grey pallor on his skin and deep lines round his eyes.

I can't stay here. I'm intruding. At any moment a nurse might bustle into the space and ask me what I'm doing. I have to find somewhere else to hide. I turn and walk away.

'Don't go,' the dying man says. His voice is like wind through a husk. He can't be a threat, can he?

I go back to the bed, let him see me.

The sight of me seems to perk him up. 'No one's been near me for hours,' he says through parched lips. 'They just leave me alone.'

His voice is in danger of cracking up, as if his throat is dry.

And suddenly I guess who he is. Time to break my rule. I check the camera is still on. It isn't much of a risk. I won't be in the shot, and only Martin knows what my voice sounds like.

'Would you like some water?' I ask him.

'Please.'

I know what to do. I wet a fresh paper towel at the sink and allow him to suck from it to moisten his mouth. I daren't raise him up and let him have a proper drink. He seems too ill for that. And anyway, I can't see a glass.

'Do you want some more?' I ask.

He nods, so I repeat the process several times. When he's had enough he waves the towel away.

'Tell me,' he asks, his voice looser, 'does it say *Nil by Mouth*?'

I look around, giving the camera time to film the room.

'I can't see anything.'

'Perhaps there's no need for anything written. You see, they've cut me off. Only one nurse ever comes near me. Even Katherine no longer visits. I'll tell you a secret: they are terrified I'll change my mind.'

'What about?'

'My successor.'

Of course, that's why Patrick brought me to see him. That's why Patrick let me into his kingdom and lied about me. They've made a deal. Patrick will become his successor if he brings me and my mother back into the fold.

'Have you made the recommendation?' I ask.

I'm not sure he understands me. Perhaps he hasn't heard, so I make it simpler.

'Is it Patrick?' I ask gently. I calculate he's too far gone to wonder how I know, and there'll be no button for him to summon help or he would have been pressing it for hours.

'Yes,' he admits. 'Yes. I've even signed the paper.' He reaches out as if to grab hold of me. 'But I must change it. I must do that now. I don't know how many days I have left.'

He looks crushed, so I do what I never could with Dad, I hold his hand. I pick up the cloth I used for the water and gently wash his face. His eyes close and he smiles.

'Tell me who you will now choose,' I say. 'I'm good with secrets.'

His eyes stay closed. For a few seconds I wonder whether he has slipped away, but with Dad it wasn't that peaceful. There's no rattle in this man's throat, no long sigh.

Then he seems to wake and he smiles at me. 'Are you an angel?'

'I'm your angel,' I say, 'but it isn't your time yet.'

The calmness leaves him. He appears agitated. 'Then I must stop this nonsense, mustn't I?'

I nod my head slowly so as not to disturb the camera. I

need this on film, but being here with God's Man it seems intrusive.

'Not Patrick,' he says, quite distinctly. 'If I go you must tell them, it mustn't be Patrick. Choosing Patrick was wicked of me. He says he's met the three targets I set, but even so ….'

My guess was right. The third target must be the money.

He tries to sit up. I manage to jam another pillow behind him so he is partly upright. Even that effort has winded him.

'Write it for me,' he begs.

I take a piece of paper from the desk and write as he dictates. *I, God's Man, wish to ensure that Patrick Barr does not become my successor.* Then I date it and add the time. I linger over the paper so the camera gets a good view of what I've written. I read it out for him. 'Is that what you want to say?'

He nods.

'Do you want to make an alternative recommendation?' I ask.

His concentration is slipping. He appears to shake his head.

'If I hold it and give you the pen, can you sign it?'

'I'll try.'

But he can't. I hold his right hand in both of mine. He is so cold to the touch. I massage his fingers and slowly warm his hand. He tries again, manages, seems pleased with his effort. When I look at the signature it's no more than a shaking squiggle, but it is signed.

'Who do I give this to?' I ask.

He doesn't or he can't tell me.

I hold his hand again. 'Have a sleep,' I say. 'I'll wait for you if I can. I'll try to be here when you wake.'

I feel his hand clasp mine, then he relaxes the grip, his eyes close, and his head lolls.

To save battery I switch off the camera.

I'm still trapped, but they will not follow me in here. They must be waiting, hoping he will be quick about his dying.

This man may have done great harm. He could have been

implicated in the story of Joshua and Hilary. They must all have known she was right in her accusation. But to me he is only a frail, dying man who has been abandoned.

Can I stay and wait for him to wake? This is probably the safest room in the building, but they know I'm here and they can't leave me here for ever. I now have real evidence and a signed piece of paper. I have the weapon I need to ruin Patrick, but if I step outside that door he and Katherine will be waiting. After all, they can wait there all day and not call attention to themselves.

Perhaps there is another way out. I start to walk round the room. Just past the bookshelves there is another door. It leads to a bedroom and a private toilet. And the bedroom has windows which open, old fashioned sash windows like at home. It will be easy to escape. I ease a window part way up just to make sure.

Now I have what I came for I itch to leave, to check there is a way through to outside. But I made a promise and I find I am no longer afraid. I go back into the main room and wait by his bedside. I'm safe so long as I stay here, I tell myself. Then, when God's Man wakes up, I'll climb through the window and make my escape.

***

An hour goes by and no one disturbs me. His irregular breathing tells me he's very close to the end. I find myself moved to be there, almost as if it is a privilege. Then there is a gentle knock on the door.

I quickly go back into the bedroom and leave the door open a crack so that I can see. I switch the camera back on. It's cold waiting here because of the open window.

It's both Patrick and Katherine. Patrick searches the main room quickly, sees the open door to the bedroom and comes straight towards it. I duck under the bed and in doing so I bang the camera on the floor. I hope it's okay. Patrick spots the open window, leans through it to check outside, then closes it. He must presume I have already escaped.

He goes back to Katherine and stands a little way off. I can see their feet, nothing more. They are too far away for the microphone to pick this up.

Patrick is agitated. 'Not here. She can't have gone far,' he says. 'The gate's locked. If she tries to climb it she'll cut herself to ribbons.'

I note that. I'm still trapped.

'She must be hiding somewhere. She's a danger to us.' Katherine's voice.

'Is this room bugged?' Patrick asks.

'Not any more. It's a long time since he has been able to harm us.'

There's a pause. Then Patrick says, 'So there is still an us?'

'I don't love you. Don't fool yourself. This has never been about love.'

Patrick doesn't reply.

'And it isn't about sex either. If you must, you must. I could cope when it was one of those tarts at the factory. I've always understood about men's needs. Your saintly father taught me all about that.'

And in that spat-out sentence I hear another truth about this place.

Then Katherine's tone changes. 'Always remember that I know you now in the same way I know all the other Saints. God Almighty himself doesn't know as much as I do about his so-called chosen ones.'

'You always think the worst of me. Leah's a fantasist, as soft as her mother, as enraptured. What she said . . .'

'Was true.'

His feet move. He must be facing her now, and very close.

'No, no, no. It's something she wanted to happen but never did. Women make a play for me. Leah dressed specially for me, wore perfume, threw herself at me.'

'It happened, it didn't happen,' Katherine says, as if weighing alternatives. 'It makes no real difference to what holds us together.'

'So what do you want of me?'

'I want the power, that's why I'll go through with this.'

'You need me,' Patrick says. 'Otherwise you will have nothing after he dies. You need me.'

'And I can ruin you any moment I choose. Never forget that.'

'Do you have the piece of paper?'

'He signed it two days ago. It makes you the next God's Man.'

'And you his wife.'

From where I am hiding I can sense Patrick's relief. It's then I understand the attraction. They are the same, united in nastiness, an alliance of evil. Together they are formidable. I don't see the kiss, but I do see the feet move so they are overlapping and I hear the long suck of its ending.

'Yes,' Katherine says, 'of course I'll marry you. Now do it, before he changes his mind.'

She leaves the room and shuts the door behind her. Patrick walks towards the bed. He's turned his back on me, so I slide out and return to my watching post by the door, making sure the camera can see everything. I watch him bend down and listen to the irregular breathing of his spiritual leader.

Then I hear Patrick talking. His voice is so low that I doubt the microphone will pick it up.

'Sorry,' Patrick says to God's Man, 'but we can't wait any longer. The plan's changed. Katherine and I agree that it is just too much of a risk.'

What can he mean? How much of a monster is he?

I know from the Macmillan nurses that when someone is dying, hearing is the last thing to go. I'm too far away to see if the old man has woken up or is still asleep. If he's woken I'm sorry I'm not there to hold his hand.

Then I know he must be awake, for Patrick is talking directly to him, whispering. 'So this is for all the beatings. This is for all the times you locked me up. This is for the way you tried to crush my spirit.'

He goes to the edge of the room to pick up a spare pillow which he carries almost casually over to the trolley bed. Then he holds it up. 'Can you see this?' he says. 'This is the will of God.'

I can only imagine the old man's terror as Patrick slams the pillow down on his face and holds it there with all the force he can muster.

***

The next morning I open the shop, then turn on the computer expecting to find nothing. I watch the sequence with Patrick and Katherine. I see Leah throw her case and then she is running. The shop bell goes. It's James. I wave him over and keep watching.

'Leah's in trouble. I know where she is. We need to go there.'

James doesn't argue. I grab the *A to Z*. He looks at me with scorn.

'Don't you have sat nav?'

'No.'

'What's the postcode?'

I read it out and he punches it into his phone.

'Come on,' he says.

My old van horrifies him. I watch him get in reluctantly. He does this quickly and then ducks down until we are out of the town in case anyone recognises him. If he'd had a pair of dark glasses I'm sure he would have worn them.

As we drive down the A64 heading for Leeds he comments, 'The usual problem with using smartphone maps in a car is that the satellite can't keep up with the speed of the vehicle. Today that's just not going to be a problem.'

I have to admit his instructions are good and we make no mistakes. An hour after setting off we drive past an area of roll-fronted premises just being opened up. They reveal cafés and restaurants, newsagents and corner shops. There is Macdonald's and there is the white painted building with no big sign to announce its status.

The area is quiet.

'Do we just go in and demand to see her?' James asks.

'No. They may have already moved her to Waterloo Terrace. We need to check the building out. From here the door and the gate seem to be the only entrances. Otherwise, the place is walled and the walls are too high to climb. You stay here. Watch the entrance. I'll check the whole site to look for another way in.'

James is not exactly a man of action. He's quite willing to sit there.

From the outside the Headquarters of the Living Saints looks like a prison. The gate is tall and razor-wire runs along the top. Through the gate I can see a building with very few windows. I keep moving. The Headquarters clearly has large grounds. In some places big trees throw branches out over the wall. In other places the wall becomes part of another building and then a whole row of houses. I keep turning left when I can. There are more houses and then I meet the high wall again. Finally I am right the way round, back to the padlocked gate and the door. These are clearly the only ways in and out. It's possible to monitor both at the same time.

I climb back into the car. 'Anything?' I ask James.

'No.'

I tell him this is the only way in and out. I want to trust Leah to sort her own problems.

'Give her an hour,' I suggest to James. 'If she's not out in an hour, we'll go in.'

***

I am filming a murder. Under the pillow the old man has woken up. He struggles but feebly. I see his legs kick out and I cannot bear it.

'Stop,' I shout.

I expect Patrick to be shocked. I expect him to drop the pillow and perhaps turn on me. I shout again and he looks round, sees me there and smiles. He doesn't stop. His hands press down harder still. His face has a look almost of serenity. The old man's legs continue to kick.

'Who would have thought he had so much breath in him?' Patrick says.

I have to stop this. I rush forward and try to grab the pillow.

But Patrick is much stronger than I am, so I lean forward and bite his arm, sinking my teeth into his muscle.

He flinches but carries on. 'Nearly there now,' he says. The legs have stopped moving and there's nothing more I can do. With blood running down his arm Patrick holds on and then relaxes, lifts the pillow slowly, leans forward and checks the old man has stopped breathing. Then he staunches the blood with a handkerchief before reaching down and smoothing the old man's features so that he looks peacefully asleep.

I've never felt so helpless.

'Sure, isn't it better for him now?' he says, turning to me.

He stands back and examines his work with immense satisfaction. For a few moments he has the look of a medal winner or a goal scorer, then he smooths his own features as carefully as he smoothed the old man, fixes his evangelical face back into place and turns to me.

'God's will,' he tells me, and smiles. 'So Leah, you will say nothing about this for two reasons. First, no one will ever believe you and second, you'll never see your mother again if you do.'

He looks down at his arm to check he is not dripping blood.

Then he stands by the man he has just murdered and calmly says a prayer over the body before he steps out of the room.

When Patrick's gone I approach the body, tell him I tried, apologise for not being there when he woke. Then I'm out of there, opening the window, climbing through and breathing in great gulps of air.

I have my piece of paper. I hope to God, yes, I hope to God Almighty that the camera was still working and that Martin has all this on his computer. And I think, I know you. I know all of you. I understand what a monster my mother gave birth to. I know what you are capable of. But you, Patrick, you don't know me and you have no idea what I'm about.

Outside the window is a courtyard surrounded by a high wall. I notice that at some stage the wall has been added to, making it taller so no one can see over. I suspect there is razor wire along the top. This is a closed cult. I wonder if I can get over the wall. Can I run for it, jump up, grab the top and pull myself over? I know what that action looks like in films, but I doubt if I can jump that high. Even if the top is smooth and undefended, have I the strength to pull myself up?

Has Patrick left me here because he knows there's no way out?

The space I'm in is closed on the left. The wall runs wide but links to the buildings. There's no way out on that side. I run to the right and there, just past a flower border with snowdrops and aconites, is the only way out, the high locked gate. I can take my clothes off if necessary, throw them over to cover the razor wire. Then I can climb over and away from this terrible place. I head that way at speed. I don't mind how undignified my exit is. In a few moments I will be over that gate and free. I'll find Martin, go to the police with the evidence we have. It's time to tell the whole story.

But the gate is in a corner, and as I run towards it Katherine steps forward to block my way.

'He raped me,' I shout, using my voice at full volume. 'But you know that, don't you? You listen into conversations. You know everything. Well, now he's a murderer too. You're marrying a monster.'

'I'm marrying God's Man,' Katherine tells me as she walks towards me and slaps me hard across the face.

I go to slap her back, but she's too quick for me. She's grabbed my arm and I'm hopeless at this physical stuff. There's no point in wrestling. She's much stronger than I am.

'Let me pass,' I demand.

We are close together, face to face, eye to eye. I'm breathing heavily. Katherine is calm and in control. 'You never really read your Old Testament, did you? With a true understanding of God,' she says, 'there is no rape and no murder.'

I stare at her, take in her calmness, the total blankness in both her eyes.

She continues, 'We are in tune with His will. We know His mind. Why does no one read the Bible all the way through? Once you have done that, and if you truly believe, any action taken in God's name is permitted.'

I refuse to be intimidated. In trying to get away from her I spin her round. But then she plants her feet and we are still again, face to face, eyeball to eyeball.

'I will marry Patrick,' she spits at me. 'We are a good match. You and I will be sisters.'

Then her focus suddenly changes. She steps back and opens the gate. I rush through before turning to face her. She's re-padlocked the gate and is standing behind it, utterly calm, for all the world like a farmer's wife looking across her fields.

'You can't hurt us,' she explains. 'God has helped us to be proof against anything you try.'

'Where are you holding my mother?' I ask.

'We aren't holding her. She's on a long retreat. She is at this moment very close to God. If God wants to take her early, who are we to prevent that?' Then Katherine walks away.

I watch her go and turn round. It's only then I see Martin and James standing in the middle of the street looking anxious.

James is filming this using his phone.

'Are you alright?' Martin asks.

No, I'm not alright. How can I be after all that? But I'm glad he's here and it's all I can do to stop myself rushing into his arms.

'Where's your case? Do you want me to get it for you?'

Oh, Martin.

Chapter 27

We hold an emergency meeting back at Isabel's house in front of a roaring fire. Leah, Julia and James are all there. James introduces me to Roz. We shake hands.

James has already set up the computer and linked it to the TV. Because the choice of the next God's Man is essentially an internal matter for the Living Saints, I select the second sequence shot by Leah, the one in which Patrick smothers the old man. The image is difficult to make out because the light isn't good and the picture bounces around, especially when Leah is running or wrestling with Patrick. The microphone must have been damaged when Leah dived under the bed because there is no sound.

We are all shocked. It isn't easy to watch. The smothering takes such a long time, longer than any film director would dare give it.

Roz especially is white-faced when she realises what she's witnessing. 'You have to go straight to the police,' she says.

Julia nods. 'This has got so out of hand. It's gross. It's gone way beyond the family.'

James adds, 'We have enough to sink him on that sequence alone, and Roz has more.'

'Your brother Patrick is a serial offender,' she informs us. 'I've spoken to three girls who tell remarkably similar stories. Given the slightest encouragement, Patrick assaults. His victims are left feeling bruised and used. They say he's rough and he has no understanding of tenderness or of consent.'

I look at Leah. She grimaces. It is her story too.

'But,' Roz adds, 'they are not willing to go on record and they are not willing to go to the police because they couldn't really describe it as rape.' She lets that sink in. 'One of them took out a sexual harassment charge against Patrick and the men who run the company dismissed it out of hand. My research corroborates Leah's story but doesn't produce much that we could use in a court of law.'

'Can I talk to them,' Julia asks, 'tell them what their rights are, offer to go to the police with them, even to represent them at an industrial tribunal?'

'I could ask them if they want to talk to you,' Roz says. 'I've already arranged to go back to the company tomorrow.'

'Is the girl who made the harassment charge still there?'

Roz shakes her head. 'But you don't really need this, do you? You have the murder. You have proof. You have to go to the police.'

'No.'

A voice I know and they don't.

'Not yet.'

The first words Leah has spoken to her siblings in two decades. They turn and stare.

'We don't have enough,' Leah insists.

They are still flabbergasted, ignoring what she is saying and concentrating only on the fact that she spoke.

'Look,' she explains, 'I've started talking again. Get used to it.'

She has their attention, so she continues.

'I was there. I heard it. I witnessed it all. I know it was murder, but looking at the pictures without sound I've realised that Patrick can make it seem like a mercy killing. The old man would have died soon anyway, if not today, then tomorrow or the day after. I'm sorry there's no sound. I must have banged the microphone when I hid under the bed.'

No one complains. She has them mesmerised.

'But after the murder Patrick made a specific threat, that I was to say nothing about this for two reasons. First, because he said no one will ever believe me and second, because if I breathe a word about this I'll never see my mother again.'

She lets that sink in.

'He and Katherine are utterly ruthless. He's capable of anything and he has our mother locked up.'

'The police will find her,' Roz says. 'We need to go to them now.'

'Will they even look? They can be funny about anything religious. Patrick is very persuasive, we all know that. What do the police do? Storm into a place in deep mourning for their dead leader and search it from top to bottom? What if she isn't there? And if, against all the odds, they actually locate her, will she really tell them she is being held against her will?'

There's silence. The rest of the family are staring at Leah.

'I asked Katherine where Izzy was,' Leah tells us. 'Katherine said she was on a long retreat. According to Uncle Joshua they have houses which they use as punishment blocks. I'm frightened for Izzy's safety.'

Julia recovers first. 'How long have you been talking?'

Leah smiles and shakes her head.

'I do have a signature on a piece of paper saying Patrick is not to succeed as God's Man, but the signature is so poor I doubt if a court would accept it.'

There's silence in the room. We listen to the fire crackling.

'If I can add my penny's worth,' James says, 'officially, as far as I can gather, Patrick doesn't exist. His birth was not registered. There are no adoption papers. He has lived his life entirely within the cult. He went to the cult school. The factory that employs him belongs to the cult. It pays him but he has no National Insurance Number. If that tells us anything, it backs up what Leah is saying. They are a law unto themselves. I would guess that the death we have witnessed is already registered. No police force will want to insist on an autopsy against the leader of a religious institution with charitable status.'

'The money?' asks Julia.

'If Izzy has given it away, it was coming to her anyway. There's nothing we can do,' James explains.

'But I am an executor,' Julia insists. 'I haven't signed any document releasing it.'

'Fight it if you want to, Sis. It'll cost you and you might win, but all you'll win is the right to sign the money over to our mother, who can then give it away whenever she wants to. That's what the will says.'

There's silence, then James turns to Leah. 'I'm sorry for what we did to you that day. I'm glad you're talking again.'

I ask if I can make a suggestion.

They turn and look at me. 'Like Leah I've seen the sequence more than once. By itself it's not enough, so I agree with Leah. But Patrick won't know the microphone stopped working. If we send him some stills from the sequence he'll think we have the whole thing, including his threats. Why don't we offer to swap the film for your mother? We need to meet him somewhere well away from the cult. Once we have your mother we then go to the police. There'll be nothing to stop us.'

'Why should he come?' Julia asks. I can tell that she's hating being here with so little to contribute.

'Because of the Living Saints' charitable status,' Leah explains. 'We threaten him with scandal and questions asked. James and Roz have given us two other weapons that we hold in reserve. If James is right and Patrick doesn't officially exist, then Patrick himself is proof that the Living Saints break the law.'

'Safeguarding,' Roz screams. 'Were there other unregistered children? What's happened to them?'

'Let Danny in on this,' Leah adds. 'Danny's strong and fit. He can detain Patrick, make a citizen's arrest. Then we go to the police with everything, and to the papers if the police won't listen.'

'Clever,' James says. 'How do we set it up?'

'I'll make the contact,' Leah asserts. 'It has to be me. And we meet a long way from the cult. We need somewhere Izzy knows but Patrick doesn't, somewhere she can't identify on a map so that he has to bring her with him.' A smile spreads over her face. 'I know just the spot,' she suddenly announces. 'It's a place where you can see a long way, a place where, if he brings others with him, we'll be able to spot them.'

'When you set up the meeting, can I come with you as protection?' James asks.

That's when she turns to me and smiles.

'No thanks, I'll take Martin.'

Chapter 28

This year snow stopped falling at the end of January, but the cold continued until early March. Warmth and sunshine then brought melt-water and the melt-water turned into floods.

I reconnoitre the area with Martin and find it's possible to approach the spot from two directions. Izzy will bring Patrick along the valley path because that's the only way she knows. We will park just past a small copse of trees and take the other way in, using the track that goes downhill.

It's only three days since the murder. To either side of us the tangled heather shows signs of last year's burning. Its silver skeletons shimmer in the spring sunshine among the green of fresh shoots. Between them the peat shines wet and lumpy. All round us the moorland stretches like a smudged line across the landscape, impossible to do justice to in any photograph, wild and endless. The bracken is curled over and deep brown, ready to shoot again. Lapwings dance in the sky. I think I hear a golden plover piping its lament, but the sound is a long way off.

We've come in two cars. Martin and I lead the way while James follows with Roz, Julia and Danny. I wonder just when they will realise which spot I've chosen. Danny was probably too young to remember. Have the other two already guessed? Has James told Roz? When Martin parked and we all got out I saw no sign of recognition. Have they ever approached the spot from this side? But any moment now we will go over a ridge in the moor and glimpse the site of that childhood picnic. If they don't know already, they soon will.

We climb to the crest and the whole of the moor is laid out before us. Two figures are already coming towards us and I can see a car parked where I would expect it to be. At this distance I can make out very little. They look just like two walkers, and I realise I never thought about other people, about the chance of ramblers being in the area. It's a great day for a walk across the moor if it wasn't for this mud. Are those two figures ramblers? Could they be Patrick and my mother? If so, Mum has lost weight, but I could be wrong. The sun is low and shapes become exaggerated.

Danny is restless. This is his thing and he continually strides out, then has to wait for the rest of us to catch up. One of the places he chooses to wait is the top of a slight incline. When I catch him up he gives me a look. James joins him and they gaze down at the natural amphitheatre of cropped grass, shaped like a green triangle in all this expanse of bracken and heather.

'Of course,' James says. 'Have you never forgotten?'

'Never.'

Julia is a few steps after James. When she recognises the arena she winces but says nothing.

The couple are closing on us quite quickly. One of them is definitely Patrick. Is the other one Izzy? I still can't be sure. It matters that we are there before them, so we speed up. We are in place on the greensward before they reach it. The sinkhole is still there, roped off. There is a warning sign.

Patrick arrives not with Isabel, but with Katherine.

'Where's our mother?' Julia demands.

Patrick and Katherine ignore her, so I step forward. 'Katherine,' I say, 'allow me to introduce the rest of Isabel's family. Here are Danny, Julia, James and Roz. Finally, this is my boyfriend, Martin. Katherine,' I explain to my siblings, 'is Patrick's fiancée.'

No hands are shaken. The two halves of the family stand apart from each other. There is a short silence, so I take over. 'Patrick, where is our mother?'

Katherine answers for him. 'She didn't want to come. She has repudiated all of you. She is now a full member of the Living Saints and therefore is not allowed any intercourse with the outside world.'

'An unfortunate word that, intercourse,' James remarks. 'Your fiancé doesn't seem to feel bound by this ban on intercourse with the outside world or, to be precise, with several young women at his place of work. None of them can remember actually giving consent.'

The barb goes home. Katherine flinches.

'I can provide names and dates,' James tells her.

'At least one of these cases will soon be going to an industrial tribunal,' Julia adds.

'Where I will defend myself and deny the charges,' Patrick says. 'These are old allegations.'

I hold the DVD out. 'This then for Isabel. Without Isabel there is no deal,' I explain.

'We don't need a deal,' Patrick asserts. 'You are free to go at us with everything you've got. We are inviolate. We have good relationships with the police.

'If you really think that, why have you come?' I ask.

'To spare our mother this embarrassment,' he patiently explains. 'The last thing she wants is an unseemly family squabble.'

'Your family disagreement is tearing her apart,' Katherine adds. 'We are, of course, supporting her as well as we can.'

'Brainwashing her more like,' James snarls.

'Have you got her locked up somewhere?' Danny intervenes.

Julia adds, 'If you have nothing to hide, why threaten Leah that if she says anything about the murder she will never see her mother again?'

My family sound rough and angry.

Patrick puts his hands up as if quelling a riot, engages his most mellifluous tone. 'Brothers, sisters, you've got this all wrong. I admit that I helped end the physical existence of God's Man. We had agreed between us that when his pain became unbearable I would do exactly that. I'm sorry, Leah, that you were there to witness it. As for the other accusations, our mother is radiantly happy. She has been restored to the bosom of her real family. She has made her peace with God.'

Katherine again takes up the supporting role. 'Do you want her questioned by the police? Do you want her to have to attend court to swear that what she is about to give to the Living Saints is freely given? I'm sure you would wish to spare her that.'

I listen to the sanctimony in their voices. Can my mother have switched to their side wholly? I remember her troubled face, her hushed whisper that she never told them about our conversation.

'It's true you can embarrass us,' Patrick concedes. 'You can create headlines. The Charity Commission may ask awkward questions. Is that what you want? After all, you are not disinterested observers, are you? If Katherine and I are here to spare our mother's embarrassment, you are here to secure the money. Go to the press if you want to, but the newspaper headlines are as likely to be about an unseemly family squabble as they are about a religious scandal.'

It's not going well. My siblings have played too many cards too quickly, giving Patrick the chance to fall back on blandishments.

A curlew fills the silence with a long liquid cry, somewhere between hope and despair. Instinctively I look up to see if I can spot the bird. Instead my eye picks out a shape moving along the path.

'Before we settle this,' I say, 'can I ask how you found the way here, to this exact spot?'

My siblings are getting restless. I turn to Danny and whisper an instruction. He raises his hand to shield his eyes, looks where I have been looking, follows the unusual movement on the path.

'Isabel showed us the place on the map,' Katherine tells us.

'So exactly where is she now?' I ask.

'At the Living Saints Headquarters,' Patrick patiently

explains. He looks at his watch. 'Right now she will be eating lunch with the others.'

There is a long silence. A light wind shivers the moor.

Julia suddenly says, 'But Mum can't read maps. It was a standing family joke. She said she always smelled her way to places.'

Patrick ignores this. He pauses, sees if we have anything else to throw at him. 'Have you any more questions before you hand over the DVD?' Patrick asks. He wants the meeting over. He's looking at the mud on his shoes.

'Just one,' I say. 'If all that is true, why is our mother crawling along the path behind you?'

Danny sets off at a run, splashing down the track. Patrick and Katherine turn to watch. My siblings surround them. As Danny reaches Izzy, she falls again. We see him crouch over her. She's partly tied up and we see him get out a knife and cut her free. Then he helps her stand up and embraces her. Finally, he leads her towards us. They are talking, and as they come nearer we see our mother's pointed finger jabbing at the air in Patrick's direction.

Then she is amongst us, out of breath, muddied up. There is blood on her wrists.

'I'm sorry,' she says, looking at me. 'I'm so sorry, Leah.'

'They tied her up,' Danny explains as soon as he is close enough. 'They forced her to show them the way, then hid her in the boot. She found the internal catch, rolled herself out.'

James is at Patrick's chest pushing him backwards. 'Rape,' he's shouting, 'rape, kidnap and murder. And you call yourself a man of God.'

But Patrick is bigger than James and pushes him away with ease. Patrick must know the money is lost, but he stands there tall and smiling, calling for Katherine.

Katherine hesitates.

James is back on his feet. 'You don't exist,' he shouts. 'You were never registered. We could, we should, finish you off. You don't deserve to live. I don't think we can be charged with the murder of someone who doesn't exist.'

Patrick's self-control snaps. There is no pretence anymore. His voice becomes rougher and sharper. 'Just try it,' he challenges, crouching down, ready to fight.

Julia is now comforting Izzy. I see James step up, then fall backwards as Patrick thumps him on the chin. Then I notice Danny walking towards Patrick and in his hand, as if he has simply forgotten to put it down, is the knife he used to cut Izzy free. There is no bravado in the way he walks, just an almost robotic sense of purpose. Katherine has also seen the knife and is screaming. Danny is shouting at Patrick, 'You're a phoney. I meet phoneys all the time. I find you despicable.'

The scene in front of me is spiralling out of control. Danny has real purpose in his strides. James, his pride wounded, is urging Danny to just do it.

'No,' Martin yells above the mayhem. 'We have to be better than they are.' He runs forward.

Danny is facing Patrick who is staring at the knife. I watch as Martin steps between them and holds out his arms to keep them apart. 'Your mother will be alright. We have to stay within the law. We have to be better than they are.' He ducks a blow from Patrick aimed at the back of his head and then yells at me, 'Tell them, Leah.'

They all look towards me.

'Martin's right,' I pronounce. 'We can't take the law into our own hands.'

James moves away. Danny stands his ground, the knife still in his hand. Martin lowers his arms but stays where he is between them.

'Besides,' I add, as if reminding myself, 'this place has a way of settling its own scores.'

At that moment Patrick shoves Martin in his back, throwing him forwards so that he cannons into Danny. The knife spills out of Danny's hand. Patrick is climbing the hill, running away from us. Then there is a roar. Something internal in the structure of the earth gives way. We watch Patrick turn towards us as he tries to keep his balance, then he is toppling and sliding backwards as if Hell has opened for him. The rope and the notice collapse as the mouth of the sinkhole gapes wide and swallows. Then the earth shakes, the lawn lurches. There's a fresh hollow in the ground and Patrick has disappeared.

We are stunned, shocked. It has been so sudden. The first to recover is Danny. He walks to the edge of the hollow and stares. Katherine follows him and stands a little way back. The earth is quite still. She is white-faced but in control. 'He's gone,' she says. 'Well, that ends everything.' With head held high she turns and walks away.

There is nothing to be done, so I watch her go. She walks steadily, never turns round. Then the low sun shines through her and she disappears from sight.

I go to my mother. 'I'm sorry,' I say. 'I tried to spare you from all this. Do you understand what I've been through? Do you believe me now?'

She isn't listening. She points to the spot and says, 'For just a second before he fell backwards I saw that look on his face. It was his puzzled look. When he was a small baby, when I handed him over, he looked at me in just that way.'

Then she howls.

I lift her up, hug her to me. 'It's over,' I tell her. 'Time to take you home.'

The howling continues. Danny takes her from me, tries to comfort her.

Julia is recovering, looking round her. 'I hope I never see this place again as long as I live.' Then she turns, looks me straight in the eye. 'I too am sorry.' She spits it out.

On the way back to the car Izzy collapses, so Danny holds her up and half carries her. Julia fusses alongside. Roz is telling James he was stupid to challenge Patrick. I find myself walking at the back of the group. Martin is in front, but then he hangs back to walk with me. The path isn't really wide enough for two people.

He is splattered with mud and rubbing one hand as if he hurt it when he fell. 'Are you alright?' he asks.

I nod, then he gives up trying to be beside me and steps back to let me go in front.

As we cross the ridge and drop down to where the cars are parked, the sun dips lower and fires the edges of last year's heather with a red tinge.

Here the path widens out and Martin is at my side again. I wait for what he will say. Will it be a quotation, a parallel from the world of literature? Will he fall back on Shakespeare?

He says nothing, but I feel his hand suddenly touching mine, which is muddy from lifting Izzy and flecked with her tears and her blood. His muddy fingers clutch mine. The March afternoon is dying quickly, and any spring warmth is already leaking away. His fingers are warm to the touch, so I clutch him back.

I expect him to drop my hand but he doesn't.

'That was a close call,' he says, 'back there.'

A shudder runs through me. When Danny and Patrick squared up to each other I saw how well matched they were, height for height and weight for weight. Two brothers. Cain and Abel. Either one of them could have killed the other.

Chapter 29

We're in our family home, sitting by a blazing fire, drinking wine and whisky. Izzy is back with us, so are Roz and Martin. It's three days since Patrick was killed.

Last night there was a hard frost. It pressed pause on this late spring. It wilted the daffodils. It spread its rime across the landscape and it furred the roof tiles of this wonderful house. It will also have stabilised the soil round the sinkhole and further cooled the body that is buried there.

Three days is a long time for my family to be together, but no one has left. No one has gone home. Even Julia has chosen to stick around.

We have been occupied with the aftermath. I went with Martin to the Living Saints. I needed to talk to Katherine. I also wanted my case returned, together with Izzy's things. We demanded the original will and we got it.

There was no fight left in Katherine and the building felt quite different. It was as if the confidence that had held that place together for so long had finally dissolved. It had the feel of a lost campaign. People were rushing round, talking loudly. Files were being moved from one room to another. We spotted cases stacked near the car park as if other people were leaving. The gate was not only unlocked but left wide open.

James and Julia went to Gouldens to re-start the sale of Dad's company. Then they visited the Living Saints' solicitors with Izzy and moved the account back to the firm Dad had originally chosen. They were relieved to find that no damage had been done, no money had yet been handed over. Izzy had come to understand what was really happening and refused to sign, even before the final act.

Roz and Julia went back to the ball bearings company, met with Patrick's victims, and told them of his death. Julia explained their rights should anything like that happen to them again, then blasted the management for rejecting a valid claim of sexual harassment. The management all looked identical, she said. They were clearly all Elders and shell-shocked by the turn of events. They'd lost two God's Men in a single week. They seemed incredibly unhappy.

I am worried about Izzy. She is back home but not glad to be back. Her sense of guilt has expanded. If only she had kept him as a baby, she continually tells us, she could have looked after him. She could have prevented him becoming what he was. She apologises to each of us for what she's put us through. She apologises most often to me. When not apologising she is withdrawn. I've suggested she goes to see her brother.

I suppose it was a kind of battle and we won. Under the influence of wine and whisky a certain cheerfulness sometimes comes over our faces. For long periods everything seems back to normal. Julia is taking her role as executor seriously. She consults Izzy, even defers to her, but I know she is organising early pay outs and I also know Izzy is insisting that I take my rightful share. The potential sums involved bewilder Martin.

Even at moments of near elation there is a problem. We have not reported Patrick missing. We have not been to the police and told them about his death. James persuaded us that it wasn't our responsibility, that Patrick belonged to the cult and that Katherine, who was after all his fiancée, should be the one to go to the police. He was their creature and we have no DNA proof that he was ever part of our family.

We told Katherine we were leaving that to her. She had been present at his death. She could give a clear account. But even as we said all this we guessed she had other things on her mind, and we wondered what else was hidden in the records of that closed organisation. Martin was particularly forceful, urging her to go to the police at once, offering to go with her, but she was non-committal. I know Martin frets about this, but I tell him we have done our duty and I dread the investigation that might follow. 'Izzy needs protecting,' I tell him, then realise I am falling back on the same argument Patrick used at the sinkhole. So the matter remains unfinished.

And I, what do I feel?

The answer is that I don't exactly know. I hated the living Patrick. It is much more difficult to hate the dead. I feel freer now. I'm glad he's gone.

Today the activity slowed down. When Izzy was in her room sleeping, I had the house to myself. I walked through it, looking and listening. The structure feels solid again. I revelled in the space after Martin's cramped flat and the cult's study rooms. I touched the chair and the iris vase. I walked round outside. I paused where we scattered Dad and wondered if he might now think I had made something of myself. Finally, I stood in the hall and pinged the jardinière. The echoes that came back were clear as water. The house was relaxed, untroubled.

Now I'm watching my family from one side of the room. I still feel more comfortable tucked into the shadow, observing. I still think words should be reserved for when they are absolutely necessary. I notice that my family is growing. We have adopted Roz. My siblings have also accepted Martin. Even Julia has begun to respect him, to ask his advice, to talk to him. He's across the room from me, in conversation with James.

The Goulden Family. We look the same as we did, but we are very different. Perhaps we have Patrick to thank for that. My eyes take in a subdued Julia and a more confident James. They skim across to Danny who has been shocked into caring for someone apart from himself. They reach Roz who is now secure enough in her relationship not to be always at James's side. Finally, my eyes rest on Martin.

I owe him such a lot. In my mind I list the things he didn't have to do. He didn't have to take me in after the rape, tip toe round me, play me music in the middle of the night, drive me up to Scotland, pay for the hotel. He didn't have to take my side, work out where the Living Saints Headquarters was and be there at the crucial moment. I've often wondered whether Katherine would have unlocked the gate and let me leave if she hadn't seen Martin and James standing there. He didn't have to put up with my family's rudeness. He didn't have to intervene when Danny went for Patrick with a knife.

He's an unsuccessful bookseller. He cares. He has courage. He's a good man and I am absolutely in his debt.

But if you add all these things together, do they amount to love?

I look at him long and hard. He's holding his own with James. He's animated in conversation, and I feel a sense of pride that he wants to be with me.

We were once lovers. Now we are both something more and something less. Now we've talked, spent time together, shared experiences. I've kissed him and held his muddy hand. Is it the right moment to invite him to stay the night? Am I ready for this? I can always claim it's because he's drunk too much to be allowed to drive home. Especially not in that old van of his.

November 2014 to September 30th 2015,
Spring Café, York

Note From the Author

If you enjoyed this novel, I'd like to send you a free, unpublished short story as a thank you for buying it. All you need to do is send your email address to candsbridge@btinternet.com. I will also keep you up to date with future publications.

You can find me on twitter @ChrisBridge313 and I occasionally blog about writing https://chrisbridge.blog

So far, I have published two novels and a book of poems:

2014: ***Back Behind Enemy Lines*** http://amzn.to/1zaUqyP. *When Anna returns to England in 1944 after serving in Normandy she is sure her spying days are over. But old age feels like being back behind enemy lines. If she is to keep her independence she must bring her intelligence skills back into play, find the gun she never handed in and face up to the ghosts that have haunted her ever since. Amazon ebook or PoD.*

2017: ***Walking Through*** A book of poems published by Graft Poetry. Email me if you are interested and I'll tell you how to buy one.

2018: ***Girl Without a Voice*** http://amzn.to/2FR2ApT *Childhood trauma robs Leah of the power of speech and forces her to be a watcher on the margins of society. But when her mother goes in search of the child she gave up for adoption, Leah is tempted out of the shadows. At first Patrick is everything she could hope for in a half-brother. Then Leah makes a shocking discovery that leaves her with a moral dilemma and the overwhelming need to do what has always been impossible for her: to take action. Amazon ebook or PoD.*

Praise for 'Back Behind Enemy Lines' by Chris Bridge

"This contemporary story pits generation against generation, is by turn suspenseful, poignant and funny. This was a world I didn't want to leave when I came to the end of the book."

Helen Cadbury: Author of To Catch a Rabbit.

"*Back Behind Enemy Lines* is beautifully written. This is an author who excels at hinting at the unsaid, allowing the reader to fill in the blanks, whose contained and precise prose marches across the pages …at times bursting apart to reveal the oceans of unhealed pain that lie deep within Anna."

Historical Novel Society Review

"Sometimes I come across a novel, that grabs hold of me and will not let go until I have completed the book and sometimes that book would do well set on the small screen as a TV drama. *Back Behind Enemy Lines* by Chris Bridge has it on both counts. This is an exceptional debut novel."

John Fisher: The Last Word Review

"Part Two kept me just as enthralled…I was up late reading into the night to get to the end of this wonderful book."

Roses are Amber Review

"Fantastic novel. I was still reading it at 3am! I felt as if I was immersed in the thoughts as well as the actions of the characters. It has so many layers. That's why I couldn't put it down. It's an important book too, because of what it says about the way the old are treated. The ending was both poignant and triumphant. Anna is such a rich character."

Jo Cole, Amazon

"Compulsive and from my own knowledge a very accurate interpretation of "what it was really like" during the war for some of our unsung heroes and heroines. Excellent seems too short a word for this entrancing read."

Mr C, Amazon

"I found this a compelling narrative that reintroduced me to a past I had never before visualised so clearly and suggested a future of challenging ageing that was both stimulating and frightening. Chris Bridge's style of writing is evocative, descriptive and shows amazing empathetic insight into the feelings, actions and impulses of each character to whom he introduces the reader. His use of words and his style of writing show an understanding of the need to keep readers engaged and motivated while at the same time conveying situations and conversations where every detail is important and no words should be missed. I shall read this many more times I am sure, both to rediscover Anna as an older person reliving her youth and using it to face her future, and to enjoy the powerfulness of the author's use of words."

Paula, Amazon

"I could not put this book down. The tension of the wartime love story behind enemy lines draws you into the novel and doesn't let you leave. It is beautifully and clearly written. The characterisation is skilfully done, there is a terrific sense of place throughout and it is clear that the author has researched the background carefully. The ending is satisfying and redemptive. I loved the book and recommend it wholeheartedly."

Carole Bromley, Amazon

"From the very first pages of this book you will be hooked. The young woman's experience in France is compelling and has a long-term effect on the rest of her life. But the author's depiction of the old woman's battle is an imaginative conclusion to a well-constructed story. I recommend this book."

Kath, Amazon

Acknowledgements

I need to thank so many people: Emma Elwess for legal advice; Emma Forbes for all she told me about elective mutism; the Tuesday night Guppy's group for their forensic examination of key passages; Patrick Scott for conversations about the nature of evil; Julie Ridge and Paul Bridge for commenting on earlier drafts; my agent, Sonia Land, for her suggestions, for the title, and for her continued support. Finally, I want to thank my wife, Sheila, for editing numerous drafts.

The Living Saints do not exist; they are a product of my imagination. But there are many similar cults which do exist and whose certainties terrify me. I am indebted to the testimony of ex-cult members, whose stories I may or may not have used in writing this novel.

About the Author

Chris Bridge was born in Hull, England in 1947. He studied English and Philosophy at Nottingham University and became a teacher after graduating. He eventually became Headteacher of Huntington School, York, and finished his school career as a National Leader of Education. He has been a regular contributor to poetry magazines and his poems have featured in the winning lists of *Hippocrates* and *Stanza* poetry competitions. *Girl Without a Voice* is his second novel. His first novel, *Back Behind Enemy Lines*, was published by Peach publishing in 2014. He lives in North Yorkshire.

27728411R00177

Printed in Great Britain
by Amazon